DADDY'S PRECIOUS PATIENT

Claimed by Daddy - Book Two

POLLY CARTER

Published by Blushing Books
An Imprint of
ABCD Graphics and Design, Inc.
A Virginia Corporation
977 Seminole Trail #233
Charlottesville, VA 22901

Polly Carter
Daddy's Precious Patient

EBook ISBN: 978-1-64563-460-7
Print ISBN: 978-1-64563-461-4
Audio ISBN: 978-1-64563-462-1
v1

Chapter 1

Leaning forward over the steering wheel, she squinted out into the tunnel of light created by the headlights. She hated driving in the country at night. Nocturnal wildlife emerging from the bushes was hard to see until the car was upon it, and animals confused by the unexpected brightness behaved dangerously and unpredictably. Her unruly mind played movies of all the potential disasters: hitting an animal and killing it, not killing it but badly injuring it, crashing her car as she tried to avoid it and killing herself, not killing herself but being trapped, maimed, alone for hours or days or forever.

Her foot eased off the accelerator; she couldn't risk an accident by driving fast in the dark. But being late could be worse. According to the dashboard clock it was 7:20 p.m. She had forty minutes, which should be enough, and arriving early wouldn't get this ordeal over with any quicker anyway.

Anxiety and dread constricted her chest and bloated her stomach. She was terrified. But that was the point of this malicious charade. The fingers of her left hand stopped tapping on the steering wheel and reached across to her handbag on the passenger seat. They would find no cigarettes there. She'd stopped smoking eight years ago, but a remnant muscle memory itched in her fingers and they clawed at her bag before admitting it was futile.

She looked at the clock. 7:25 p.m. Switching on the radio, she scanned the channels for any in range. On the first of the only two accessible, a falsetto with a speech impediment over a thrumming drum machine told her life was for 'dancing and trancing'. Trancing? Ugh. Happy music felt too much like another slap across the face or punch to the gut anyway. She tried the other one. A melancholy lady with a tearful twang declared the misery of living with a man was bliss compared to the misery of living without one.

"No," she yelled aloud, banging the off button. Her palms were clammy and her shaking hand slipped as she replaced it on the steering wheel. Pressing a button on the door next to her and lowering the passenger window, she let in a blast of night air, but it was colder than she'd expected. It chilled her lungs and took her breath away. Clamping her mouth tight to quell the chattering of her teeth, she closed the window, turned up the heater and checked the time.

7:30 p.m. In just over half an hour, she would be on her way home. She wouldn't be there longer than ten minutes, and less if possible. Maybe two minutes. She'd obeyed the order to come; she wasn't doing anything else—no matter what. Then it would be over. Until next time. *Please, dear God, don't let there be a next time. I'm not sure I can take any more.*

Outside, the tall trees had given way to low bushes and scrubby country as the road reached the coast. She slowed as she approached a T-junction and, seeing no lights in either direction, turned right and headed north toward the isolated beach to which she'd been summoned. As the road veered even closer to the ocean, the outlines of sand dunes were visible in the light of the rising moon. At least the sky was clear and the moon almost full. She would not be in total darkness, and she'd brought a torch as well as her phone.

She glanced in her rear-view mirror at the bundle in the middle of the seat behind her: a change of clothes, a thick jacket, a warm blanket, and a lunch box with peanut butter sandwiches, an apple, a chocolate bar and a flask of hot chocolate. Her heart ached with anguished longing. He must be frightened, confused and cold. What kind of a monster could be so cruel? And how could that evil have been any part of creating such innocence, sweetness and goodness?

Calculating she was nearing the designated turn-off, she scoured the roadside for a track down to the beach. One disappeared between the dunes, then another, but the one she sought had a marker: a small wooden sign, nailed to a post beside the road, bearing the word 'Covington' in red paint. According to the directions, it was twenty-five kilometres beyond the T-junction, and her odometer told her she had come twenty-three. She slowed the car down to fifty kilometres per hour, then to forty, then thirty as she neared the twenty-five-kilometre mark.

As the car slowed, her heart rate quickened, exacerbating the growing tightness in her chest and belly. What if she couldn't find the meeting place? What if this was another act of cruelty and no sign existed but she was going to spend hours searching for it in the dark? *No. No. No.* She repeated the word over and over, as though it were a magic mantra capable of protecting her from the manifestation of her worst fears. It couldn't be a lie, a trick. Hadn't the last week of loneliness and worry been enough? She must find the sign. She must be waiting when they got there. She had to rescue him. He needed her and she needed him. Desperately. Her battered, broken, crushed heart couldn't take any more. He kept her alive and gave her life meaning. She would take him home and this time keep him safe forever, no matter what.

Covington. The sign appeared out of the darkness, its blood-red paint glimmering in the headlights. Her relieved *Thank God* filled the car as she expelled a stale breath and allowed her grateful lungs to draw in a fresh one. She braked until the car was barely moving and turned off the road onto the track. The wheels slipped on loose sand. *Please don't get bogged.* Inching the car forward and picking out the firmest parts of the track, she followed it as it cut its way between two dunes before curving behind the one on its right. It stopped just above the beach and widened into an open, flat area where visitors, mostly fishers and surfers, could park or turn around.

Facing her car toward the beach, she switched off the engine, closed her eyes and gave herself a second to enjoy a rare sense of achievement – she'd made it this far, and on her own – before bracing herself for the next challenge. Not expecting to be long, she decided to leave everything but the torch in the car rather than risk losing any of her possessions in the sand. Her phone had no reception anyway, so she dropped it with her car keys into her bag, took the torch out and shoved it into her pocket, and stowed her bag under the passenger seat.

The icy wind blasting off the ocean was so strong she struggled to open the door, and the air so cold once she was out she shivered despite her thick jacket, jumper, long warm tights, woolly socks and boots. She switched on her torch and flashed it in each direction. She was alone on an isolated moonlit beach.

Cold joined the fear, anger, and hatred churning through her. Her stomach heaved and, for a moment, she thought she was going to vomit, but she swallowed hard and kept it down. She couldn't fall apart. Not for her sake, she didn't matter, but she had to stay strong until she got him to safety.

Steeling herself against the icy, salty wind stinging her eyes and matting her hair, she trudged across the sand towards the sound of wild waves hitting the shore. This was madness. A new thought revived her panic. Was it a lie, a trick, after all? Had she been lured here to be murdered on this deserted beach? There was no one to come to her rescue, and it might be days, weeks even, before anyone found her body, or her car, hidden as it was from the road.

She paused, wondering if she should leave as fast as she could? Or had the monster been telling the truth? And, if this suffering and misery were punishment, would it be deemed sufficient? Would they be allowed to leave unharmed?

She tucked her hair down into her jacket and pulled the hood over her head, her ears already throbbing from the cold wind drumming into them. She knew she should keep moving to stay warm, but her body was shaking and her legs threatening to collapse as she plonked herself on the sand facing the sea. She pulled her knees up and hugged them to conserve warmth. She should have brought the rug with her, but hadn't and couldn't summon the will to fight her way up the slope to the car to fetch it.

Staring out across the dark ocean split by the silver light of the moon, her eyes searched for anything that wasn't water, her ears strained to hear anything that wasn't the crashing of waves. The sea whipped into a frenzy by the wind was as cold, as violent, and as cruel as her tormentor. Bile rose up and burned her throat and mouth as she shivered on the sand. She closed her eyes tight. *Please, let him be safe. Don't let any harm come to him.*

When she reopened her eyes, a dim shape had appeared behind the waves further down the beach. Her heart leapt. He was here. In a few moments, he would be ashore and she would bundle him into her car and get him home and they would be safe. For tonight.

She rose to her feet as fast as her frozen muscles and joints could manage, and lumbered towards the object. It seemed to be a small launch moving parallel to the land. She forced her legs into a stilted jog. It was too big to come ashore. It would have to stop and anchor so its passenger could be ferried ashore in a dinghy. Her eyes squinted into the moonlight in case he was already coming, but she couldn't see a second craft. She shone her torch but the beam died a few metres across the waves.

Oblivious to the agony, she pushed her aching legs onward, stumbling on the uneven sand, her lungs burning from exertion and cold air, but she couldn't make up any ground. The boat was as far ahead as ever. She waved her torch to signal her position, but no answering flash reassured her she'd been seen. She laboured on, leaving the car further behind. She wondered if she'd come in on the wrong track. Perhaps she was supposed to take the track after the sign, or two or three or four tracks after. Doubt and panic snarled her insides as she tried to keep going, to keep the boat in sight, to catch up to it.

At last, with no idea how far she'd come or how she could go any further, she saw the boat swing to face the beach and edge closer to shore. Glancing towards the dunes, she spotted what might be a track. So, she had come in at the wrong place. Her tired, frozen face managed to break into a shaky relieved grin and she slowed to a walk. It would take them a few moments to lower a boat and row to shore. She still had to endure the terror of him coming through the waves and then it would be over.

Her gaze returned to the boat the instant it was lit up by a flash so bright it stung her eyes. The accompanying explosion unbalanced her, momentarily knocking the breath from her body and toppling her onto the sand. Scrambling into a kneeling position, she stared in disbelieving horror at the red, yellow and orange flames dancing on the water. The acrid smell of smoke wafted into her nostrils as her mouth opened wide in an anguished scream which rose from her toes, forging itself right up through her body and splitting her face as it burst forth.

She crawled towards the burning boat, ready to fight her way through the freezing, turbulent water to save its precious cargo. Another small explosion stopped her. The boat lilted, its stern dipped, its bow rose, and it disappeared into the black water accompanied by the hissing of doused flames.

It was gone, and she was left staring at an unsympathetic ocean that had already forgotten the boat was ever there. Mesmerised, she watched the waves rushing to the beach, tumbling over each other, spraying her and rushing away. Her jacket afforded some protection from the salt water spraying over her, but her tights were damp and her face burning. She closed her eyes and shut her mind.

Awareness of how cold she was brought her back. It was ridiculous kneeling here, freezing in the dark, and she had no idea why she was. She searched for an explanation. Unable to find one, she stood up and forced her frozen legs towards the dunes. Reaching the edge of the beach, she turned and made her way parallel to the sea until she found a track leading to the road.

Her hands were frozen into fists, her head ached, and her legs were so numb she could only be sure they were still attached to her body because she was moving. She needed help before she got any colder. She would get to the road, flag down a passing motorist and ask for a lift home. Her heart lightened at the thought of home. A niggle told her she was forgetting something, but she was too cold, too tired and her head hurt too much to try and remember. Later would do. First she needed a hot bath and dry clothes to get warm, and she would eat, too, and have a hot drink.

With thoughts of a warm, snug home and a bed to crawl into keeping her occupied and giving her hope, she dragged herself along the last bit of sand and out onto the road. Across from her was another road joining it to form a T-junction. Excellent. There were three directions from which a car could come. That help was bound to arrive any moment was her last thought before her legs crumpled and she pitched forward into a senseless heap.

Chapter 2

Gavin loved driving in the country at night, especially when the moon was round and the sky was spattered with stars. It required extra vigilance, but the eerie quiet of the dark and the surreal effect of the headlights on the landscape stirred his imagination. Usually, he would allow his mind to grab onto and follow any passing fancy. A tree might lean menacingly out towards the road, and he would be transported to an alien planet where he was rushing to prevent an extra-terrestrial army of tree-people from attacking the earth. Or a pair of red eyes might shine in his lights before disappearing into the bushes with a silent *follow me*, and he would find himself adopted into a wolf pack, helping them guard their territory against a neighbouring pack or defending themselves against brutal men with guns. Tonight, however, his imagination was under strict control. If he let go of his hold, it wouldn't take him on marvellous adventures; it was stuck fast in one harrowing story that was wrecking him.

He'd already been off work for ten of the fourteen days he'd been granted to sort himself out, and planned to spend the remaining four on his own in an out-of-the-way shack by the sea. If, by the end, he were still as haunted, if the silence and ocean hadn't laid his poignant ghost to rest, he'd see a professional counsellor. He understood doctors couldn't always deal easily with the death they encountered. Every one of his patients who died took a piece of his heart with them, and every one to whom he helped restore the miracle of life gave him a new piece with which to patch it. As long as he had heart left to lose, he'd continue. If ever he didn't, he'd give it away and find another career. So far, at least until recently, he'd managed the roller coaster.

And then... his stomach constricted, his throat tightened and his eyes squinted as his teeth rubbed together as he felt his guard slipping and his mind breaking loose. If he didn't rein it back, it would spin him round and round on the carousel of self-doubt, guilt and grief. His hands gripped the steering wheel as he tried to slow his breathing and calm himself. He'd hoped by now to be dealing better with what was, after all, one death in the many he'd faced in his time as a doctor.

It wasn't even the first time he'd seen a child close its eyes for the last time; straight out of medical school, he'd done a stint at Raphael Children's Hospital. He'd seen the tragedy of tiny lives snuffed out before they'd barely begun, and watched the souls of grieving parents shatter knowing there was no medicine that could heal them. He knew when he became a doctor that he couldn't avoid death, but he could avoid the deaths of children. Accepting he wasn't cut out for paediatrics, he'd accepted a position as surgical registrar at Metro Dora Hospital, and if he'd stayed in the Surgical Department instead of moving to the Emergency Department a year ago, an arbitrary ambulance break-down wouldn't have forced him face-to-face with the agony he'd sought to escape and in the most horrific way imaginable.

He'd managed to deal with his grief before, and he had four days left to deal with his latest experience. Not to get over it, he'd never do that, but to find a way to live with it so he could face returning to the hospital. Feeling his heart racing, his chest hurting and his body shivering, he recognised the panic that attacked him whenever he thought about being in Emergency. It wasn't abating, so maybe he was finished as a doctor. Maybe this was it, and he should leave everything behind and keep moving forever.

He had switched to automatic pilot when his mind had wilfully reopened the door to the room in which he'd hidden that terrible memory, but was brought back to the present by something in the headlights: a shape on the side of the road. An unlucky animal, by the look of it. A big one. It was an odd shape, though, and it didn't look right. He braked hard, but still couldn't make out what it was as he crawled by. He stopped, reversed and pulled up behind it so it was illuminated by his headlights.

Clothes! He jumped out and rushed around. A woman. Automatically, his hand went to her neck. She had a pulse, but it was slow and her skin was cold. Hypothermia was a danger. Using his phone torch, he checked her eyes. She seemed to be unconscious, but he couldn't find any blood or lumps on her head to suggest she might have sustained a head injury. In such a remote location, his first thought was that she must have fallen from a passing vehicle or been hit by a car, but a quick check revealed no other obvious injuries, so how and why she was here was a complete mystery. Right now, though, getting her warm was the priority.

He opened his rear door, picked her up and lifted her into his car. She was a heavy, dead weight, but he was a big man, tall and broad, who'd found exercising and weight-lifting useful meditations to help deal with the stress of his work. She stirred and mumbled incoherently as he lay her on the rear seat. That was a good sign; she didn't appear to be in a coma. He checked her breathing and pulse—still slightly depressed. He fetched a jacket from the boot and spread it over her, and cranked up the car's heating once they were on their way. In twenty minutes, they'd be at the shack and he would be better able to assess her condition and decide whether warmth and bed rest would be sufficient first aid. He had the medical bag, which lived permanently in his car so, if he hadn't overlooked anything and her condition didn't worsen, he should be able to take care of her until morning. The nearest hospital was two hours away, a trip he was happy to avoid unless it was essential.

Arriving at the shack, he took his torch and started the generator, then unlocked the front door and checked there was a bed made up before fetching in his unexpected patient. Her breathing and pulse hadn't deteriorated, and her skin wasn't as chilled as it had been when he'd found her, but her clothes were damp and would have to come off sooner rather than later. After covering her with all the blankets he could find, he lit the fire, which had thoughtfully been left in the grate, and hung four towels in front to warm while he brought in his luggage and medical bag.

Back with his patient, he tapped her cheek, gently shook her shoulder and called to her. Her eyelids fluttered and she mumbled as she tried to turn away. He called to her again, but she wouldn't wake. Under the electric light, he was able to see her clearly for the first time. Her skin was pale but not grey or clammy. He raised her eyelids again and discovered her eyes were brown. He guessed her age to be about thirty.

Bending down, he noted her full lips as he put his nose to her mouth and smelled her breath without detecting any trace of alcohol. He wondered what her story could be: who was she and how had she come to be lying, with no injuries he could find, on the side of the road in the middle of nowhere on a cold night? He reached under the rugs to check her left hand and saw it was ringless. Was it possible she had no one to look after her?

Always conscious of the person behind the patient, he was touched by the vulnerability of the stranger thrust into his care. He reached out one finger to gently brush strands of long damp hair from her face as he called to her again, but a small squirm was the only response. Banishing thoughts and feelings stirred by her beauty and mystery, he set about attending to her.

He removed her boots and socks; then, keeping her as covered as he could, he reached under the blankets and manoeuvred her tights down over her feet. He knew from when he'd carried her that she was tall and well built, and he got an even better sense now of the length and firmness of her legs. She wriggled but her eyes didn't open. He fetched a warm towel and, as she was still too cold to put it over her lower limbs without risking dangerously pushing cool blood up into her abdomen, he wrapped it over her lower belly and the tops of her thighs, and tucked the blankets tightly over her bottom half.

That half done, putting his arm behind her shoulders, he raised her up and undressed her top half. She fidgeted and her muscle tone was normal, not floppy. His brow furrowed, puzzled as he was by her state of consciousness. She wouldn't wake, but she seemed more like a sleepy child being undressed than an unconscious adult. It appeared she had some aware- ness of the outside world but was either not able to join it or refusing to do so. He reached behind and undid her bra and slid it down over her arms.

He was a doctor. He had seen countless women in various states of undress and hundreds naked, and had never once failed to maintain his detached clinical professionalism. His heart could connect with their humanity, but never before, not once, had he reacted romantically or sexually to a patient. This time, however, a stirring in the depths of his belly as he spread another warm towel over her naked chest and felt the soft, fullness of her breasts warned him that something about this woman might be different.

He covered her with blankets and walked away, silently chiding himself, blaming the shock of finding her by the side of the road for his coming dangerously close to reacting to her as a man instead of a doctor. After giving himself a stern talking to and putting to flight all thoughts of her other than as a patient, he undid his medical bag and removed a digital sphygmomanometer, stethoscope, thermometer and small metal dish and put them on the bed next to her.

Her blood pressure was 100 over fifty, low but within the normal range. Sliding his stethoscope under the warm towels, he could hear her heartbeat was strong and regular and there was no apparent congestion or obstruction in her lungs. This time, as his hands touched her breasts to move them aside so he could get his stethoscope underneath, he was aware of nothing but the sounds of life within her.

Before removing the thermometer from its sterile tube, he pulled on a pair of surgical gloves and took a jar of gel from his bag. He couldn't put the thermometer under her tongue; even if he could open her mouth to get it in, the risk of her biting down and shattering it was too great. In other circumstances, he could have slipped it into her armpit, but the possibility of her having hypothermia hadn't been entirely ruled out so it was imperative he get as accurate a reading as possible, and with a simple thermometer, that would be obtained rectally.

"I need to take your temperature," he told her in case she could hear. "I'm sorry if it is a little uncomfortable but I will be as quick and gentle as I can. First I need to roll you onto your side and then I'm going to take your panties down." Apart from the same incoherent mumble he'd heard before, she didn't resist as he rolled her onto her left side, positioning her bottom close to the edge of the bed and tucking her knees up so she was in something resembling the fetal position. Nor did she react as he lifted the corner of the blankets over far enough for him to be able to see, and slipped her panties down.

"Oh," he audibly gasped as her full, sumptuous globes came into view. *Crikey. That's the best-looking arse I've ever seen. For fuck's sake, Gavin. Stop it. What the hell is wrong with you?* Taking a deep breath, he walked around in a small circle castigating himself as he pushed away his unprofessional thoughts for the second time. He needed to be a clinically impersonal doctor and attend to his patient.

Taking the sterile thermometer from its case and opening the jar, he dipped the thermometer in and pulled out a blob of gel. He took some of the gel from the thermometer onto the end of his gloved right forefinger then used his left hand to hold her right cheek open while he put the gel from his forefinger on her tight entrance. "This might feel a little uncomfortable but it will be over in a minute," he said soothingly as he slipped the thermometer in. "Shh. Keep still," he added as she moaned and flinched at the invasion. He covered her but left his hand under the blanket to stroke her while he waited to remove the thermometer. He gazed at her, wondering why she wouldn't wake. So far he'd found nothing to explain it and, although he'd initially feared hypothermia, he was less worried that was the problem.

When sufficient time had elapsed, he raised the blanket and parted her cheeks again. She fidgeted, her bottom squeezing against the discomfort of the foreign object and then relaxing open. He watched fascinated, shocked by an unexpected urge to grab a cheek in each hand and push and rub them together or, even better, to bury his face in that delicious flesh.

"Hold still, little lady," he murmured. "I'm going to take it out now." Almost imperceptibly, her bottom raised a little towards him. "Good girl." She sighed as he slid the thermometer out and checked it. 35.4°C. He frowned. Not dangerously low, especially as her blood pressure was also a bit depressed, but he would be happier if it was above 36°C. Deciding to keep her as warm as possible and recheck her vital signs in an hour, he removed the now-cooled towels from her abdomen and put them back near the fire. After adding more wood to the cheerfully crackling blaze, which was already beginning to heat the shack, he took two fresh warm towels and covered her with them and tucked her in. She wriggled again, but this time it was purposeful—she was making herself more comfortable. He thought he might even have caught the merest glimmer of a contented smile as she sighed and settled.

As the fire was bringing warmth to the room, so that small reassurance that she was relaxing and feeling more comfortable despite refusing to wake up brought warmth to his heart. He put a chair beside her bed and sat down to watch over her. He had checked her as thoroughly as he could in the circumstances and his experience and intuition told him she was not physically injured and that she hadn't had an epileptic incident. She'd been cold, but he'd found her before her temperature had sunk low enough for her to develop hypothermia. She might well have been in trouble if he had not happened on her, but he had and now she was warm and safe.

His best guess at the moment, in the absence of any apparent physical trauma, was that she either had a pre-existing brain condition, or she'd had some sort of psychological episode. For tonight, he'd let her sleep and keep an eye on her temperature, pulse and blood pressure, and maybe she would wake in the morning. She looked like such an angel, sleeping peacefully. Physically she was quite big and strong, but there was a fragility about her expression and the way she had her hands up near her face that reminded him of the innocence and defencelessness of a child.

He left her long enough to make himself a steaming mug of hot black tea and fetch the supper he'd brought with him, then sat in the chair by her bed while he ate. The more he looked at her, the more waif-like she seemed, and the more he felt the need to protect her. He reached out and stroked her hair, and the almost-smile appeared again as her head moved a fraction like a kitten rubbing against the hand petting it.

"Hey," he called softly. "Do you want to wake up? I've got hot tea if you'd like a cup. And food, if you're hungry." But she nestled down further into her bedding, almost as though she'd shaken her head and hid her face.

He opened his mouth and, without realising he was going to, started slowly and quietly singing the lullaby his mother had sung.

"Hush little baby don't say a word,

Daddy's gonna buy you a mocking bird,

And if that mocking bird don't sing, Daddy's gonna buy you a diamond ring.

And if that diamond ring turns brass, Daddy's gonna buy you a looking glass…"

Chapter 3

A stirring from the bed jerked Gavin awake. The shack was warm from the fire he'd kept burning during the night, and enough sunlight was slipping in through the cracks in the curtains to enable him to see his patient, now motionless again. He stood up and stretched. The chair wasn't the most comfortable place he had ever spent a night, but at least he had slept for a few hours on and off. In between, he had taken her blood pressure and temperature twice more, and both times the readings were higher than the initial ones and within the normal range. He checked his phone. 7:15 a.m. It was definitely morning, and his mystery woman had slept all night.

She stirred again and moaned, her eyelids fluttering but not opening.

"Hey," he called softly, squatting down level with her face and trying to ignore how her unguarded beauty made his heart ache. "Hey, little lady, are you ready to wake up now?"

Her only response was a deep sigh, but she stirred again and he was pleased her movements were more pronounced than they had been the previous night. He felt she was on the verge of waking.

"My name is Gavin and I'm a doctor," he explained in case she could hear and understand. "We are in my friend's shack. I picked you up off the road last night. I don't think you are injured, but you've been sound asleep since I found you. You can wake up now. It's morning. You've slept all night, and you are quite safe. I'm going to fetch you a glass of water, and then I'll make you a cup of tea while you wake up."

Her eyelids twitched and her brow furrowed as though she was trying to understand.

Gently squeezing her hand with his left hand, he used his right one to tap and stroke her forearm. "That's a good girl. Wake up. I'll be back in a minute. I'm just going through to the kitchen." He put her hand down and walked away from the bed. "I'm leaving now but I'll keep talking to you, so you won't be alarmed if you wake and wonder where you are… So, this is Gavin talking to you from the kitchen and pouring you a glass of water... Okay, the glass is full, so here I come." Back in the bedroom, he put the glass on the bedside table. "I'll leave this here in case you wake and want a drink. I'm off to make you a cup of tea… And here I am, Gavin, talking to you from the kitchen. You don't know me but I'm a doctor. I found you on the road last night and brought you here. I'm making tea and toast." As he made breakfast and continued with his running commentary, he kept nipping to her door to check on her. She hadn't woken or touched the water, but he was heartened to see her legs stretching under the covers one time and her arm appearing from beneath another.

"Here we are then." He put a breakfast of tea and toast on the small cabinet next to her bed. "Are you waking up now?" He saw her start and then freeze. She must be awake and realising that she didn't know where she was, who he was and what was happening.

"My name is Gavin. I'm a doctor. I've brought you a mug of tea. Do you drink tea? I can get you something else if you'd prefer. There's water here, too, and toast. Do you want to sit up and have a drink?"

A tiny whisper emerged from where her face was buried in the blankets. "Am I sick? Is this a hospital?"

"No. This isn't a hospital, although I am a doctor. I've examined you and haven't found anything physically wrong with you, but you have been deeply asleep. Can you drink your tea, do you think? Shall I help you sit up a bit? You can tell me if you feel any pain anywhere."

He pulled the cushion off his chair, put it at the head of the bed, and took hold of her shoulders.

"I don't have any clothes," she said in a voice still barely audible.

"No. I'm afraid I had to take them off. You were very cold and your clothes were quite damp, except for your panties which you still have on. I hung the rest by the fire. I'll fetch them for you." He left the room briefly, returning with her clothes. "Here. They're warm and dry now."

She had pulled herself up into a half-sitting position while he'd been out of the room and was looking at the doorway.

"Oh," they gasped in unison as their eyes met for the first time. Gavin smiled tenderly, then quickly coughed and nodded in a clinical manner as she blushed and looked away. He put her clothes on the bed next to her.

"How are you feeling? Do you have any pain anywhere?"

She kicked her legs around under the covers and waved her arms about. "No. Everything seems to be okay."

"Excellent. I'm sorry about removing your clothes, but you were very cold and I had to warm you as quickly as possible. I'll turn away while you slip on your jumper. Can you manage, do you think?"

"How do I know you're actually a doctor? That you didn't drug me and kidnap me, and… and…"

Gavin pointed to his bag. "Well, there's my medical bag and the instruments I used to check your blood pressure, chest and temperature. I promise you, I really am a doctor on holiday, and I was on my way here when I found you. There was no drugging, no kidnapping and definitely no anything else. You were lying on the side of the road. Do you remember how you got there?"

She flinched and grimaced, then shook her head—hard—and looked up at him with a confident, defiant smirk. In an apparent abrupt change of disposition, she ran her tongue across her lips, leaving them wet and glistening, and smiled suggestively.

"Are you sure we didn't play doctors and nurses when we got here and that's the real reason my clothes were in the other room? Damn. I would hate to think I'd been asleep for that. How about a rerun?" Without taking her eyes off his, she lowered the covers to display her full breasts. "Did you like these?" She cupped one hand over each and squashed them in and pushed them up to form a large cleavage. "Do you think they are my best asset?"

Gavin licked his dry lips as he slumped into the chair, and crossed one ankle over his other thigh. "What I think is that you should put your jumper on rather than risk getting cold again, and then drink your tea and eat your toast before they go cold."

She pouted, but he interrupted her with a grin and a wink before she could protest.

"Doctors orders. Quick now. No arguing. See how you are after. If you're feeling up to it, you can have a hot shower and finish getting dressed. Then we'd better think about getting you home."

"Oh, all right." She picked up the jumper he'd put on the

bed next to her and smiled invitingly again. "But I think it would be much more fun if you were getting undressed." His only response was a slight raising of his eyebrows. She sighed and pulled the jumper over her head.

"I couldn't find any identification on you last night," Gavin began once she was settled and sipping her tea, "so I have no idea who you are, or what you were doing, unconscious, in the middle of nowhere at ten o'clock on a cold night. Do you remember what happened? How you got there?"

She flinched again, and a puzzled expression momentarily robbed her of her bravado, leaving her seeming much younger and more fragile.

"What is it?" he asked. "Did you remember something? Do you know who you are?"

As she had previously, she transformed in an instant, pulling herself up so she was sitting taller and straighter and looking directly at him.

"Of course I know who I am. I haven't lost my marbles. My name is… Fiona Stafford-Allen, but I prefer Fi. And you? Do you have another name apart from Doctor Delicious?"

He grinned. "Gavin. Gavin Minchin. So, Fi, do you know what day it is?"

"Yep. Unless I was asleep for longer than one night, it is Wednesday the 23rd."

Gavin nodded. "And do you know how you came to be lying on the side of the road?"

She frowned and pulled her knees up under the blankets. "Ahh, not exactly, but I think the fog is clearing. Give me a bit longer."

"Okay. How about a bit more about you, then? What else do you remember? Are you married?"

"Nope. I'm most definitely single and available, any time you want to avail." She smiled and patted the bed next to her.

He held his hand up in a gesture of refusal. "Thanks for

the offer. I'm not saying it isn't tempting, but I think I'd best not."

"Doctor patient thing? Or is there someone waiting at home for you?"

"No. I'm single too."

"Ooh, goody."

He held his hand up again. "Seriously, I think we need to talk first."

Fi clapped her hands. "First!" she repeated, but he broke in, "Nuh uh uh. We need to talk is all I was saying. The 'first' just slipped out, but I didn't mean anything by it. Now, if you think you're up to it, I want you to have a shower and get dressed. While you're in the shower, you might be able to remember more about what happened. Then we'll get you home. Someone must be wondering where you are. And it's odd you have no phone, wallet, handbag or any of the things people usually carry. I'll leave you alone to get out of bed. The bathroom is out this door and to the left. I'll put a clean towel in there, and my bathroom things: soap, shampoo, toothpaste and toothbrush. I always have an unopened toothbrush with me which you are welcome to." Knowing she was still mostly naked from the waist down, he ducked out quickly as she threw off her bedding.

While she was in the bathroom, he cleaned the ther-mometer and put it in its sterilising sleeve, replaced his instru-ments in his bag, took the mugs and plate from the bedroom into the kitchen and washed them, folded up the dry towels hanging in front of the now dying fire, and was sitting by the embers when she emerged, fully-dressed, from the bathroom.

Seeing her upright for the first time, he stood up and watched as she walked toward him, her freshly washed hair hanging over her shoulders in dark, wet, ringlet-type curls. He'd been right about her being above average height; she was tall and shapely, with broad shoulders and hips, narrow waist, large breasts, rounded belly, well-padded bottom and strong firm thighs.

But if she was Junoesque, he was Herculean: more than a head taller, at least one axe-handle broader, barrel-chested, and thighs and calves like tree-trunks. Instead of stopping, she walked up to him until her body was pressed against his and looked up. Stepping back, he took her shoulders in his hands and guided her into the chair next to his.

"I made a pot of coffee. Are you a coffee drinker? Or would you prefer another tea?"

"Coffee's fine, thanks. White. No sugar."

The galley kitchen was in one corner of the living room so he was able to continue their conversation while he made the coffee.

"How was the shower? How are you feeling? Do you have any pain? Any dizziness or anything?"

"Nope. No pain. No dizziness. I feel fine."

"Are you sure?"

"Cross my heart, Doc." She drew a large cross over her heart with her finger, earning her a raised eyebrow from Gavin. She smiled. "Hey, I'm being serious. I checked myself over in the shower. No bruises. No bumps. No sore bits. I feel great. No kidding, this is the best I've felt in ages."

"And how's your memory? Did the shower help with that?"

She screwed up her nose, squinted her eyes and looked up to her left, then sighed, relaxed her body, and leaned forwards towards him.

"Not really, but I'll tell you what I know, okay?"

He nodded.

"My name's Fiona. I've told you that. And I'm single. I work as an exotic dancer at the TwoCans Club in town. Do you know it?"

He shook his head with a chuckle. It was both an answer to her question and a comment on her information.

She snorted. "Yeah, yeah. Not the best name is it? Apt though," she added looking pointedly down at her ample chest. "But before you go turning your nose up and acting all superior, it's a job. It pays my bills."

Gavin put his hands up defensively. "I have no intention of either acting or feeling superior. It was the name of the club that made me laugh. Honest. So, you're an exotic dancer." He smiled. "And a pretty good one, I'd imagine. I reckon you would be quite the draw card."

She winked at him. "Play your cards right, Doc, and who knows? Maybe I'll treat you to a private show."

He chuckled, but his eyes narrowed and his tongue flicked out to wet his lips. "Okay. Well, we'll see. So, you're Fi. You're single, and you're a dancer at a nightclub. Do you know where you live?"

Her face clouded and she looked at her mug as she thought about his question; then she took a mouthful of coffee, looked at him uncertainly and nodded. "Yeah, I live with my mother." Her face contorted again into a puzzled frown, and her hand shook so violently as her whole body shuddered that she almost spilled hot liquid over herself. Gavin leapt forward, took the mug from her and put it on the floor, and squatted next to her.

"What? What is it?"

For a moment she stared at him blankly, her eyes wide and wet. Standing up, he took her hand and pulled her up into his arms, stroking her hair and murmuring reassuringly. "What is it, baby? Pain? Do you hurt?" He moved his head so he could see her face. Her bottom lip was trembling and a tear spilled over. He wiped it away and bent his knees so he was at her eye-level. "Tell me where it hurts."

She looked into his eyes for a moment as though seeing him for the first time, then pulled away and sat down, studying the hands she had clasped in her lap. Gavin returned to his own chair and, when she looked across at him again, her tough exterior had returned.

"Nah, I'm fine. There is something I'm not remembering. It's sort of right here, if you know what I mean." Closing her eyes, she put her hands, palms toward her, in front of her face and jiggled them in frustration, then opened her eyes, dropped her hands back into her lap and exhaled loudly. "But I can't quite grasp it, like when you wake up and know you've dreamed something but it's like a wraith that slides away from you if you try and grab hold of it." She relaxed her shoulders and scratched her head. "It'll come to me. It's not important."

"It's not important knowing what happened to you last night?"

"Nah. I'm fine. Not hurt. I'll remember soon and it will turn out to be nothing. I probably did something stupid. But, if I did, I must've got away with it. Let me try again and I'll see if I can remember anything else."

She closed her eyes and Gavin waited patiently. "Hey, Doc?" she said at last, opening her eyes and looking at him. He nodded. One side of her mouth turned up slightly as she spoke in a singsong voice. "What I do know is that I was on my way to the beach, and now here I am, somewhere near the beach I take it. And here you are. And we're both single. And alone. And I've always had a thing for doctors. And orders. And, I know I've only just met you, but I get the feeling you like giving orders. Am I right? You being a doctor and all."

Gavin's eyes narrowed again, and his bottom tooth rubbed against his canine as he gazed at her without speaking. "You might want to be careful, little lady," he said gruffly at last. "I don't only give orders. I enforce them. Strictly. Now unless you're sure you can finish anything you start, I suggest we pack up and I'll drive you home."

Without taking her eyes from his, she uncurled herself from

her chair, padded over, sat down straddling his legs, and hooked her arms around his neck.

"I'm a great finisher, Doc." She brushed her lips against his, and when he didn't respond, pulled back to see him looking at her with the hint of an amused grin. She bent down and pressed her lips harder against his, forcing her tongue into his mouth. For a brief moment, he continued to resist; then, with a throaty growl, he clutched her to him, one arm around her waist and the other sliding underneath her hair and grasping a handful against the back of her head. He pushed her tongue out of the way with his own and clashed his teeth against hers.

"Are you sure you aren't going to regret this?" he asked in a low voice, pushing her from his lap as he stood up while still keeping his hand in her hair and his arm around her waist so she stayed close against his body.

"What about you, Doc? Not worried about the patient-doctor thing, then?"

"You're not my patient. I did no more than administer the same first aid anyone could have. My only concern is that you remember enough about who you are to know that you are okay with this."

"Oh, I do. I remember plenty. And I know I get off on big strong men, with big hard hands. And belts even more so. Mix that up with a game of doctors and nurses and I'm all in. Come on, Doc, fulfil my fantasy."

Without releasing his hold on her head, Gavin raised the hand that had been around her waist and gently stroked her cheek. "Okay, baby, I can't deny you are incredibly sexy and my cock is begging to be let loose. But I don't take my pleasure with women without being sure it is completely reciprocal and no one is going to get hurt."

Fi smiled flirtatiously. "I don't mind a little hurt, Doc." She stopped and froze. "No punching or shit like that, though," she added quickly, shivering violently and turning her face away.

"What?" Gavin barked, his protective instinct instantly aroused by the cold shadow he'd seen pass across her eyes. "Has some bastard hurt you like that before?"

Using the hand he had on her cheek, he guided her head gently back so she had to look at him. She shrugged. "Maybe. But that was a while ago."

"Hitting women is inexcusable," he said, his eyes flashing. "I've never hit a woman and never will."

"What, not even a little consensual spanking of naughty girls?" The fleeting troubled vulnerability had vanished in an instant, replaced once more with enough chutzpah to quell his misgivings and send hot blood gushing to his groin.

"Well, maybe that. How did you guess?"

"I can smell it. Besides, I don't believe you could be letting these go to waste." She took hold of his hand and lifted it up to study it. "Mmm, look how big it is." She licked her lips and then raised it to her mouth and slowly drew her tongue along the underside of his middle finger while looking brazenly into his eyes. "That's a hand that could have a girl squirming over your lap in no time."

He cleared his throat. "You could be going the right way to find out. Do you make a habit of encouraging strangers to spank you?" he asked, apparently casually as he stroked some wayward strands of hair from her face.

She grinned. "I have a healthy sex life with a bit of kink on the side, if that's what you mean. Does that bother you?"

He chuckled and shook his head. "Not at all. I see no difference between women indulging in and enjoying as much sex as they want and men doing it."

"How come you're not married?"

Her sudden and unexpected question took him by surprise. "No good reason. I didn't allow myself much time for distractions while I was studying. When I qualified, I met someone. We were together for a long while; then came to the amicable conclusion that we didn't want to grow old together, so that was that. What about you, now that you've opened that can of worms?"

Fi laughed, and then screwed up her face as she looked for the answer. She sucked in her breath as her eyes popped wide open before her face contorted in pain.

"What is it?" Gavin pulled her to him, holding her head against his chest as he stroked her hair. "Is it that bloke who beat you, baby? I'd like to get my hands on that jerk and give him a taste of his own medicine. I'll never let anything bad happen to you again. Ever. I promise."

She looked up at him in surprise and, as though he'd been as startled by what he'd said as she had, he released her and took a step away, his face troubled. He ran his hand back and forth over his short, cropped hair, then scratched at the beard stubble on his face.

"What is it about you?" he asked quietly, almost to himself. "We need to get out of here before it's too late. I'm going to pack the car."

"No." Fi grabbed hold of him as he walked away.

He smiled tenderly and a little sadly. "Yes," he said in a voice that told her his mind was made up. "Come on. We can talk in the car."

"Oh. Okay." Her face crumpled in disappointment, then she dropped her head as a small smile played about her lips. "I need to go to the bathroom first," she said quickly, leaving him to watch her walk away, a look of bemusement on his face, not with her but with himself. He shook his head and went to the kitchen to clear away and pack the few things he'd had a chance to unpack.

Chapter 4

"Doctor!"

Hearing Fi in distress, Gavin rushed to the bedroom to find her lying on the bed in her bra and panties.

"What happened? What's wrong?"

"I don't know. I came over hot and faint. I had to take my clothes off and lie down before I fell down."

He put his hand on her forehead. "You do feel a bit warm." He fetched his bag from the adjoining room, put it on the chair next to the bed, opened it and took out the thermometer. "Open your mouth." She shook her head, clamped her jaw and pointed to her bottom. "Are you saying I should take it rectally?"

She put her hands protectively in front of her face and spoke through clenched teeth. "I'm afraid of putting glass in my mouth."

"Is that true?"

"Yes. Honest."

"Okay, take your panties down?"

She moved her hands from her face. "You do it."

He sighed and regarded her suspiciously. "You'd better not be messing with me."

"Or?"

Taking hold of her panties, he pulled them down and over one foot. "Or I'll tan your backside. Lie on your side."

As she got herself into position, he put on gloves, and put some gel on his finger and then on the thermometer. "Ready?"

As he parted her cheeks and applied the gel, she sucked a breath in through her teeth as a tremor ran through her body.

"Relax." She exhaled, but her muscles tightened automatically in response to the intrusion as he inserted the thermometer. Satisfied it was in, he removed his hand so her cheeks could close. "Okay?" She nodded, her eyelids down and her face half hidden. "Good. I'll take your blood pressure again while we're waiting." He wrapped the cuff around her upper arm and turned on the digital reader. The machine hummed as it inflated the cuff and then slowly released it. "Blood pressure is fine." He removed the cuff. "Okay, keep still while I get the thermometer."

Watching him, she reached behind with one hand to pull her cheeks apart and raised her bottom up. He pursed his lips and withdrew the thermometer.

"Perfectly normal." He pulled off his gloves and packed away his instruments.

"Are you sure? Maybe you didn't leave it in long enough. Maybe you should try again." She pushed her bottom towards him.

"Or maybe I should make good on my promise to warm your bottom."

Rolling her from the side of the bed, he sat down, swivelled her around and across his lap and started spanking her conveniently bare bottom hard and fast. "That was a complete put on. You pretended to feel unwell to get me to play doctor with you, didn't you?"

"Ow. No, I…"

But he spanked her harder. "Don't lie to me."

She squealed and kicked her feet in the air. "Oh, ow. All right. All right. I did." Her body contorted, arching and writhing in its effort to avoid the flurry of stinging blows raining down on both cheeks. "I'm sorry. I won't do it again. Ow. Please stop."

He did stop, but instead of letting her up, tipped her further forward, and with one arm across her back holding her in place, he reached over and picked up the jar of gel, opened it and dipped his finger in. "Spread your legs." She obeyed. He parted her cheeks and pressed his finger against the hidden entrance, hearing her sigh and feeling all resistance drain from her as he pushed his finger in then slowly withdrew it before pressing it back in.

"You like having your little rose penetrated, don't you, baby?"

His breathing was ragged and he could feel beads of perspiration forming on his upper lip. One trickled down the side of his face from his temple as he watched his finger moving in and out and her hips rising and falling in concert. His whole face flushed and damp with perspiration and his breathing hard and fast, he withdrew his finger all the way, lifted her off his lap so she was standing, stood up himself, pulled her into the bathroom and lowered the toilet seat cover.

"Bend over."

With her hands resting on the cover, she watched him over her shoulder as he lathered his hands with soap and water and then rubbed the soapy water between her bottom cheeks, slipping his finger in and out as he scrubbed her.

"Don't move. Naughty girls don't only get their mouths washed out with soap."

She moaned and shuddered but stayed in place despite the soap stinging. After rinsing off the soapy water, he patted her bottom dry and led her back to the bed.

"Now then." Holding her eyes with his, he piled two pillows at the end of the bed, undid his belt, slid it out of his jeans, folded it in half, and snapped the halves together so it made a loud crack. "Lay yourself across the pillows."

Her cheeks were flushed and her lips red and dry as she silently lay across the pillows adjusting her position so her bottom was perched as high and round as she could make it. Folding her arms in front of her, she rested her head sideways on them so she could watch him in action. An electric bolt shot through her as their eyes met and she saw the white-hot desire in his.

"Give it to me," she mouthed.

His lips parted as he sucked his breath in, raised his belt and brought it down with a crack across her waiting bottom. She squealed, her shoulders arching up. *Crack!* He lashed the belt across her again leaving a second pink streak. This time she uttered only a small grunt.

"You were a naughty girl, making me worried, weren't you?"

"Umph," she grunted again, suppressing a mischievous giggle as the belt made a third mark across her cheeks.

"And who spanks naughty girls?" He laid the belt across her candy-striped bottom once more then paused, waiting for an answer. She opened her eyes wide in a caricature of innocence.

"You?"

Smack! Down came the belt. She cried out and one foot twitched up.

"Their daddies. That's who, isn't it?" *Crack!*

"Ow. Yes."

"Say 'Yes, Daddy. I'm sorry, Daddy'." *Crack!*

"Ow. Ow. Yes, Daddy. I'm sorry, Daddy."

"Are you sorry you tricked me?" *Crack!* Each lash was now falling across a previous one, and her whole upper body snapped up in response to the latest stinging stripe.

"Ow. Oh. Ow. Please. Yes, Daddy. I'm sorry."

"Good." He tossed the belt onto the floor. "Stand up and take off your bra." His eyes devoured her as she released her heavy, dark-tipped breasts and stood completely naked before him. She flinched as though to shield herself. "Stand up straight. You are so goddamn beautiful you make my eyes hurt." He moved closer and cupped one of her breasts, allowing it to overflow, then trailed his finger down to the small, dark bush between her legs.

"You don't shave?"

She shook her head. "I used to." The flash of pain crossed her face again and she looked away. "He made me. He did it. It hurt."

Gavin smiled tenderly, and gently raised her face with a finger under her chin. "Poor baby. Well, Daddy thinks you are absolutely perfect exactly as you are and is not going to make you do anything you don't want to. Okay?"

She nodded and shyly looked away.

"What a mystery you are." He stroked her hair and fondled her breast. "I can't decide if you are a sad little girl or a dangerous wild woman." He chuckled and, as she tilted her head back up to him, his expression changed to one of deadly seriousness. "But unless you have any objection, I plan on being around long enough to solve that mystery. I have a hunch I might be exactly the man you need to look after the little girl and control the wild woman. What do you think?"

A deep sigh rippled through her and she surrendered her body, leaning limply against him as he bent his head and gently took possession of her mouth. When the kiss ended, he drew back far enough to look into her eyes. "I'm going to take that as meaning you have no objection. Part little girl, part wild woman—and part witch, I think, who has cast a spell on me, and I'm not letting you go. I'm going to stake my claim and make you mine right now."

He fetched a small plastic packet from his medical bag and tossed it on the bed next to him as he stood in front of her again.

Without taking his eyes from hers, he pulled off his jumper and T-shirt in one motion watching her intently as he revealed his muscular arms and massive, broad chest with its covering of coarse black hair thinning across his sculpted abdomen before disappearing below his jeans. He remained motionless until her eyes finished roaming over him and returned to his face. The tension in her body was visible in the roundness of her eyes, the flush on her drawn cheeks and the tautness of the tendons in her neck. He lowered his head slightly and looked at her from under his eyebrows as his lips curled in a hungry leer and the tip of his tongue protruded. Slowly, he undid his jeans. Fi's eyes followed as he pushed them down his long, hard, strong legs until they were over his feet and on the floor, then travelled back up to the only piece of clothing left covering his body.

His fingers hooked into the sides of the waistband of his snug boxer briefs, and he paused as she stared at the bulge and the thick hard bar pointing straight up, it's glistening tip peeking over the top. She looked up at his face and his grin became broader and more predatory as he pushed the briefs down and his erection burst forth.

"You sure you want what Daddy's got to give you?" he asked as he retrieved the packet from the bed, opened it with his teeth, removed the condom and slid it over his shaft.

She paused and for the briefest moment looked like a scared rabbit caught in a car's headlights. Then, with a defiant toss of her long hair, she cupped her breasts and pushed them towards him as she gyrated her hips and then ran her hands down her belly and between her thighs, inserting one finger into her wetness, withdrawing it and sliding it down her tongue.

"I want it all." She looked directly into his eyes.

With a deep, throaty growl he took hold of her, one hand once again under her hair and clasping the back of her head and the other behind her, between her legs, cupping her cheeks and pulling her hard against him. His mouth opened and covered hers, his tongue exploring her lips and gums before plunging in between her teeth. She responded as ardently, her arms locking behind his head and her body straining against his.

Without taking his mouth from hers, he walked her backwards until her legs were against the bed, then pushed her away from him and down onto her back. Kneeling on the floor at the end of the bed, he took hold of her feet and pulled her to him, pushing her knees up, parting her legs and hanging them over his shoulders so he could bury his face in the swollen wetness between them, his long tongue simulating the work his cock would soon be doing. As he withdrew his tongue and used the tip to seek out and tease her mysterious, secret button, she writhed and moaned, clutching the bed with her hands and tossing her head from side to side. He grinned as far as he was able with his mouth full, thinking how, if he didn't know better, he might think he was torturing her.

It was a torment, though, as the pleasure became so intense she could hardly breathe and her body felt it was about to explode. Showing her no mercy, he relentlessly licked, sucked and worried her until, when death seemed the only possible escape, the battle was lost. All fight flowed from her, swept aside by a rising swell of exquisite tingling warmth. Her eyes popped open, staring sightless at the ceiling as the wave carried her to shore, dumping her at the last moment so she cried out again and again, and then lay gasping for breath.

Before she had time to recover or realise what he was about to do, he had flipped her onto her belly, her legs dangling down off the bed, opened her cheeks and started licking between them. She gasped in shock, trying to pull away, but he took hold of her legs and pushed them up so her feet were off the floor and his arms were wrapped around them holding them tight so she couldn't move.

Her mind groped for context as she felt the tip of his tongue push its way in. Had this happened to her before? She couldn't remember. If it had, had she welcomed it? Had she enjoyed it? Was she horrified and revolted? How should she react? She froze, her muscles tightening to stop him penetrating further while she tried to think, but his gently probing tongue robbed her of the ability to resist. With a deep sigh of submission and acceptance, she relaxed and opened to him as the sensation he was creating permeated her brain. It wasn't driving her mad like the other had done before releasing her in waves of pleasure. It was infiltrating her with a peace so powerful it robbed her of her will, completely taking over her mind, and gently absorbing and dissolving her power.

She lay motionless, paralysed by the unexpectedly soft, warm, voluptuous sensation flowing through her body, melting her muscles and transporting her beyond conscious awareness. She heard herself moan as though she was hearing someone else, and from that distant place she felt him lean up and slip his finger in to take the place of his tongue and then slide up the bed planting tender kisses all over her on the way.

Reaching her ear, he whispered, "Roll over," removing his finger as she complied. As he moved over her, he paused at the entrance to the core of her being so he could look into her eyes as he claimed her for his own.

She put her arms around his neck, and their hearts soared in unison as their eyes locked and they each read the message the other held for them. Groaning with the heavy weight of undreamed emotion, he buried his face against her neck and squeezed his hips forward to enter her. She moaned at the intense pressure as he forced her wide, straining to reach the innermost part of her, and tightened her hold on him as though her life depended upon it.

So completely moulded were they that not even a breath could have found its way between them, and for a long moment, they clung motionlessly to each other as though they'd found the only truly safe place in the world and neither wanted to break the spell.

Slowly their awareness receded back onto the carnal plane, and in seeming unison their bodies came back into focus. Gavin sucked on Fi's neck and then nipped it gently as he began slowly to ride her, gentle strokes that quickly became a passionate fury. Matching his arousal, her breathing increased and she gripped his buttocks and bucked beneath him, pulling him hard into her with each thrust as he licked and sucked her ear and muttered endearments.

"This is it, baby. You're mine now. No one will ever hurt you again. I promise. If any man does so much as try, I'll cut his balls off."

Tears of joy welled in her eyes as he pushed her harder and faster. Her breathing became more and more laboured until she stopped suddenly, her body rigid, and cried aloud as the tension crested, wrecking her again and again. The pulsing contractions of her internal muscles sent Gavin into his own frenzy. He thrust harder, faster, deeper and she helped him on, pushing her hips up to meet him until his body convulsed and he moaned in blissful agony, his face contorted in ecstatic agony and his body rocking to the rhythm of the pumping of his seed.

Chapter 5

The day was all but over by the time their bodies were finally sated and exhausted. They had made love and dozed for hours until they could do it no longer and were lying wrapped in each other's arms in the afterglow.

"I think I might be getting hungry," Gavin said, nuzzling her hair. "How about you, baby?"

She nodded her head, and stroked and kissed his chest. "I think I am a little, but I don't know if I want to get up. It feels safe here—like nothing can touch us."

"Nothing is going to touch us even if we get out of bed and have something to eat. I promise."

He moved to get up, but she clutched at him. "No, please."

Gavin tilted her head so he could see her face, concern written in his own expression.

"Whatever it is, I'm going to be there to protect you and look after you. This is not a drive-by. I don't deny it's sudden and completely unexpected but, unless and until you say different, you're mine. I didn't just say that before; I meant it, and I was also deadly serious about taking care of you from now on. Are you afraid of the guy that beat you? I told you, if he comes near you I'll cut his balls off. And I have the instruments to do it, don't forget." He smiled as though he was joking.

She smiled back, a tiny ghost of a smile behind which the lurking terror that occasionally almost surfaced was still faintly visible.

Gavin stroked her face with one finger, a look of deep tenderness and worry etched into his eyes.

"I think it's time we got you home. I probably should have taken you this morning."

"I'm glad you didn't." Fi pressed her face against him again. "I don't want to leave."

"But you still haven't remembered how you got onto the road last night, have you?"

She shook her head and screwed up her face. "I think I've remembered a bit more, but it doesn't make sense. I feel like Elly was there, but she can't have been." Her voice broke. "She's dead."

"Who's Elly?"

"She was my best friend. She died. She had a little boy who died and then she killed herself." An almighty sob racked her body and left her trembling. Gavin held her as tight as he could against him until she regained control.

"It's okay, baby. Daddy's here now. How old was her little boy?" His voice was hard and tight.

"Seven."

"What was his name?" His body trembled and he had to fight to get the words out.

"Joey." She looked up at him and saw the muscles in his cheeks hard as rock as he ground his teeth. "Why? What's wrong?"

He managed a small smile as he shook his head and pulled her closer so she laid her head back on his chest, and he stroked her hair while he breathed deeply until he had calmed himself.

"I work in the Emergency Department at Metro Dora," he began quietly, as though telling her a bedtime story. "Death is part of my job, but I hate it. Maybe slightly less so with old folk who welcome it, but even then there's always someone who suffers. And the truth is, few people want to die whenever it happens to them. There's always some other pleasure that can be wrought from life: another sunrise, another bird song, another child to welcome into the world, another piece of history to witness.

"So, much as I have to accept death is a part of life, it always hurts. I'd managed to cope, until..." His voice broke and he stopped. Fi looked up, concerned, but he took a deep breath and continued still staring over her head. "A little boy came in. Seven. Same age as your friend's boy. That's why I asked his name, but this kid's name was Tyler." His voice rose in angry despair. "He'd been brutally assaulted, and was on his way to the children's hospital when the bloody ambulance broke down pretty much right outside Metro Dora. All our ambulances were out, so they had to bring him in while they waited for one. We did our best. I tried to stabilise him, even though I knew he wasn't going to make it. Hell, he wouldn't have made it to Rafe's anyway." He paused and rubbed his eyes with his free hand as if to rub away the picture in his mind. "He managed to raise his hand a tiny bit in a silent plea for me to hold it as his life slipped away."

Two heart-wrenching dry sobs convulsed his body and this time it was Fi who cradled him in an attempt to share his grief. "I couldn't shake the memory of that kid's face or the anger boiling inside me at both my complete inability to do anything for Tyler, or to the arsehole who attacked him. If I'd got my hands on him... I'm not normally a violent man—but I might have made an exception in his case.

"Anyway, it must have been interfering with my work because my boss suggested I take some time off. I've been on the road, and on the run, for the last two weeks. I'm due back Monday, but was wondering whether I should forget that and turn this into an endless road trip instead. Now I guess I have to take you back anyway, so maybe that's a sign, eh?"

She looked up at him again. "Do you believe in signs?"

"Believe is a pretty strong word. I only *believe* things I know to be absolutely true, and there are precious few of those in this strange world in which we live." He shrugged and ran his free hand over his head. "But sometimes I think we can get some small comfort from imagining a bigger picture. Does that make sense?" She nodded. "And sometimes it gives us an excuse to not take responsibility for decisions we make." He chuckled. "See? There I was wondering if I should go back and face up to what happened and try and work through it and find some peace—a long and tough journey—or if I should keep driving and hope to outrun it. Now, it's like the decision has been taken out of my hands, only it's not about *me* anymore; it's about you. I have to get you home so we can put the pieces of *your* puzzle together. For a start, it's weird you have no phone or bag. I think we should get back as soon as possible."

"No," she cried out, her body curling up. "No. I don't want to. I'm scared."

"Oh, baby," he said gently, kissing her over and over. "There's no need to be scared. I'm here to protect you, and I'm not going to let anything bad happen to you. We need to find out what's going on and fix it. It might well be post-traumatic stress from what happened to your friend. It sounds like a terrible and painful experience, and I know all about not wanting to face deep wounds. But we have to, and I know we can work through it together." He twisted himself again so he was looking into her eyes. "You have a big, strong daddy now who's going to take care of you. Okay, baby?"

She rubbed her face on his chest, then tilted her head just

enough so she could see him with one eye. "Okay. Does that include spanking me?"

He nuzzled her hair and winked at her. "If you deserve it."

"Or want it?"

"Absolutely, naughty girl," he said with a chuckle. "So, we're agreed?"

She nodded, and they sealed their pact with a long, slow, kiss filled with infinite tenderness and a new and growing love.

A little over an hour later, they'd showered and dressed, eaten, packed, tidied up the shack, and were on the way to where he'd found her.

"I don't think it was too much further. We must be getting close," Gavin said when they'd been driving about fifteen minutes. "I think it was less than thirty minutes from the shack. I'll see if I can recognise any landmarks, and you see if you can recognise or remember something,"

Fi gasped, grabbed her head with both hands, clenched her eyes tight and tipped her head forward with a moan.

"What is it?" Gavin's face was contorted with worry. "Have you remembered something?"

Fi dropped her trembling hands. Her face was drawn and ashen as if she'd seen the ghost of someone she loved.

"Sort of. I keep getting flashes of being on the beach looking at something in the water and feeling sort of happy, I think. Then I was cold, so cold I could barely move, and running, or trying to run, to the road. I think I was looking for someone. That's all." She stopped and stared at him, then blurted out, "No wait, I do remember something else. When I got to the road, it was a T-junction and I was glad because I thought I would have more chance of a car coming because there were two roads."

"Oh. Yeah. That's right. I remember seeing it. It should be only a few minutes away if my calculations are right."

The sun was well along its arc to the horizon and the sky turning orange and pink when Gavin pulled up at the T-junction and parked. Together they walked across the road.

"There's a track here, so I reckon this is where you came up from the beach. Let's go down and see if we can find anything."

Taking her hand tightly in his, Gavin led her along the track and onto the beach. It was deserted, and they found no sign that any human had been there other than one set of footprints leading up from below the tide line.

"These must be yours leading to the road," Gavin said pointing to them. "Looks as though any others have been washed away. I'll have a quick scout in the dunes, but unless I spot anything else, we may as well head off."

She didn't answer, just stood, motionless, her eyes fixed on a point across the waves. A look of horror started silently creeping over her face and, as she opened her mouth to let out a silent scream, she crumpled onto the sand, clutching her head and slapping it as though to drive away her thoughts.

Gavin was on his knees beside her in an instant. "My God, Fi. What is it? Tell me. Breathe, baby. Long, slow breaths. Come on."

She gulped some air, then managed three deep breaths. Her body relaxed slightly. She shook her head again, as she did each time she was trying to capture the memory that remained beyond her reach.

"What?" Gavin pressed her. "Anything coming back?"

"No words or pictures, just a feeling that something really terrible has happened. Like being in the worst ever horror movie but only being able to hear the music without knowing what's going on." Her face was contorted with the agony of grief, and the frustration of not being able to remember what had caused such heart-shattering despair. "It's about Elly, though. I'm sure it has something to do with her. Maybe this is where she killed herself?" She looked up at him, suddenly hopeful that the veil of darkness shrouding her memory might be lifting.

"It didn't happen recently, though, did it? Her suicide, I mean."

She shook her head furiously. "No. No. No. It was six months ago. I remember going to her funeral. It was the saddest I've ever been in my whole life, and I still miss her like crazy. But this place could have something to do with her death, couldn't it?"

He nodded seriously and stroked her desperate face. "It could do, baby. It might be too painful for you to remember the details, but perhaps being here is triggering the shock again, and when the emotions are too strong for you to bear, your mind blanks out the memory. I don't think we can achieve anything else here. We should get you home. Being in a safe and familiar environment might allow the memories you're suppressing to come back. Give me your hand. I shan't let go of you."

As he spoke in a voice that demanded to be obeyed, he stood up and held out his hand so he could help her to her feet, then wrapped his arm around her shivering shoulders and supported her as she made her way, mutely and unsteadily, back to the car. Once she was strapped into the passenger seat, still shaking so violently her teeth were clacking together, he fetched some pills from his medical bag and got into the driver's seat.

"Take this," he said, offering her one with a bottle of water. "It will help you relax. You might even be able to doze."

At first she didn't move other than to look up at him with wide, staring eyes.

"Take it," he ordered again, and this time she obeyed, as a

robot might obey a verbal command. "Good girl. I've got your address in my GPS, so you can lean back, close your eyes and concentrate on your breathing. Don't think about anything else. I'll put on some music."

Gavin started the engine, turned up the heater and as the first sublime notes of Eric Satie's *"Gymnopedie"* floated through the car, he pulled out onto the road. Once they were moving, he reached over and took her cold hand in his, squeezing it tenderly. Gradually he felt the tension leaving her as her hand warmed and the music and sedative lulled her into a peaceful sleep. Carefully releasing her hand, he smiled sadly and tenderly at her, his heart filling to bursting. With the fear and pain temporarily wiped from her face, she slept with the peacefulness and innocence of a child. Whatever it was that had robbed her of that, he would find it and fix it. He touched her face as he made her that silent vow, then put both hands on the steering wheel as he sped them forward to face their demons head on.

It was dark when he pulled into the driveway at the address Fi had given him. She'd slept most of the way, and her breathing was deep and even. Switching off the engine, he ran his finger down her cheek and spoke softly. "You're home, baby." When she didn't stir, he got out of the car and closed the door carefully behind him checking he hadn't woken her, then walked to the front door of the neat but unremarkable, suburban brick house. The steel, security screen-door was locked, and it made a tinny, rattling sound when he knocked on it.

A few moments later, the wooden door behind it opened inward as the porch light above him sprang to life, bathing him in illumination.

"Yes?" A middle-aged woman was looking warily at him.

"Hello. Mrs Stafford-Allen? My name is Dr. Gavin Minchin. I have your daughter, Fiona, with me..." Gavin began, but was interrupted by the sound of a car door and footsteps coming up the path. "I'm afraid she's suffering from shock and has lost her memory," he explained quickly in a low voice. "Please don't be alarmed if she seems vague. It's probably best just to agree with her, for the moment, whatever she says rather than risk disturbing her further. Maybe tomorrow…" He stopped speaking as Fi staggered drunkenly onto the porch, and he put his arm around her to ensure she didn't fall.

"Oh, sweetheart," the older woman said, her face immediately full of concern. She unlocked the security door and opened it. "Are you all right? Come in, you poor love. Where have you been? What's happened?"

Gavin stood back to allow Fi to enter first. "Hi, Mum. This is Gavin. He's a doctor," she said groggily, stumbling in and giving the other woman a quick hug before disappearing into the rest of the house, steadying herself against the walls as she went.

The colour drained from the woman's face and she turned wide-eyed to Gavin before hurrying off. Gavin closed and locked the front doors and by the time he joined the women in the lounge room, Fi was apparently asleep on the couch. The woman standing over her, looked at him.

"What's going on? What's wrong with her? Is she hurt?"

"No, she doesn't seem to have been physically injured. I think she's had some sort of shock and temporarily lost some of her memory. I found her on the side of the road last night when I was driving up the coast but she can't remember how she got there. I was hoping you might know, or that being home and feeling safe might give her the strength to remember."

"Was she alone? Did she tell you she is Fiona? What else did she tell you?"

Gavin noticed Mrs Stafford-Allen had turned quite pale as she bombarded him with questions.

"She told me her name is Fiona Stafford-Allen, that she's a dancer at the TwoCans Club, that she's not married and lives here with you. She also told me that her best friend's son died a few months ago and then the friend, Elly, killed herself. She was obviously traumatised by their deaths, and I think they might be linked to her current amnesia."

"Oh. oh." The woman collapsed into a chair clearly distressed by what he'd said. "No. That's not right."

Gavin squinted at her. "What's not right?" He stopped as Fi stirred restlessly, her face contorted and she moaned. "Look, I think it would be best if we put her to bed and I give her another sedative. Then we can talk. I'll explain what I know and maybe you can shed some light on what's going on and we'll see how she is in the morning. Is that okay? There's no need to worry. Honestly. Physically, she's fine, and she seems to be slowly getting her memory back. Another good night's sleep might be all she needs to recover it all. If you show me her bedroom, I'll carry her in."

"Her bedroom…?" The woman stared at him as though she'd never heard the words before, then seemed to collect herself, stood up and rubbed the palms of both hands down the sides of her dress. "This way."

Gavin scooped the barely-conscious Fi into his arms, and carried her to the bedroom. He waited while the bedclothes were turned back, then lay her on the bed and walked to the door. "I'll go out to the car and get the sedatives."

Mrs Stafford-Allen followed him as far as the bedroom door, ready to close it behind him. "Okay. You go and do that. I'll get her into bed. Knock when you get back if the door is shut."

Gavin smiled to himself as he went outside. He admired and respected a mother wanting to protect her daughter's modesty, and wasn't about to let on how the two of them had spent most of the day.

He dawdled around outside for a few minutes and by the time he returned to the bedroom, the door was open and Fiona was tucked up in bed.

"Daddy," she murmured as he approached the bed.

"It's Gavin, Fi. Dr. Minchin. Could you fetch me a glass of water, please?" he asked Mrs Stafford-Allen, as he opened the bottle of sedatives and tipped one into his hand. When the water arrived, he held Fi's head up and helped her take the pill.

"Daddy," she murmured again.

"Hush now, precious." He pushed some wayward hair from her face. "You're home, safe and in your own bed. Sleep now."

Within a few moments, the sedative had combined with the events of the past 24 hours and she was fast asleep.

"We can leave her now, I think," Gavin said to the woman hovering nearby. "I don't think she'll wake till morning."

"Would you like a tea or coffee while we chat?"

"I'd love a cup of tea," Gavin replied with a weary smile, suddenly exhausted himself. "White, no sugar. I'll be out in a minute."

Alone with the sleeping woman, Gavin knelt by the bed and stroked her cheek and hair. Once again, with all the cares of her waking life lifted, her face had that childlike innocent beauty that so touched his heart. Softly, so softly even she would have had difficulty hearing had she been awake, he sung:

Hush little baby, just sleep tight,
Daddy's gonna love you all day and night,

And if that love is not enough
Daddy's gonna love you twice as much

. . .

Satisfied she was fast asleep, he tiptoed out of her room, leaving the door ajar in case she woke, and went into the lounge room.

Mrs Stafford-Allen was waiting and held out a mug of tea as he joined her.

"Thank you, Mrs Staff..." he began, but she put up her hand to stop him.

"Two things, Doctor Minchin," she said in a clipped voice. "First, my name's Moira. Mrs Stafford-Allen is way too big a mouthful. And the second thing is," she paused, "that's not Fiona."

Chapter 6

Gavin started visibly, almost spilling his tea. "What did you say?"

"The lovely girl you brought in, the one asleep in the bed through there? That's not Fiona. It's Elly." Tears pooled in her eyes, spilled over and rolled down her plump, pink cheeks. "My beautiful, beautiful daughter, Fiona, died six months ago."

"Elly?" Gavin put his cup down on an occasional table, and paced around the room, vigorously rubbing his hand over his head. "That's Elly? And it was Fiona who died?"

Moira fetched a handful of tissues from a box on an oak sideboard, wiped her eyes and blew her nose.

"Yes. Fiona had terminal pancreatic cancer. She… she… suicided when the pain got too bad."

"I'm so sorry, Mrs… Moira. And your grandson?"

A heartbroken sob racked Moira's stout body and she collapsed backwards into a chair. "Fiona was my only child, and she didn't have any children. She planned to, but then…" She shook her head, noiseless sobs shaking her body. "I don't have a grandson, Dr. Minchin."

"Please call me Gavin." Sitting on the end of the couch next to her chair, he reached over and rubbed her shoulder. "It's a terrible, terrible thing for a mother to bury her child." He paused. "I wonder why Elly made up the story about Fiona having a son called Joey."

Moira's head jerked up. "Joey is her son, and the closest thing I'll ever have to a grandson of my own. He's such a sweet little thing. He doesn't deserve that nasty Les Sutton for a father."

"Who?"

"Les Sutton. Elly's husband, God love her."

Gavin jumped to his feet, his head reeling from this second huge shock, and stared at her. "Her husband? She told me she wasn't married. She isn't wearing a ring."

"She's separated. She talked about divorce, but Les told her he'd sue for sole custody of Joey if she tried it. He's wealthy, well, he says he is, and can afford a good lawyer, and she doesn't have any money. He's a dreadful bully and she's always been such a timid little thing, so he has no trouble putting the fear of God into her."

Gavin paced again, wringing his hands, and shaking and rubbing his head as he tried to sort out all this new and disturbing information.

"So, have I got this right, then? The girl I brought here is Elly... Elly?"

"Elly McInnes. Well, she was McInnes before she married. She's Elly Sutton now."

"Right. So she's Elly and she's married to, but separated from, Les Sutton, and they have a seven-year-old son called Joey?"

Moira nodded.

"And Fiona, was your daughter, and she passed away after discovering she was terminally ill? And they were best friends?"

Moira nodded again. Gavin said nothing as he stopped and

ran through all the information in his mind again, then raised his head. "Which one is… was the dancer?"

"Fiona. Les would never let Elly do anything like that and she would be way too shy anyway."

"Shy?" The perplexed frown creased Gavin's face again as he remembered his day with Fi, or rather, Elly. Then Moira's comment about Les registered. "You say Elly's husband is a bully? Do you think he ever hurt her physically? She hinted she'd suffered physical abuse, but now I'm not sure if she was talking about herself or Fiona. It looks like something has triggered dissociative fugue; she seems to have lost her own recent memory and taken on the persona of Fiona."

Moira winced. "Oh my God. Is that serious? Is she going to be all right? Is she hurt?"

Gavin patted her arm. "She doesn't seem to have any physical injuries at all, but she can't remember what happened the night before last. If her memory doesn't return, we can run some tests. And there are treatments. Cases like hers are pretty rare, but the amnesia doesn't usually last long, and it is possible for the memory to return suddenly and completely with the right stimulus."

"What do you think could have caused it?"

"I don't know, but maybe it has something to do with her husband and his abusing her. She meant herself, did she, when she said that? She wasn't talking about Fiona?"

"She would have been talking about herself there, although it does look like she's mixed up their lives." Her face grew angry and she clenched her fists. "I know Les is cruel and I always suspected he might have hit her but she would never admit it to me. I think she was too afraid."

"Could she have meant Fiona?"

"No. I have absolutely no reason to think my daughter had a boyfriend who was bullying her. I'd like to have seen one try." She smiled. "It's a jumble, isn't it, dear? And your tea has gone cold. How about I make us both a fresh one, and I'll tell you what I know? I might be able to fill in some gaps." She picked up the cups and started for the kitchen, turning before she disappeared through the door. "And you can tell me how you came to arrive at my door tonight with Elly who apparently thinks she's Fiona. And where's Joey?"

Left on his own, Gavin paced to and fro, chewing his lip. As blindsided as he'd initially been by the discovery of the true identity of the woman he'd brought here, he could see that it might at least answer one mystery: her apparent changes in personality. With the small amount of information Moira had given him so far, he guessed the hurt, scared and shy persona was Elly being herself, while the sexy and confident one was her mimicking her friend, Fiona.

"So, I might answer your question first," Gavin said when he and Moira were seated again with mugs of fresh tea in their hands. He gave her a quick rundown of how he'd found Elly on the side of the road and taken her to the shack, and what she'd been able to tell him. He omitted anything that might hint at how they'd spent the day, but Moira's expression softened as his story went on. When he finished, she patted his knee.

"You've already grown fond of her, haven't you? I'm not surprised. She's a lovely girl. I just hope you're a better man than the jerk she married. You seem like you are. She deserves a good man."

"You're quite perceptive, I see." He chuckled at his compliment's ambiguity. "About my feelings, I mean. But I also hope I'm a better man than her husband is by all accounts." He shrugged. "I know I've barely known her twenty-four hours, but I would be lying if I said I wasn't strangely drawn to her. She seems so fragile and vulnerable, like she needs protecting. I wasn't sure what from before, but I'm beginning to think it has a lot to do with her husband. It would help if you could tell me more about her. I might be able to sort out which bits of what she's told me go with her and which with Fiona. I'm still a bit muddled."

Moira nodded. "Elly enrolled at Fiona's school when they were both fifteen, and they became best friends immediately. Elly didn't have a father; he apparently disappeared shortly after she was born. Her mother, Jenny, was sweet, too, like Elly. I think she desperately wanted to marry, but always seemed to find creeps who used her, abused her and then left her for someone else. She was busy with men and, unfortunately, drugs, so Elly spent as much time as she could here. Fiona's dad, Jeff, was still alive then, and Elly adopted him as her surrogate father. He passed nearly three years ago. We were all devastated."

"I'm so sorry." Gavin's face expressed his sincere sympathy.

Moira smiled a sad smile. "Thank you, dear. At least I have the memory of a happy marriage. We had thirty-one wonderful years together. It's so much more than Jenny had."

"What happened to Elly's mother?"

"She died of a drug and alcohol overdose when Elly was nineteen." She squinted up at her eyebrows as she did the mental calculation. "Nine years ago now, I guess. They said it was accidental." She drank some tea, then put her mug on the small table next to her and straightened her skirt.

Gavin shook his head in disbelief. "Poor little Elly. She's had some burdens to endure. No wonder she seems a wee bit fractured." He grinned. "When she's not being Fiona, that is."

Moira smiled. "Is she really acting like Fiona? The girls were chalk and cheese. Fiona was always brash and full of confidence. She could stand up for herself, and didn't let anyone push her around, but she had a kind heart. Elly brought out all her natural protective and mothering instincts. I think the only time Elly felt safe was when she was with Fiona. After they left school, they went travelling, then rented a flat together when they came back. Elly got a job in an office, but Fiona never wanted a nine-to-five job. She was a photographer." She pointed proudly to three framed black and white photographs hanging on the walls. "Those are hers."

Gavin went to each in turn, looking closely and nodding appreciatively while Moira continued. "She did wedding photos to earn extra money, but she wanted to be recognised as an artist. She'd already been in three exhibitions, two with other people and one solo. She was beginning to make a real name for herself." A sob broke her voice and she stopped.

"I'm not surprised," Gavin said standing in front of a photograph of an empty bench by a river. "They are superb. I particularly like this one. It's so poignant, both welcoming and yet sadly empty at the same time." He paused trying to articulate the emotions it had evoked. "It makes me think of that phrase *the passing parade.* The river flows by, and people come and sit on the bench and look at it, and then they move on and are gone forever, like the individual drops in the river. The bench just sits there, day after day, a mute sentinel, but someday it will be gone too." His voice tailed off as he realised he'd been thinking out loud and his insensitive words must have been painful. He sat back down next to Moira and saw the tears running down her cheeks. "Oh, I'm so sorry..."

Moira leaned across from her chair and patted his arm. "Don't be." She took a tissue she'd tucked up her sleeve and mopped her tears. "They're tears of happiness as well as sadness. Yes, my wonderful daughter is now but one of the drops in the river that has flowed past and into the distance. But, thank you. She would have been so pleased you understood what she was saying. It's called *Magic Shadow Shapes.* Do you know "*The Rubaiyat*" by Omar Khayyam? It's a quote from that. *We are a row of magic shadow-shapes that come and go...* Something like that."

"I don't know it, I'm afraid, but I'll definitely look it up.

Thanks for the tip. Fiona sounds like a special person. I'm not surprised you and Elly loved her so much."

Moira smiled. "Thank *you*, dear. Yes, she was special. Especially to her mum."

"I'd love to see more of her work some time, if I may. I don't suppose you want to part with any now, considering... but if you do find one you would be prepared to let go, I would love to buy one to hang at my place. I promise it will get a good home."

Moira seemed at a loss, so Gavin prompted her to return to her story.

"You were saying about Elly... She had no father, her mother died when she was nineteen, so she only had you and Jeff and Fiona."

"More or less. Yes. She was working in a small office, so she knew the people there, but I don't think she made any what you would call friends."

"Boyfriends? She is very attractive." Gavin tried to make it sound like a dispassionate observation, but Moira's crinkle-eyed glance told him she'd seen through him.

"She is. And she's a genuinely nice person. Sweet. And trusting. I think that's partly why Les was so easily able to manipulate her. I don't actually remember her mentioning a man until she met Les."

"Fiona introduced them?"

"Not really introduced. Fiona was working in a bar to fund her photography—behind the bar then, not dancing. Elly used to meet her there sometimes at the end of Fi's shift and they'd go home together. I gather Les was a regular and he started talking to her and buying her drinks. Fiona tried to convince her to stay away from him, but he was good-looking in a flashy way, older and a smooth talker."

"He's older than her?"

"About ten years, I think. So he must have been thirty when

they met. He had his own fancy car and house and gold jewellery." Moira's face expressed disgust at the picture her words evoked. "Flash as a rat with a gold tooth, as Jeff used to say." Gavin chuckled at the description. "He probably looked like security to Elly who'd had so little in her life. Maybe nothing would have come of it, but then Fiona met Hank and started spending a lot of time with him, and Jenny died so Elly probably felt quite alone. It was only about six months after Jenny died she married Les, and Joey was born not much more than year later. She might have been happy with Les initially, but it didn't take long for her to be afraid of him. Mind you, she never said anything bad about him, but she looked more and more miserable and we knew she was afraid for Joey. Then Fiona and Hank broke up, and Fiona and I managed to convince Elly to leave him.

"Les was furious, and when Elly said she wanted a divorce, he threatened to take Joey away from her, so they're still married. He insists on having Joey sometimes, but I'm fairly sure he only does it to upset Elly. He's been trying to force her to go back to him." Moira paused again, and her eyes filled with tears. Gavin reached out his hand to her but she brushed it away, wiped her eyes and sniffed loudly before blowing her nose in the tissue she was still clutching. She tried to speak, but no words came. She paused, took a deep breath and tried again.

"It started as soon as he found out Fiona was sick, and got worse after she died. He's even threatened to harm Joey and told Elly it will be her fault if he does. Poor Elly has been living a nightmare, so if she's finally flipped, I'm not surprised." Her voice broke again and she started sobbing. "Why couldn't it have been that arsehole who got cancer and died? Why did it have to be my beautiful girl?"

Gavin leaned over and rested his hand on her arm, waiting for her sobbing to subside before he spoke again. "There's no answer to that question, is there? Life can be monumentally unfair. Can I get you a glass of water or anything?" She nodded and he went to fetch one, making sure he took his time, pretending not to be able to find his way around the kitchen so Moira could have a moment to herself.

When he returned, she was sitting up, her eyes red and swollen, but she managed the glimmer of a smile as he handed her the glass. She sipped the water and then patted the hand he'd laid back on her arm as he sat down in his spot at the end of the couch.

"Did neither Elly nor Fiona have any siblings?"

Moira shook her head. "Elly has an older brother, but he'd disappeared long before she arrived here and we never worked out what the story was there. Elly doesn't seem to know. Jeff and I only had the one child. We didn't think we were even going to have that, and then Fiona popped up out of the blue when I'd decided I was too old to get pregnant. It was the happiest time of our life, Jeff and I."

Her voice broke and she buried her head in her hands. Gavin waited, sensing there was nothing he could say and his silence would be more comforting. At last she looked up, the expression of grief in her eyes one with which he was all too familiar. "This probably sounds terrible, but as much as I loved Fiona, I wish now she'd never been born. The pain of losing her is too great. Most days I don't think I will survive it, but unfortunately I do."

Still Gavin said nothing, offering her only silent, understanding companionship as she wrestled with her grief. When she'd calmed herself again and was searching for the thread of her story, he prompted her.

"And is that where things are at the moment with Elly and her husband?" She nodded. He leaned back, closed his eyes, chewed his lip and thought for a moment in silence. "So she doesn't live here?"

"No, she's at the flat she shared with Fiona before she married Les. Fiona kept it when Elly moved out, and Elly moved back when she left Les."

Gavin nodded. "Can you think of any reason she would have been at that remote beach on her own at night? Or how she might have got there? Does she have a car? Well, even if she does, we didn't see one. Do you think Joey is with Les?"

"All I know is, she popped in for a cuppa on Saturday. She was distressed because Les had insisted on having Joey for a week of the school holidays and was taking him on a fishing trip. Elly hates it when Joey is alone with Les. She doesn't trust him." She shook her head as though to shake out the bad feelings she got from thinking about Les. "Anyway, Elly said she was getting Joey back on Tuesday—yesterday, so he should be with her."

Tiny hairs all over Gavin's body flew to attention.

"Having said that," Moira added, "it wouldn't be the first time he mucked her around and kept Joey longer just to taunt her. It's hard not to worry, though."

Forcing himself to relax, he leaned over and patted Moira's arm again. "I'm sure Elly will be able to explain tomorrow. She seems to be regaining her memory, so I'm hoping that, by morning, she will have remembered what happened. Meantime, I'm sorry I gave you a shock turning up like that. I had no idea."

Moira put her hand on top of his and laughed. "I'm not sure which one of us got the bigger shock. You should have seen your face when I told you she isn't my daughter and her name's not Fiona." Gavin grinned and snorted and they smiled at each other, but Moira's smile quickly faded. "She will be all right, though, won't she? Her and Joey are all I have now."

Gavin managed a small reassuring nod. "I think she'll be fine. We'll know more tomorrow." He stood up. "But right now, I'm more concerned about you. I've kept you talking for ages.

I'm very grateful, but I'm sure you must be ready for bed, so I'm going to get out of your hair. I know Elly will be safe, but if you'll allow me, I'd like to sleep in my car in the drive so I'm here when she wakes. I have no idea how disoriented she is going to be."

"I'll allow no such thing," Moira told him firmly, then smiled at his surprised expression. "You will sleep on the couch. I'll fetch you a couple of blankets and show you where the bathroom is. Have you eaten? I had an early dinner but if you've been driving, you wouldn't have had time to eat."

Gavin looked a little embarrassed. "No, please. Don't worry about me. I'm fine."

"So you haven't eaten. I'll make you a sandwich, and then leave you to it."

A short time later, sitting on the couch in his boxer briefs and T-shirt eating his sandwich, a pillow and blankets next to him, Gavin sifted carefully through the information Moira had given him.

The tragedy of Fiona's death had devastated both Moira and Elly, and Elly was married to a man who had physically beaten her at least once, and who was emotionally abusing and physically threatening her in a terror campaign to force her to return to him. No wonder her mental state was so delicate, especially taking into account her unhappy childhood.

But there were still three important questions: Where was Joey? How had Elly come to be lying on the road? What had tipped her over the edge emotionally making her forget she was Elly and want to be Fiona instead?

Finishing his sandwich and laying back along the couch, the pillow under his head and the blankets covering him, Gavin hoped the morning would bring some answers. As concerned as he was about Elly, and as much as he had truthfully vowed to do whatever he could to take care of her and protect her, it was the face of a little boy that was haunting him as he tried to sleep. He hadn't been able to help Tyler, and although that pain might lessen with time, he could never again be the person he was before he'd felt it. Now another little boy in trouble had crossed his path, and he desperately wanted, needed, to help him. He had to find Joey.

Chapter 7

It took Gavin a moment to remember where he was when he opened his eyes the next morning. He could hear the kettle boiling, which was odd because he lived alone, and he usually slept in his bed, not on a couch. Then it all came back in a rush. His mind immediately went to the bedroom and his beautiful Elly asleep in there—if she *was* still asleep. Jumping up, he pulled on his jeans and went barefoot into the kitchen to find Moira, in a dressing gown and with her greying curls still tousled from bed, making coffee. She looked up as he appeared in the doorway, her eyes even more puffy than they'd been the previous night, but she managed a small smile.

"Good morning, Gavin. I looked in on Elly; she's still asleep. Would you like some coffee? Or tea? I like coffee in the morning and tea at night. Coffee keeps me awake, and I'll take all the sleep I can get."

"The coffee smells so good, I'd love a cup if I may, please. Same as tea. White, no sugar."

"Of course you may." Moira took another mug from the cupboard, poured him a piping hot, freshly brewed coffee, added some milk and handed it to him. They each took a sip from their mug.

"The couch wasn't too uncomfortable, I hope."

"No. Not at all; it was absolutely fine. In fact, I slept better than I thought I would—nothing to do with the couch." He smiled.

Moira chuckled softly. "No. It's fine. I'm not going to take offence. I slept too. Eventually." She sighed deeply. "Grief is exhausting."

"It is. Have you got anything to help you sleep? I can get something for you if you need it."

"Thanks, love. I'm okay for the moment. My GP prescribed me some when… when… at the time, but I try not to use them. As much as I love being unconscious, I hate feeling groggy the next day. And sometimes in that state, not really either asleep or awake, it's hard to control my thoughts." She stared into her cup, then looked up and spoke briskly. "What's the plan for the day then?"

Gavin grimaced to show his uncertainty. "I guess first thing is to see how Elly is when she wakes. If her memory has returned, we can make a plan once we know what we're dealing with. If she still thinks she's Fiona and it was Elly who died, we'll have to find some way to jog her back to reality."

"I was thinking, while I was laying there awake in the wee hours of the morning… What about if you visit Fiona's grave? It has a headstone with her name on it."

Gavin's face, tilted down and clouded with thought, brightened. He looked at Moira from under raised eyebrows and nodded, sucking air through one corner of his closed lips. "That's an excellent idea. It's definitely worth a try, but I'm still hoping it won't be necessary."

"The thing I kept thinking about last night was why does she think Joey is dead? Even if she had decided she was Fiona and it was Elly who'd died, why is she saying Joey is dead too?"

A chilly invisible hand squeezed Gavin's heart. It was the question he'd deliberately not been allowing himself to ask, translating it instead into an urgent need to 'find Joey'. But Moira was right, and he had to face the fact that knowing her son had died somehow could well have been the reason for the collapse of Elly's emotional reality. If she believed she was Fiona, she only had to suffer the death of her friend's son, not the agony of her own child's death.

He shook his head sadly. "I honestly don't know, Moira. She obviously doesn't want to be herself right now, and if she acknowledges Joey is alive and needs caring for, it would make it harder for her to hide in the shell of Fiona's persona. Making up the story about him dying could be a convenient way to relieve herself of her parental responsibility, but we shan't know for sure until she recovers her memory or we speak to Joey's father. We'll see who she thinks she is when she wakes and decide what to do from there, I think."

"I'll know by what she calls me. I knew something was wrong last night as soon as she called me mum. She never does that. Jenny was Mum, so she started calling me Moy, and Joey calls me Nanna Moy, bless his cotton socks."

Her voice stopped abruptly and their heads turned to the door as they heard footsteps approaching. A still groggy Elly appeared wearing the slightly-too-small pyjamas Moira had dressed her in the night before. Gavin's eyes, which had lit up at the sight of her beautiful sleepy face, roamed down over her breasts bulging above and between the buttons of her top, and then over the curves of her hips and thighs accentuated by the tight material stretched across them. He discreetly cleared his throat, looked away and wriggled as his jeans became suddenly too tight in front.

Seemingly unaware of the scrutiny, Elly collapsed into a chair at the kitchen table, rubbed her eyes, forced a yawn and then contemplated Gavin and Moira who were both staring at her, holding their breaths, waiting to see who she was.

"Hey, Mum," she said, and their hearts sank in unison.

Moira flicked a glance at Gavin, whose features had set in a grim mask. Imperceptibly, he shrugged.

"Hi, Fi," he said, giving Moira the lead for which she'd silently asked.

"Good morning, sweetie," she said with a tight, fake smile. "How are you feeling this morning? Would you like a cup of coffee?"

"Yes, please. Thanks, Mum." Despite her calling Moira 'Mum', she seemed hesitant and diffident, and Gavin suspected he was seeing Elly, even more so when she turned to him with a look of shy puzzlement. "How come you're here? How did I get here?"

He joined her at the table, sitting in the adjacent straight-backed wooden chair and took her hand. She didn't pull it away, but stared down at their clasped hands as though she couldn't quite comprehend what it was she was looking at. She glanced up at him as he spoke.

"I brought you last night, but it was late when we got here, and I was pretty tired, so Moira kindly let me sleep on her couch. Do you remember coming in last night and going to bed? You fell asleep in the car on the way home."

Elly screwed up her face as she tried to find anything in her brain apart from a messy fog. Moira put a mug of coffee in front of her, and she picked it up with her free hand and sipped it, then rested it on the table without taking her fingers from around the handle and shook her head.

"No," she said at last. "I must have been asleep. I vaguely remember driving home, I think, and leaving that place I was at. Was that your place?"

Gavin nodded. "Yes, it was my friend's shack by the beach,

remember? I found you on the side of the road the night before and took you to the shack. We spent yesterday there while… while you recovered, and then came home. We stopped at the beach on the way. At the T-junction where I found you."

Her head was bowed for a moment as she listened so he couldn't see her expression, but when he'd finished and she raised her head, the timorousness of Elly had been replaced with the confidence of Fiona. She gave him a small wink to acknowledge she remembered perfectly well what had taken place in the shack.

"Yeah, I remember now. Well, up to stopping at the beach and walking down to the sea. We were looking for something, weren't we? I can't remember if we found it. Or the rest of the drive home. I guess I must have crashed."

She stood up and went to Moira, wrapping her in a big hug. "Hey, Mum. How are you? You look tired. Are you okay?"

"I'm fine, dear," Moira replied as evenly as she could in a slightly shaky voice. "Now, why don't you go and get dressed and I'll make us all some breakfast. You'll stay for breakfast, won't you, Doctor Minchin?"

"I'd love to if you're offering. Thanks."

"Okay, well you two go and finish dressing and I'll cook us something to eat."

Once in the lounge room and out of sight of the kitchen, Elly swung around to Gavin, put her arms around his neck and stood up on her toes to kiss him passionately on the mouth. He looped his arms around her waist and returned her kiss, albeit slightly less vigorously.

As the kiss ended, Elly put her hand down to cup the front of his jeans and arched an eyebrow at him. "I have no idea what all that stuff about remembering was, Doc, but I do remember how we spent yesterday, down to the last dirty, delicious detail. I bet you didn't tell Mum about that, eh?" She clicked the side of her mouth twice and winked at him. He took her intrusive hand in his, removed it from his groin and raised it to his lips.

"No," he agreed with a lopsided grin. "I most certainly did not."

She pressed her hips against his and suggestively moved them in and out and around, but he took a step back and looked at her sternly. "Behave yourself. Do as your... Moira said and go and get dressed, or you'll get a painful reminder of how my belt feels across your bare arse. We'll have breakfast, and then there's somewhere I want to take you, unless you've got anything else planned for the day."

He saw her thought processes pause as she had to consider her life beyond the present minute. It was clearly too confusing. Her expression cleared and she smiled up at him.

"Nope, I can't think of a thing I have to do. Where are we going?"

"It's a surprise. Now go and get ready. No need to dress up. Casual is fine."

It didn't take long for Gavin to slip on his jumper, and socks and shoes. He took the bathroom bag he'd fetched in from the car the previous evening into the bathroom, and cleaned his teeth, washed his face and ran a wet hand over his head. Ready, with his things together on the couch, he went back into the kitchen to wait for Elly whom he'd heard go into the bathroom after he'd vacated it. She joined them a few minutes later wearing a long-sleeved, red T-shirt that was at least two sizes too small and struggling to pull up the zip on a pair of blue denim jeans.

"Looks like I'm going to have to go on a diet. I can't believe all my clothes are so tight."

"Why don't you wear the clothes you had on yesterday,

love?" Moira suggested. "I folded them up and put them on the chair. They still look quite clean and presentable."

"Okay," Elly agreed, returning to her bedroom still muttering about diets and being fat.

"You've kept Fiona's things?" Gavin asked.

Moira nodded. "I know I should get rid of them, but I can't."

Gavin shook his head. "There's no 'should' when it comes to grieving. You can make it harder on yourself if you do things before you're ready because you think you should. One day you'll know it's time and it's what you want to do. Or it will never be time, and that's okay too."

"Thank you." She shot him a grateful smile as she put the plates on the table, put a piece of toast on each one and scooped the poached eggs from the pan. "It's odd, isn't it? Elly must have looked into a mirror by now, but she still thinks she's Fiona."

"The mind is a mysterious thing," he agreed.

When Elly rejoined them, she was wearing her own clothes and had brushed her hair. She pushed it back out of the way, and Gavin and Moira exchanged a quick glance. Fiona had short-cropped hair, and yet Elly could still believe she was her dead friend while pushing her own long curls behind her shoulder.

"Mysterious is right," Moira murmured.

Conversation around the table was difficult. Moira was finding it impossible to address Elly as her lost daughter; Gavin still knew so little about either girl it was hard for him to know what to say, and his own recent trauma at the hospital made it difficult for him to talk about his work; and Elly was clearly having problems, slipping between personas without any conscious awareness of attendant memory. In the end, they talked about the weather, what a lovely morning it was and how it might rain later; how good the eggs and coffee were;

and how lovely the garden, visible through the kitchen window, looked.

As the meal went on, Moira found it more and more distressing having to pretend her daughter was at the table, and the sigh she released when they finally laid their knives and forks on their plates and drank the last of their coffee was one of relief. She jumped up and collected the plates together.

"Leave this to me to clear up. I know you have something important to do, Gavin. Why don't you two get on with that? Come for lunch afterwards, if you like, and let me know how you got on."

Elly looked questioningly at the other two, but they pretended not to notice. Gavin took his cue and rose to his feet. "Okay. We'll see how it goes, and thanks for the lunch invite. I'll give you a call and let you know what's happening if we aren't going to make it back."

"Yes, please," she said. "I'll give you my number."

"I'll get my things," Elly said, standing up and walking toward the door. "I've got Mum's number, Gavin," she called back over her shoulder.

"Okay," he replied, not taking his eyes from Moira's as he slipped his phone from his pocket. With Moira's number added to his contacts, and quick directions to Fiona's grave in Fellstone Field, the city's biggest cemetery, he folded the blankets and put the pillows on top, and was waiting by the couch when Elly reappeared looking perplexed.

"I can't find my bag or phone or anything. I didn't leave them in your car all night, did I?"

"No, honey. You didn't have anything with you when I picked you up. Remember? That's why we stopped at the beach on the way back here—to see if they were there."

"Oh, okay." Elly still looked confused but shrugged it off and joined him at the front door.

"See you later, Mum." She hugged Moira who was seeing them off.

"See you later, love." Moira returned the hug while looking over Elly's shoulder and soundlessly mouthing *good luck* to Gavin.

He nodded understanding and reassurance. "Thanks for the couch and breakfast, Moira. I'll be in touch soon."

Chapter 8

"So, doc, where are we going?" Elly said brightly as she fastened her seat belt. "To your place for a bit more of what we had yesterday, I'm hoping." She winked at him. "This seat *belt* is giving me ideas, if you catch my drift."

He chuckled and patted her thigh as he started the car and began reversing out of the drive. "As tempting as that is, we have other things to do first. Maybe later."

Elly pouted at him. "Hmmph. What things?"

"I want to visit a friend. And maybe we can get some ideas about where you left your bag and phone and how you came to be on the side of the road, hey? Think of it as a quest. What do you say?"

"I wouldn't mind getting my phone back. And bag." She frowned. "I don't know about the rest. Is it even important now? I'm perfectly all right. What does it matter how I got there? I'm sure I'll remember sometime and it's bound to be something stupid I'll be mortified about."

"I'm sure you're right," Gavin said. "Let's not worry about that for now. We can focus on finding your phone, but I need to drop in and see someone first."

"Well, that sounds very mysterious. Are you going to say any more?"

"Nope."

Gavin turned the radio on to keep them distracted for the twenty-five-minute drive to the cemetery. As they got closer, he watched Elly to see her reaction. At first there was nothing—she was humming along to a song, playing with her fingernails and looking out the window. As they neared the entrance to the cemetery, though, he saw her tense, her movements became jerkier, and her voice started to break so she had to stop singing. He pulled into the car park and she turned to him with a frown.

"Why are we here?" She sounded breathless, as though her heart were racing. Gavin placed his hand over hers and squeezed.

"I need to visit someone special. Do you mind? It's a lovely walk through the gardens anyway. Come on."

Hesitantly, she got out of the car and let him take her hand. He didn't want to frighten her, so took a circuitous route to their final destination, feeling her relax as he took a different path to the one that would lead them directly to Fiona's grave.

"You look sad," he said. "Is your friend here? The one who died?" He felt her begin to tremble.

"Yes."

"Would you like to visit her while we're here? I know how much she meant to you."

Elly turned to him and he could see her eyes welling and her bottom lip trembling. He put his arm protectively around her shoulders and held her against him as he guided her down the path that led to Fiona's grave. He could feel her getting heavier and having more and more difficulty moving her feet. Then she stopped and pointed to a headstone a short way in front of them. He kept hold of her.

"There." Her voice was so quiet he barely heard her. "Can we go now?"

"No." His voice was soft but determined. "Come on. I want to see what the headstone says."

For a moment, she looked about wildly, alternating between glaring at him and trying to run away. His heart was pounding. He had no idea if this would work, but he had to try. Gripping her even more tightly, he urged her forward.

"Come on, *Elly*. I'd like to pay my respects to Fiona."

"No, no, no," Elly began to wail as they reached Fiona's resting place.

"*Fiona Stafford-Allen*," he read without looking at Elly. "*Beloved only child of Jeff and Moira*." He turned to Elly who was staring at the headstone, her face as white as though she were staring at Fiona's actual ghost. "Even after her death, you still need your beautiful friend to protect you, don't you, my darling, Elly?" he said. She stared up at him with huge, wet, stricken eyes. "But Fiona doesn't have to protect you anymore. That's my job now." He paused and when he spoke again, his voice was louder and firmer, as he looked directly into her eyes. "I want to say 'thank you, Fiona' for taking care of Elly. You are a good and true friend, but you can go back to your rest now. I promise I will take over and look after and protect Elly for the rest of her life." His voice fell again as he stopped talking to Fiona and spoke to Elly. "What do you say, Elly? Can you trust me and let Fi go? I'm here for you. I won't let anyone hurt you."

As he was speaking, he saw all the confusion, fear and torment flash across Elly's face as she wrestled with her delusion and the underlying truth she was avoiding. Her mouth slowly opened wide in an expression of horror as the cocky confidence of Fiona receded and Elly was unable any longer to hide from herself. A low eerie moan was dragged up from the centre of her being as she collapsed onto the ground and started ripping out handfuls of grass. Gavin dropped to his knees next to her and caught her to him, holding her so tight she couldn't move.

"Fi's dead. She's dead. Dead. Dead," Elly repeated over and over.

"I know, baby, but you're not alone. I'm here. I'm with you. I'm here." With one last look of terror, she collapsed on him sobbing uncontrollably. "Oh, baby, baby, baby," he crooned, not trying to stop her. Fiona's job was finished; she'd returned to her grave, and he knew it was Elly, and only Elly, in his arms. His face was contorted with his own distress. He hadn't cried, or released his grief and anger over Tyler before now, but he felt as though some of it was somehow pouring into Elly and she was crying for him too. They were moulded together by their suffering, unaware of anything beyond themselves and each other, lost in their own bubble of tragedy.

By the time Elly's sobs were subsiding, Gavin's legs had gone to sleep and his back was aching, but he didn't move. He waited patiently, knowing Elly needed time, stroking her hair until at last she lay still.

"Hi, Elly," he murmured. "Would you like to get up now?" Her face was still buried in his lap and he couldn't see her, but her head moved the tiniest bit and he took it as assent. "Come on, then. Here, I have a nice clean handkerchief. Would you like to wipe your eyes?" He managed to retrieve the hanky from his pocket without disturbing them too much and handed it to her. It disappeared under her hair and her head bobbed as she wiped her face, and he heard her sniffle and blow her nose, then sniffle again. Sensing she wasn't going to be able to find the impetus to move on her own, he pushed her up far enough that he could extricate himself and stand up on numb legs. She stayed kneeling with her head bowed.

"My legs have gone to sleep," he said with a chuckle. "I

need to see if I can get to that bench and sit down for a moment or I might fall down. Can you give me a hand?"

He held out his hand and felt a surge of relief when she reached up and took it. He helped her up but she still wouldn't raise her head to look at him. Together they stumbled the couple of metres to the bench, Gavin reaching it as his legs buckled under him. He sat with a thud, and Elly plonked herself next to him.

"Arrrgh." He waved his legs around to get the blood flowing as quickly as possible and the painful business over with. Hearing his mournful cry, Elly looked up at him, and it was as though she were seeing him for the first time and he her, but also as though they knew each other intimately and had a profound and unbreakable connection.

"Arrrgh," he complained again, but this time less intensely as he shook both his legs and chuckled. "Don't look so worried. They're nearly back to normal. Gawd, I hate that, don't you?"

She smiled and nodded, her big brown eyes still staring at him as though she was afraid he'd disappear if she looked away even for a second. As the pain in his legs receded, their eyes met and were held with such an intense magnetic force they couldn't tear them apart.

"Oh, Elly," Gavin murmured at last, taking her by the shoulders and pulling her toward him so he could press his lips to hers in a slow sweet kiss of recognition, like lovers who've been parted for an age and are finally reunited. When the kiss ended, he took her hands in his. "Do you feel okay?" She nodded. "Do you know who you are?"

"Elly McInnes." She looked surprised by the question.

"Do you know who I am?" He noted she'd used her maiden name but didn't comment.

"Gavin Minchin." She blushed. "Doctor Gavin Minchin."

Gavin hid a small grin. "You remember being at the shack with me yesterday?"

She nodded, her blush deepening. "Some of it," she said in a soft voice. "I think there are some blank spots." She pulled one of her hands away and pressed it to her head.

"Do you remember being at the beach on Tuesday night?"

"No. My head hurts. I can't think."

He gently squeezed the hand he was still holding as his thumb caressed it. "Never mind. Why don't you tell me about Fiona? Moira told me how you met her in school when you moved here with your mother, and how she took you under her wing."

Elly nodded. "She was the best friend I could have ever had."

"She sounds like she was a special person."

"She was the most special person in the world, clever and creative and strong and... everything I wished I could be." She paused, and looked down at her shoe as she swung her leg under the bench. "Sometimes I tried to copy her."

Gavin nodded. He'd seen her do it. "In what way?"

Elly gave a long sigh as she sought the words to do justice to her friend. "She was so... so... so vibrant. So alive. So fearless." She paused and gave a little self-deprecating snort. "I was such a timid mouse, scared of my own shadow, but when I was with Fi, I felt bold. I watched her prowl through life, taking what she wanted, but also stopping to help others, often stepping up but never backing down. She wanted to be a photographer, so she bought a camera and had some business cards printed and... that was it. She was a photographer. I would never have the courage to do something like that.

"And she was so exotically beautiful: long almond eyes, and cheek bones so high and sharp they looked like they could cut you. She kept her hair in a short pixie cut that accentuated her long neck, and willowy, graceful body. And she had this way of walking that was more like swaying. I felt like a dunderklumpen next to her."

Gavin leaned over and nuzzled her hair with a chuckle. "Prettiest dunderklumpen I've ever seen."

"I certainly didn't feel like that. Fi never meant to keep me in her shadow, but if I was with her, men never noticed me. They couldn't take their eyes off her. She could have any man she wanted. She'd flick her fingers at whichever one she chose and he'd come running. And she loved sex. I think men could sense that and it excited them. She'd tell me about all the things she did. At first I was shocked, but she made it sound so exciting and thrilling. I wanted to try doing them too."

"And did you?"

Her head suddenly swung around and she stared at him. "Oh no."

"What? Have you remembered something?"

"Les."

"Your husband?"

She leapt up. "I have to go. I was supposed to meet him."

She ran off down the path and Gavin jumped up to give chase.

"Elly. Wait. Slow down. Wherever you have to be, I'll take you."

"I'm late, though," she called over her shoulder. "I'm late. He'll kill me. He'll kill me. He'll kill me."

Catching up close enough to grab her hand, Gavin pulled her to a stop, and bobbed his face as she tried to look away so she couldn't avoid his eyes. "Listen to me, Elly. No one is going to hurt you. No one. Least of all Les. Now where do you have to meet him?"

She didn't answer immediately, then her eyes opened wide and she blanched. "At the beach. I was supposed to meet him at the beach on Tuesday night to pick up Joey. Oh my God, Joey!" Her face crumpled. "I was supposed to pick him up. Where is he? Where is he?"

Gavin took hold of her shoulders so she couldn't run away.

"If you were supposed to collect Joey on Tuesday and you didn't show, my guess is he's still with Les who's probably been trying to contact you, but you haven't had your phone. Can you remember where you left it?"

"In my car." She sounded certain.

"And can you remember where your car is?"

"Yes." Her happy smile faded and she looked at him, her brow furrowed again in confusion. "It's at the beach. I went there. I did go to where I was supposed to, and... and... and..." She screwed her eyes shut and spoke slowly. "I remember getting out of my car and walking along the beach. And then I vaguely remember running up the track to the road. I needed to get to the road, but I can't remember why or where my car was then." She stopped and opened her eyes. "And then I remember... Oh." She blushed, and started shaking as she turned away from him.

Realising she might feel shocked by what she remembered of their sexual encounter if it had been out of character for her, he interrupted. "But we didn't find your car at the beach. And you didn't have any keys with you."

"No." She scrunched her nose and pursed her lips, then her face cleared as the memory returned. "I know. I parked in the car park and walked quite a way up the beach, so my car wasn't where you found me. It's back further. In a car park. I think I left the keys in it. But how will I get it now? What if it's been stolen? And my phone's in it too. What if Les' has been trying to call? I have to call him. I have to get Joey. Les said he'd bring him to me there, but he didn't."

Gavin pulled out his phone and handed it to her. "Call Les. Do you know his number?" But she'd already snatched it out of his hand as he unlocked it for her and was tapping out a number. She held it up to her ear and paced as she waited for an answer.

"Les. Where are you? Where's Joey? I went to the beach. I

did. I promise. But you weren't there. I don't have my phone. Where's Joey? I need to get Joey. Call me. Or leave a message." She ended the call and handed the phone to Gavin.

"We should go and find your phone and fetch your car. Will you be okay to drive it back on your own, or should we see if we can get someone to come with us?"

"I'll be fine. Promise. I can follow you."

"Are you sure?"

Elly tried to walk away but Gavin was still holding her hand. "Yes. I'm sure. Honest. I just want to find Joey. I have to get him back. I hate him being with Les."

"Right. Then let's go find him." With a new sense of purpose, they hurried back to Gavin's car, Gavin calling Moira on the way to let her know they wouldn't be coming for lunch.

Chapter 9

"You okay?" Gavin asked, taking his eyes off the road for a moment to glance at Elly. She'd become increasingly quiet as they neared their destination, and he'd noticed she was starting to fidget and her hands, balled into tight fists, were shaking.

She nodded but her teeth were clenched.

"Breathe," he said.

"What?"

"I can see you're hardly breathing. Take some deep breaths in through your nose and out through your mouth and try and relax. Like this." He demonstrated and nodded for her to copy him. After a few breaths, he saw her hands were clenched a little less tightly.

"We'll be there soon. Close your eyes and focus on the music. Try not to think. We'll find your phone and you can contact Les and arrange to fetch Joey. Okay? I'll tell you when we get to North Coast Highway so you can watch out for where you parked your car."

She nodded, rested her head back against the seat and

closed her eyes, but the worried expression on her face remained.

As the car approached the T-junction where they needed to turn right, Elly felt the car slow and sprang up.

"It's twenty-five kilometres from here, and there's a wooden sign with *Covington* painted on it in red. I remember. That's where the track to the car park is."

Gavin looked at the odometer. "The last two digits are thirteen now, so they should be thirty-eight when we get there."

Even though it was going to take nearly fifteen minutes for them to reach the sign, she didn't take her eyes off the side of the road ahead. "How far?" she asked.

"We've only come four kilometres," Gavin replied with a tender smile, "so twenty more yet. Do you remember driving here?"

"Vaguely." She screwed her face up. "I remember looking out for the painted sign, and I remember looking in the back of the car. There was something on the seat. I can't remember what, but I remember seeing it in the rear-view mirror."

"So long as it wasn't your dog, I guess." He grinned to show he wasn't being serious.

"Gosh, no." Her immediate shocked reaction as the implications of his comment registered were quickly replaced by a tiny chuckle, acknowledging his attempt to lighten the moment. "I don't have a dog. Although Joey has been at me to get a puppy. I keep promising I will but it's never seemed a good time."

"A puppy sounds like a good idea. Every boy should have a dog to go adventuring with. Right. The odometer is on thirty-five, so we must be getting close." He took his foot off the accelerator to allow the car to slow down.

"It's still a bit further." Elly was leaning forward, staring intently out the windscreen. "I slowed down about here, too, I think, but it still seemed to take ages to get there."

"I can speed up a bit, but we don't want to miss it. Although, we'll know we've gone too far if we reach the T-junction where I found you."

Elly nodded without taking her eyes off the road in front. A few minutes later, she caught sight of a small splash of red amongst the browns and greens of the vegetation.

"There it is. See? There. There's the sign. And the track next to it."

"Yep. I see it." Gavin braked, left the road, and they bumped along the short sandy track through the dunes and then behind the one on the right and into the makeshift car park. Elly's car was exactly as she'd left it.

"There it is," she cried as it came into view. She leapt out as soon as Gavin pulled up next to it and, with shaking hands, wrenched open the door, sat in the driver's seat and leaned across to retrieve her bag from under the seat. She pulled out her phone and tried to switch it on. "Oh no. The battery's flat."

"Have you got a charging cable? There's one in my car."

As Gavin fetched the cable, Elly glanced into the back of her car. "Oh my God. It's Joey's things. Look, his jacket and a blanket and food. He must have been with me. He must be lost in the bush. We have to find him."

Handing her the cable, Gavin stopped her from leaping out of the car as her terror threatened to turn to hysteria.

"We don't know that. Let's check your phone and see if there's any information there, and then you can try Les again. Don't worry. We'll get this sorted. We'll find Joey, I promise." *And woe betide them if anyone has hurt him.* He was growing increasingly concerned for the little boy's safety while rigidly maintaining a calm exterior so as to not further panic Elly.

Elly plugged her phone into the charger, retrieved the car keys from her bag and started the engine, and opened her messages. "Oh, that's right. There's no reception here! That's why I left my phone in the car. The last message is from over a week ago when he was organising for Joey to stay with him, and the last call was Tuesday."

"Tuesday was when you were supposed to be doing the handover?"

"Yeah. That's probably why he called." Her face screwed up. "But I can't remember what he said. I know I was supposed to meet him here. I came but I can't remember what happened."

"Why don't we try a re-enactment and see if that jogs your memory? You must have parked your car here and then got out. I'm guessing you walked down and then along the beach to the track where you went back up to the road. Why didn't you come back for your car, though? Here. Pretend you've just arrived. Try and do everything exactly as you did before. Do you remember putting your bag under the seat?"

"Yeah. I was afraid I might drop something in the sand. I put my phone and keys in it." She switched off her engine, dropped her phone and keys into her bag and pushed it under the seat.

"What happened next?"

"I got out. It was so windy I could barely open the door."

Out of the car, she made her way down to the foreshore with Gavin following.

She walked a little way, then sat down. "I sat here. I must have been waiting for something. I was watching the ocean. It was dark but it was a full moon so there was some light." She shivered violently. "And it was cold. Oh my God, it was so cold. And windy. I was freezing. And scared." Her voice took on a far-away quality and her eyes glazed as memories rose to the surface. "And then I saw something... a... a..." She shook her head, abandoned the attempt to recall what it was and moved on. "I was so happy. But it wouldn't stop, so I chased it." She took off and Gavin silently followed, not wanting to interrupt her in case the memory vanished. "And I ran and ran, and I thought I was going to lose it and then I stopped here and then…" She looked at him in horror; her eyes glazed over and rolled back into her head, and she fell down in a dead faint.

"Elly," Gavin called, quickly laying her flat. He took his jacket off and shoved it under her legs to elevate them, then shook her shoulders and called to her again. "Elly. Elly." He let out a sigh of relief as her eyelids fluttered and she moaned; it looked like she might come round quickly. He patted her hand, shook her shoulders again and called in a louder voice, "Elly. Elly. Wake up."

Her eyelids flew open. "The boat. It blew up. He killed him. He killed Joey. He's dead. Oh, Joey, Joey, Joey." Her moaning increased in volume, and she started thrashing about, her head waving wildly from side to side.

Gavin quickly slapped her cheek hard enough to shock but not hurt her. "Elly. What are you talking about? Talk to me. What the hell happened here?"

And then it all rushed out in an almost unintelligible flood. "Les told me to come here to fetch Joey and he was on a boat and would drop him off and I got here and saw the boat and ran after it and it exploded and knocked me over and there was a fire and it sank and I ran out onto the road and then… and then… and then…"

She looked up at him, her face so contorted with grief it shredded his heart.

"Slow down, baby. You came here to meet a boat? Your husband was dropping Joey off here from a boat?"

"Yes. Yes. But the boat blew up and sank. He killed Joey to punish me."

As he listened to her, Gavin's hands absentmindedly mimed grabbing Les by the throat and throttling the life out of him. When she finished speaking, he pulled her to him and held her so tightly she couldn't move. "Did you see Joey, though? Think, Elly. Did you see Joey? Did you see anyone on the boat?"

Her body froze for a moment, then she breathed again. "No. But Les said he'd be on board and he was going to drop him off here and…"

"Hush." Gavin spoke harshly, feeling her losing control again. "You don't know Joey was there. It might not have even been the boat you were waiting for. Didn't Les say he'd meet you where you left your car? And even if the boat did have something to do with Les, it doesn't mean Joey was on it. Surely the man is not sick enough or evil enough to murder his own son."

"But he warned me over and over again that if I didn't do what he said, if I didn't go back to him, he'd take Joey away from me—one way or another…" Her teeth were chattering so hard, he could barely make out what she was saying.

"Come on, precious. You're getting cold. We can't do anything here now anyway. Can you stand up? We should get your phone somewhere it has reception and see if Les has left you any messages."

He helped her to her feet, picked his jacket up off the sand and wrapped it around her, and then put his arm around her shoulders. She looked up at him, helplessly, with stricken eyes, and he bent to kiss her lips. A kiss of comfort and reassurance. He slid his lips from her mouth gently across her face, leaving tiny kisses as he went until he reached her ear, and nuzzled gently in her hair. "Do you think you can walk, baby? If I hold you."

Elly leaned against him, her head up and her eyes closed as she surrendered to his voice and his touch. "Yes."

"Come on then. Let's get out of here."

Hooking his arm over her shoulder and holding her tightly around her waist so she was supported against his hip, he was able to take some of her weight so she could manage more easily across the sand.

"What are we going to do now?" she asked when they reached the cars.

"Hop in." He opened the driver's door of her car for her to get in, then went around to the passenger side, pulled her bag from under the seat as he got in, and handed it to her. "Start your engine and plug your phone in, then send Les a message saying you want to know where Joey is or you are going to report him to the police. Your phone can't send it yet, but it will as soon as it's in range. My guess is Les won't want you to go to the police, even if he doesn't think he's committed an actual crime. He sounds like someone who might have enough skeletons in his closet to not want to draw attention to himself."

Elly gave a nervous snicker as she sent the message. Les had never given her any details of his business dealings, but she had sometimes wondered if they were entirely within the law.

"I'm sure Les had something to do with that launch I saw. That's why he made me come here. He wanted me to see it explode and think Joey had been killed."

"I think you're right." Gavin clenched his fists and thumped them on dashboard, turned to her and took her hands in his. "I'm sure that cu… scumbag—sorry, baby—set this up to hurt you. And if I have anything to do with it, you won't be the one most hurt."

Her eyes opened wide and she shuddered. "What do you mean? You can't go near him. He's dangerous. I couldn't bear it if he hurt you too."

Gavin smiled reassuringly, squeezed her hands, raised one to his mouth and brushed his lips back and forth over it while he looked at her. Then he leaned forward and kissed her, long and slow, before drawing back. "Don't worry, my precious, precious, girl. Your Daddy is big and strong and tough, and he's not about to let the bad man hurt him or anyone else." He smiled and Elly giggled and blushed, but she had to look away, her heart pounding; she'd seen something in Gavin's eyes she'd not seen in a man's eyes before, least of all her husband's—that she was cherished and he was on her side. A medley of relief, joy and disbelief skittered through her as she allowed herself to feel a little less alone.

Gavin squeezed her hand again to ensure he had her attention and spoke matter-of-factly. "The most important thing right now is to get somewhere your phone will have reception. It's probably about a ten to twenty-minute drive either way, but I don't want you fiddling with your phone while you're driving, so I want you to follow me back to the shack where I know there's reception. We can find out what's going on there rather than stopping on the side of the road somewhere. Give me your phone and charger. I'll take it with me so you can concentrate on your driving."

Gavin led the way, travelling slowly and keeping a close eye on Elly in the car behind. When they arrived, he waved her past so she could park her car out of the way beside the shack. She jumped out and ran to him, snatching the phone he held out to her and opened her messages.

"There's one here from Les on Tuesday night. Eight-thirty. Just a smiley face. The one before that is the one from over a week ago." She frowned. "Nothing since." She checked her calls. "He rang me on Wednesday."

Gavin's mouth set in a tight line. "So there's no doubt he was behind the boat then. That's why he sent that emoji at 8:30. It was just after you'd seen the boat burn. He must have known, or guessed, you'd seen it. He really is despicable. No reply yet to the message you sent him?"

"No, but it's gone."

"Try calling him."

Elly rang, but it went straight to voicemail. "Where's Joey? I'm supposed to have him. Give him back." She babbled into the phone before starting to cry. Gavin took the phone and ended the call.

"Blow your nose, sweet. We need a plan, and I want you to trust my judgement. I honestly don't believe Joey was on the boat you saw explode. If I know anything about men like Les, it's that they love having a son. They think the father has to have high levels of testosterone to produce a boy-child, and therefore a son proves their masculinity. They're wrong, but I'm counting on Les' vanity and ignorance to keep Joey safe."

Elly looked doubtful.

"Think about it rationally for a moment. If he had hurt Joey, he wouldn't have a son to brag about, and he'd have lost his hold over you, let alone having the police after him and probably going to jail. No, I don't believe that anything he thinks he might gain from harming Joey would be worth what he'd lose. I'm sure he'll be in touch and soon. He'll want to gloat. He'll call again. I'd borrow money and bet on it. In the meantime, though, we have to work out what we're going to do while we're waiting to hear from him. Do you want to drive back to the city? We could go to his place and see if Joey is there. Or we could go to your place? Or mine."

Elly mutely shook her head, but wouldn't look at him.

"What then? There's no point sitting here." He grinned and rubbed his belly. "Besides, I hate to sound callous but I'm getting hungry. Breakfast was a long time ago."

"I don't want to go back yet. I was supposed to pick Joey up here. What if Les and Joey are still around here somewhere, still waiting for me? I can't go back without knowing where Joey is."

Gavin scratched his head. "I doubt they are here, but if you don't want to leave until we've heard from Les, we can stay for a bit. I tell you what, we're both hungry. There's a little settlement not much further up the coast where we get supplies. We'll go and get some lunch and you can bring your phone. It's still not fully charged, so you'd best plug it back in. We don't want it to go flat. Hopefully, we'll hear from that scumbag and you can arrange to collect Joey. Come on. We'll take my car."

Elly looked grateful. "I'm sorry… I'm being silly…"

"No, you're not. I understand perfectly. Come on. Lock your car, and let's get going." They switched cars and Gavin pulled out of the drive and headed up the coast.

"It's been a traumatic and emotional couple of days for you, hasn't it, precious?"

"Yes."

"Try not to worry about Joey, as hard as that is. I'm sure he's okay and we'll hear soon. How about taking your mind off him for a moment and telling me something about your marriage? I was more than a little surprised to hear you had a husband."

He smiled to take the sting out of his words, but Elly immediately blushed. "I'm sorry, I…" she began, but he put his hand on her knee and shushed her. "There's no need to apologise. Honestly. You weren't deliberately hiding it from me. But I'd be interested in hearing now. Moira said you met in the bar where Fiona was working."

Elly let out a long tremulous sigh and nodded. "Yes. I was nineteen. Les was thirty-one, and super good-looking. Like I said, men usually never took any notice of me when Fi was around, so when this handsome older man started flirting, it was exciting. I'd watched Fi with men and thought I could be like her." Her voice faltered. "I guess she was a better judge of character than me though. She told me Les was no good, but I couldn't see it. He flattered me, bought me presents, showed me off to his friends. I was so silly and romantic. I thought I'd found my perfect true love. After Fi met Hank she was always with him, so I was glad to be with Les or I would have been on my own a lot anyway. When he asked, demanded I marry him,

I thought his insistence that he needed me with him all the time was proof of his love.

"So, we got married. Then he begged me to quit my job. Said it made him feel less of a man, like he couldn't support his wife." She shrugged. "So I quit, which meant I didn't have any money of my own and he didn't give me my own money. I had to ask or beg him whenever I wanted any." She paused, bit her trembling lip and looked out the window, sighed and looked down at her hands resting in her lap. "That's when I found out I was pregnant. He had forbidden me from using birth control after we were married, and he never would. But I was stuck at home and not working anyway, so a baby seemed like the next thing to do. And he seemed so happy. It was like when we first met again. He bought me flowers and was nice to me at first, but as I got bigger, he started looking at me like I was disgusting. He was hardly ever home, and I didn't have any money or friends, apart from Fi, so I just stayed home by myself.

"Right from the start, he assumed the baby would be a boy. I said to him once *What if it's a girl?* and he said *It'd better not be.* I convinced myself he was teasing, and then I had an ultrasound and we knew it was a boy so it didn't matter. You were right about him showing off about having a son. He brought all his mates around, and they had expensive champagne and cigars. But after that, he lost interest. He never picked Joey up, or held him, or played with him, or helped look after him, and he'd fly into a rage if Joey cried and yell at me to keep him quiet."

"Did he hit you?"

Elly watched the thumb on one of the hands in her lap rubbing at the forefinger on the other. "No. Hardly ever. Only maybe if he'd had a particularly hard day and was tired and maybe Joey was more restless than usual, or I'd said something stupid and annoying... or..."

"Or you didn't want sex?"

She nodded. "But he always felt really, really bad and was depressed afterwards. He hated himself so much, I couldn't be angry with him. He'd lie on the couch not speaking, not eating, not washing, until I said I forgave him and knew he didn't mean to do it. Then he'd buy me flowers and things would be okay for a while."

Gavin grimaced and mumbled under his breath but didn't voice his reaction out loud, instead steering the conversation further along. "What did Fi think?"

"She hated Les. Absolutely hated him, and it was mutual. He tried to stop me from seeing her, but she'd come around when he was out. When he came home, he'd grill me about what I'd been doing. Fi made me promise not to tell him but I wouldn't have anyway because I knew how angry he'd be."

"It must have been hard, baby." Gavin reached over and sympathetically squeezed her leg. "Is that why you left?"

"No. I wasn't going to. I still thought I was in love with him and that he loved me. And we were married and had Joey." She paused briefly. "I believed him when he said we could be happy if I tried harder. And I did try harder." She looked at Gavin as though daring him to contradict her. "Honestly. But it seemed like the harder I tried, the angrier he became. He stopped saying he loved me and that I was beautiful. I'd lost all the weight I put on when I had Joey, and was thinner than when we met, but he started calling me an ugly, fat pig. He'd tell me I was stupid and useless and didn't know how lucky I was to be married to a man so far above me." Her voice broke on a sob in her throat and Gavin reached over to her again.

"Hush, baby. You don't have to talk about it if you don't want to."

She didn't look at him, but her voice was grimly determined when she spoke again. "I do want to. I've never said most of this out loud to anyone before. Fi knew what was going on, that Les was bullying me and I was unhappy, but I never told her the details. It actually feels good now." She paused, thinking. "Sort of like cleaning something disgusting out of a cupboard that you knew was there but pretended wasn't or couldn't bring yourself to face, or something like that."

"Uh-huh. I think I get the picture."

Elly gazed out of her side window at the ocean visible beyond the low scrub, and Gavin watched the road and waited for her to resume her story which eventually she did.

"I might have stayed forever, I suppose. Maybe I could have gone on lying to myself if it had only been me." Her hands clenched into fists. "But it wasn't. Joey was there too. Les kept telling him he had to be a man and be tough, and if Joey cried, Les would get angry and lock him in his bedroom until he stopped. If I tried to come between them, Les would go for me, then storm out and not come home for a long time, and he was always drunk when he did come back. Then one day when Les was trying to lock him in his room, Joey was struggling and accidentally kicked him. Les punched him and pushed him into his room and locked the door. He grabbed me around the throat and told me never to tell anyone, then went out slamming the door. I packed Joey's and my things and left. That was over a year ago."

"He hit Joey? The bastard. Where did you go?"

"We went straight to Fi's. She and Hank had split, and she was always at me to leave Les so she was really happy when we turned up. I never told her Les hit Joey. I knew she'd say something to him and I was afraid of what he'd do, not to her, to me and Joey. He hated her, but he couldn't bully her. I think that was a big part of why he hated her so much. And because he knew she saw through him and didn't respect him. He couldn't big note himself and show off in front of her."

"Did he bother you? After you moved?"

"Not too much while Fi was there. He asked to see Joey and I let him. I thought it was important for Joey to have a dad, and if I wasn't around he would be nicer to him. Fi talked me into applying for a divorce, but when I told Les he flew into a rage. I was so scared. I honestly thought he was going to kill me. And he told me if I applied for a divorce, he would get the best lawyer in town and get full custody of Joey and I'd never see him again."

She paused and Gavin nodded to show he was still listening. He tried to clear his throat, but unable to dislodge whatever was stuck, he gave up.

"Then Fi got sick," Elly said at last, infinite sorrow replacing the hard edge her voice had had when she'd talked about Les. "Before she died, she made me promise I'd stay in the flat and not go back to Les."

"And that miserable coward took advantage of you being alone?"

Elly nodded.

"My God, what sort of lowlife preys on the mother of his son when she's just lost her best friend and is at her most vulnerable? That disgusting excuse for a man doesn't deserve to live."

"No!" Elly looked at him in shock, and he looked back with a sad half-grin.

"Don't worry, baby. I don't have it in me to kill anyone. I promise. Not even a piece of scum like him. Do you still care for him? Are you in love with him?"

"No." Her denial was hot and certain. "I hate him. And if he died tomorrow, I would dance on his grave." She paused and fidgeted. "But…"

"You don't want to escape from one violent man only to find you're with another one?"

Her head was bent and she wouldn't look at him, but she nodded. He reached over and touched her hair.

"Don't worry, precious. I promise you on my life that you have nothing to fear. I *promise*. Okay?"

She turned a slightly reassured face to him. "And I don't want anything like that on my conscience."

Gavin nodded understanding. "Okay. I won't hire a hit-man to take care of that bastard then."

She grinned, knowing he hadn't seriously been contemplating taking out a contract on Les, but was trying to lighten the mood.

"And, now", he said, slowing the car down as they reached the outskirts of the small seaside settlement. "Let's have some lunch, get anything we need, go back to the shack and decide what we're going to do next."

"Shall I try calling again first?"

"Sure."

But there was still no answer.

Chapter 10

"**O**kay, baby," Gavin said, once they were back in the car and doing up their seat belts. Despite sitting outside in the warm sun across the road from the ocean, and having a plate of the "Best Fish and Chips in the State" to share, lunch had been short. Elly was on edge waiting for her phone to ring, and Gavin too preoccupied with Elly's distress to relax.

"Are you ready to head home? We could go to Les' place and see if they're there."

"How can I leave though? What if...? What if...?" Her voice faded away, unable to say *What if he is at the bottom of the ocean?* out loud. "What if Les *is* going to bring him here?" she finished lamely.

Gavin enveloped her hands in his. "You can't go on like this. We have to sort it out. Quickly. We'll go back to the shack and wait for a little while, but if we've heard nothing in an hour, we're going to his house to see if he's there. If he's not, we're calling the police."

"No! Last time I threatened to call the police, he said if I did he'd hurt Joey, disfigure him for the rest of his life so it would remind me forever it was my fault. And now I've left that message. What if he hurts Joey because of me?"

Her body was trembling violently and her breathing rasping. Gavin pulled her to him as best he could in the front seat of the car.

"Hush, baby. Hush. I'm going to look after you, I promise. I don't want anything bad to happen to Joey either." *Not after Tyler* swept like hot wind through his mind. They were both shaking as they clung together, Elly shivering with fear, and Gavin raging with anger and a flaming desire for vengeance.

Neither spoke on the trip back to the shack. Gavin put music on to help calm and distract them and, once inside, he made tea, but neither could settle. The room filled with the echo of Elly's heart pounding with terror as she curled up in a chair, while Gavin's thumped with frustration at not being able to march head-on into battle as he paced back and forth, but he couldn't force Elly—her psyche was far too fragile.

The sound of her phone ringing startled them both.

"Put it on speaker," Gavin muttered urgently as Elly's face told him who was calling.

"Les," she whispered into the phone. "Where's Joey?"

"Ah, my love," came a sneering voice from the other end. "You've finally deigned to return my call, have you? You were supposed to have the kid yesterday. I guess you conveniently forgot or weren't that bothered. I let my lawyer know. He's added it to his 'unfit mother' file."

"Where's Joey?" Elly whispered again.

"Aren't you going to thank me for the little fireworks show the other night? And you accuse me of not caring. Have you any idea how much effort that took to arrange just for your benefit?"

"Is Joey all right?"

"Aww, poor little Elly. Were you worried I might have turned him into the boy on the burning deck and sent him to the bottom of the sea?" He laughed, and Elly flinched as though the blow were physical. "You can't have been that worried if you didn't even bother to call yesterday."

"I couldn't. You've been drinking. You shouldn't drink when you're looking after Joey. Where is he? Let me speak to him. Are you at your place? I'll come and fetch him. Is he all right?"

"He's fine, ya dopey bitch. Except that you're turning him into a little sissy with all your fussing. He needs a man around. He's my son and he should be with his father. And you should be with your husband. You're still my wife. I have rights. You're coming home."

"No." Elly's eyes, crazed with panic, looked at Gavin, who, unable to keep still, had resumed silently pacing while keeping his eyes fixed on her. He put his finger to his lip and shook his head, then smiled encouragement and squinted his eyes in a slow blink.

"No? I've warned you before, Elly. I want my son living with me, under my roof. And my wife. Now you haven't got your ugly lesbian girlfriend to suck your pussy, you're coming back. It's time you had cock in you again, and there's not another man in the world who'd want you. And I expect a little gratitude. You owe me for the years you've leeched off me. And I intend to collect."

"I need to know Joey is with you and he's okay. Let me speak to him. Please," Elly begged.

"Joey, say 'hello' to your mother. Hurry."

"Mummy? I want to come home, Mummy."

"Stop your whining, and give me the phone." Elly and Gavin heard Joey start to cry. "For fuck's sake, listen to your son, Elly. You may as well have had a girl because he sooks like a little girly-wirly." His voice went quieter as he spoke away from the phone. "Stop snivelling, ya little piece of garbage." And then was louder again. "You've ruined him. You're a useless wife and a completely crap mother. Look what you've done to my son—turned him into a sooky crybaby. This has gone far enough. Pack up your flat. I'll be there at 1:00 p.m. tomorrow to fetch you and bring you home, and a truck will pick up your stuff."

"I want to come now and see him. Please, Les."

"We're still at Richo's. We'll be back tomorrow. Just do as I say. Be ready at 1:00 p.m., and don't mess with me, Elly, or you'll never see your idiot son again. That's a promise. Oh, and we need to have a little chat about you wanting to call the cops. I didn't like that." The phone went dead.

Elly was frozen in place. Fearing her consciousness might be overwhelmed again, Gavin pulled her to her feet and took hold of her shoulders.

"Don't be afraid, Elly. That bastard is a bully. He doesn't deserve a kid. He shouldn't be allowed near children, but he's not going to harm Joey because that would get him into trouble and bullies are about saving their own skin while making other people miserable. We'll get Joey back tomorrow, I promise." He tilted her head up so she could see the determination and sincerity in his eyes.

"Maybe I should just go back to him," she said dully. "It's my fault Joey is in danger. I shouldn't have left. If anything happens to him, I will never forgive myself."

"Nothing is going to happen to him." Gavin pulled her into his arms and held her tightly. "And there is no way that slime bag is getting you back unless you truly want to be with him. And I don't believe you do. He was completely wrong in what he said—about no other man wanting you." He drew back so he could look into her eyes. "I want you, Elly." He looked over her head and clenched his jaw as he fought for control, then returned his eyes to hers. "And I need you. More than you know."

Her surprise jolted her out of the shock of Les' cruel words. "Need me?"

He looked away again, but she could see his neck throbbing with tension. He nodded. "Trust me, baby. Let me help you. Don't even consider going back to that monster. He won't change. He'll more likely be worse because he feels more powerful now Fiona isn't around. He'll never stop punishing you for humiliating him by walking out. And it's not even as though you living with him will keep Joey safe; he knows the best way to hurt you is to torment your child. No. You're not going back. I'm going to protect you."

"Are you going to keep me prisoner, too?"

"No. No. If I thought you truly wanted to be with Les, I'd drive you to his house and drop you off myself. But I don't. I think you want to get him out of your life and, as you don't seem to have anyone else, I'm going to be with you while you stand up to him and show him he can't bully or control you any longer. Once you're safe, you can leave me if that's what you want to do. It's not what I want; I want you to stay."

"Really?" She frowned. She'd been subjected to Les' controlling abuse for so long, she'd almost forgotten her teenage dream of finding a good man like her surrogate father, Jeff, and having a normal family. Was it possible Gavin was such a man, and it wasn't too late for her and Joey?

"Cross my heart." He bent and kissed her gently, resisting the urge to crush her against him and brand her as his with an urgent and forceful possession. She didn't resist the pressure of his lips, and as he felt her begin to relax, he gathered her to him and held her head against his chest as tenderly as he might cradle a tiny hurt and frightened bird. "Now my precious, precious, girl. We can't do anything about Joey until tomorrow, so what do you want to do until then? I can take you home to your flat and stay with you there. Or you can stay the night at my place. Or I'm sure Moira would look after you if you'd rather go there. And I reckon she'd let me sleep on the couch again."

"Can we stay here? I don't want to go back yet. I feel safe here."

"Of course we can, if that's what you want."

"All I want is for it to be tomorrow so I can get Joey, and if I go back now, I'll go mad waiting. It seems more unreal here. It's almost like I can half pretend it's not happening."

"Okay, then I will make it my job to keep you occupied. And if you feel afraid, hang onto me. I'm not going to let anything bad happen to you or Joey. Understood?"

Elly managed a sad smile and nod of assent.

"Good. Then as I am your doctor and you are my most precious patient, I am prescribing a walk on the beach. Exercise and fresh air will do us both good. And we're going to take towels in case we want to swim."

It was cool by the sea but the sky was clear, the mid-afternoon sun shining and, with barely even a whisper of wind, the ocean placid and glassy in the sheltered bay. As they walked, Elly combed the sand for shells, scooping up the prettiest and showing them to Gavin: an almost perfect rust-coloured fan shell; an abalone, plain on top but shimmering like oil on water underneath; a counter-shaded violet snail, carried from the open ocean to the shore at the mercy of the currents; four pipis, two with the tell-tale tiny holes of death; and a moon snail, now as dead as the pipis on which it had feasted, sucking through the holes its radula had made in their shells. She'd spotted a sea urchin and stooped to inspect it when Gavin stopped and dropped his towel.

"I'm going in. You coming?"

"I don't have any bathers."

"Me neither. You can leave your underwear on if you want,

but there isn't another soul for miles. When was the last time you went skinny-dipping?"

Elly blushed, and shook her head with an embarrassed giggle.

Gavin squinted his eyes and looked at her sideways. "I hope you're not trying to tell me you have never swum naked in the ocean? You do swim though?"

Elly nodded. "Maybe not that well. I haven't done much swimming since, since…"

"That doesn't matter. I'm an excellent swimmer and I give expert mouth-to-mouth." He grinned and winked at her, and she couldn't help smiling back. "You game then? And if you're shy, I promise I won't look. And you're not allowed to look at me, either," he declared, taking off his jumper and T-shirt and flexing his enormous biceps and wiggling his pectoral muscles at her so she couldn't help laughing.

He stripped off his jeans, shoes and socks. "You better come in because I'm going to sit under the water holding my breath until you do." He pulled off his boxers and, with a whoop, ran down into the ocean, crying out as the shock of the cold water hit him, then belly-flopping into a wave and disappearing below the surface.

Despite his having told her she couldn't look, her eyes had followed his huge, fit body, admiring the sculptured muscles in his thighs and buttocks, and his long, strong back as he ran. She shuddered as she compared it to Les' forty-year-old, doughy body, already showing the deleterious effects of too much fatty food and alcohol and too little exercise. Pushing that image from her mind and picturing Fiona telling her, with a laugh, to get a move on, she stripped down to her underwear, paused, then seeing Gavin had his back to her, slipped out of her bra and panties and ran to join him, bobbing quickly under the water so only her head was out, her desire for modesty outdoing her shock at the cold.

"Aha." Gavin burst unexpectedly through the surface next to her. She jumped up in fright so she was out of the water from her waist up, then quickly tried to swim to deeper water without exposing herself.

"Doesn't this feel wonderful?" Gavin asked, accompanying her and turning over so he was floating on his back. "I love the feel of the sea, and being completely immersed in it. It feels not only refreshing and revitalising, but cleansing too."

Now in water deep enough to preserve her modesty, Elly closed her eyes, and allowed herself to surrender fully to the sensation of being surrounded by the ocean. The cold water *was* refreshing, and it did feel as though it was washing away her pain and fear, and invigorating her with a new strength.

"It's wonderful," she said breathlessly when she opened her eyes again. "It feels so good. I'd forgotten how much I love being in the ocean."

"Can you dive under? And stay for as long as you can, focusing on the stillness of the water and being suspended." Giving her a demonstration, he disappeared beneath the surface, then reappeared a minute later, smiling. "Now you. Pretend you're a fish or a mermaid."

Elly took a deep breath and sank, rather than dived, imagining what it would be like to be a marine creature and live in the sea. Gavin was right. It was heavenly, and she found herself twisting and turning her body, feeling the sensuous pleasure of the water moving over her. She finally surfaced again when her lungs rudely reminded her she didn't have gills. Taking a deep breath, she looked at Gavin and realised she was happier than she'd been in longer than she could remember. If only Joey was there with them, her happiness and contentment would be complete. A small stab of panic rose threateningly as she thought of Joey, but she forced it down as she swam to Gavin. He would keep them safe. He'd promised and she trusted him.

He opened his arms as she reached him, and she slipped

her own arms up and around his neck, pressing her softness against his hard body as he encircled her waist, holding her close and kissing her lips. For that brief moment, nothing existed for either of them other than the sensuous feel of the cool, healing water on their skin, their naked flesh pressed together, and the exploration of each other's mouth. Their hunger for the other was beyond sexual; it was a need to connect with another human being at the deepest level, the need to assuage loneliness, and the need for a safe haven in a world of pain and sorrow.

Elly shivered and Gavin released her. "Come on, baby. We'll get cold if we stay here. I'll race you to shore."

He turned and flopped clumsily into the water in a pantomime of inept urgency. Elly laughed and threw herself onto him, and they rolled over and under the water, then surfaced, laughing and spluttering.

"Why you..." Pretending to scold her, he lunged at her but deliberately fell short. Elly leapt on his back as he disappeared under the sea and they wrestled and tumbled until, out of breath, they struggled up, now so close to shore the water was only thigh deep.

"Come on." Gavin took her hand in his and they ploughed through the water and then ran up the beach to their clothes. Elly immediately grabbed her towel and covered herself, while Gavin turned his back to allow her privacy. Once again, Elly's eyes were drawn to his physique, roaming freely over the curves of his muscles. Feeling her eyes on him, he turned and, with his palms up, he made a small downward gesture with his hands and an upward tilt of his eyebrows as he invited her to study his naked body. She licked her lips, momentarily unable to drag her eyes from his, but seeing her hesitate, he looked down at himself and then back up at her with a second silent invitation. Unable to refuse, and marvelling at how he could be so utterly gorgeous seemingly without conceit, she lowered her eyes. She'd never been so close to a body like his before, and her eyes followed the lines of his tight, rounded pectorals and the four ripples of his abdominal muscles where they stopped, unwilling to descend further.

"You must work out," she murmured, longing to run her hands over his undulating contours.

"I do. I find it relaxing. Plus it really helps when I have to rescue sleeping damsels from the side of the road."

Hearing the smile in his voice, she looked up to find him regarding her with relaxed amusement. Everything about him seemed to be the complete opposite of Les. Gavin, who could justifiably be proud of the work he'd put into keeping himself fit, stood naked in front of her without inhibition and without pretension, while Les who made no effort to look after his body, vainly strutted his in front of her with all the self-importance of a bantam rooster.

"I'd love to draw you," she said.

"Oh, are you an artist?"

"No. No," Elly stammered quickly and dismissively. "I used to draw a bit. That's all."

"You are welcome to draw me any time you want. I would really like that. It would be fun. No one has ever drawn me before."

Again, Elly was struck by the contrast. Gavin seemed to be genuinely encouraging her, while Les had ridiculed her drawings and told her to stop wasting her time and his money.

"Would you draw me all the way down? Anatomically realistic?" He grinned. "That's what they call it, isn't it?"

Elly felt her cheeks burn, but couldn't stop herself from wanting to look at the anatomy to which he referred. She licked her lips and dropped her eyes again, following his body down to his warming and now semi-tumescent penis. She stared at it, forgetting to feel embarrassed, intrigued by how different it was to Les', bigger and somehow more generous looking, more inviting, and surrounded by a thick bush of black hair which she found most exciting of all. Les' whole body was always completely shaved, and she had come to find his hairlessness repugnant.

She was glad Gavin was so different; his huge, hard body with its natural hair was manly, earthy and indescribably sexy. She looked up at the handsome, chiselled face watching her with a half-smile. He dipped his head slightly and looked at her from under his eyebrows in a confident acknowledgement of her appraisal, then his eyes narrowed and he ran them quickly over her body, hidden by the towel and then back up. Understanding his silent request for her to return the favour, with a sharp intake of breath for courage, she let go of her towel with one hand so it fell away.

Instantly, Gavin's eyes swept greedily over her then back to her face to check she wasn't afraid. She managed a tiny smile and shrug of her shoulders, which he understood and acknowledged with a small nod of his head before dropping his eyes again to feast them on her heavy breasts tipped with generous dark brown nipples, her soft round belly and womanly thighs between which was a plump mound, its curly black pubic hair not completely obscuring the beginning of her slit, visible and beckoning like the pathway to a hidden cave of treasures.

Gavin had seen her naked the previous day, but it was like seeing her again for the first time. Yesterday, when she had flaunted her body, it had not appeared out of character for the overtly confident and sexual Fiona, but Elly was different. In fact, he realised, her sexuality was a complete mystery to him. How much of her lovemaking the day before had been her true nature and her own desires and needs, and how much had been adopted from her friend?

She fidgeted, uncomfortable with having her naked body studied so intently. He looked back up into her face and smiled encouragingly. "You are absolutely magnificent, Elly. Do you know that? So beautiful you hurt my heart. You definitely should be sculpted or painted." Elly blushed with pleasure at his sincere praise. "Will you do something for me, baby?" he asked. "Turn around."

She shuffled her feet and swivelled on the spot, then closed her eyes as she imagined Gavin studying her body from this angle. His hand running across her bottom seconds later, made her jump; she hadn't heard him move.

"Spectacular whichever way I look at you," he murmured, nuzzling into the back of her neck. "But you're skin's cool despite the sun. Pull some clothes on, and let's get back inside."

She turned around to see him tie the towel around his waist, pull his jumper over his head and pick up the rest of his clothes. She copied him, but pulled her panties on before wrapping the towel around her, and followed him off the beach and across the road. After brushing the sand off their feet and legs at the door, they went in. It was almost as if this was the first time they had been here alone together. All trace of Fiona had disappeared, and with her the ease with which they'd come together, passionately and without reservation.

"You go and wash the sand and salt off," Gavin said. "I'll have a shower after."

The previous day, they'd showered together, but today he was, in the strangest of ways possible, with a different woman. When they'd made love, Gavin had thought he'd understood his partner's desires and was happy they matched his own. Sex with her had been exciting and fulfilling, and he'd thought she felt the same, but now he couldn't be sure. What of it had been Elly, and what Fiona? He had to tread carefully; it would be so easy to frighten her.

When they were both clean and dressed, he made tea and they drank it in uncomfortable silence, staring at their empty cups when they'd finished, the spectre of the previous day hanging between them. Anxious to break through the barrier that separated them, Gavin stood up, took her cup with his and put them both on the kitchen sink, then took her hand and pulled her to her feet.

"I want to hold you in my arms. Come and lie down with me," he said, gently leading her into the bedroom.

Chapter 11

Piling the pillows together to make a support for his back, he lay down and tugged her hand lightly so she would lie next to him. With his arm around her holding her close against him, she tucked her head down on his chest to hide her face but stretched her arm over him. With his free hand, he stroked her hair, then put his hand under her chin, tilted her face up and kissed her lips.

"You okay?"

She nodded, but he could see the uncertainty in her eyes.

"Do you remember what happened here yesterday?" His voice was soft and casual, and he didn't look at her but watched his fingers brush some hair from her face. When she didn't answer, he laid his head back and stared up at the ceiling, waiting.

"Some," she said quietly at last, putting her head back on his chest. "I don't know if it's all. I can't understand..." She paused, but he didn't reply, just waited to see if she'd say anything more, and at last, raising her head slightly, she did. "It's almost as though I'm watching myself in a movie. I can see it's me, but it doesn't feel like me. Or rather it sort of does, but not completely. It's weird. More like a memory of something Fi did and told me about than something I did myself." She gave up trying to make enough sense of it to explain it to Gavin, and with a long sigh of frustration, dropped her head back.

"Tell me what you do remember," he said. "Start from the beginning. Were you aware of me finding you and putting you in my car?" She shook her head. "Do you remember anything of that night after you ran to the road?"

She shook her head again. "Not clearly. It's all fuzzy. I was freezing and lying on something hard. I guess that must have been the road. Then I had this feeling, it might have been real or it might have been a dream, this feeling of warmth. Then nothing again."

Gavin nodded. "You're doing great. I think there were moments when you drifted back towards consciousness but instead of waking, you went back to sleep almost immediately."

"How come I was asleep?"

"My best guess is that the explosion and your belief that Joey was on the boat when it burned and sank was more than your mind could take. The dissociative amnesia allowed you to immediately forget what you thought you'd seen, and then when you were cold and alone and frightened, sleep was another refuge."

"But I didn't just forget who I was."

"No. When you couldn't sleep any longer and had to wake up, it seems your mind went one step further. Dissociative fugue is when as well as losing your memory, you develop another layer of protection by creating a new persona. Instead of being Elly who couldn't remember a few hours of her life, you changed the story so you were Fiona, and Elly was the person who died. That way you could distance yourself from your grief. You had still, as you thought, lost Joey, but your pain was no longer that of a mother, and Fi, being a stronger personality, was more able to deal with grief. At least, that's what your mind hoped."

"And us?" she asked quietly. "Didn't we… I mean, did I… Did you… Did I really…?'"

He engulfed her in both arms and held her against him.

"You were uninhibited. Sexually… adventurous, shall I say? Very confident and comfortable with your body—and mine. I seriously hadn't intended… hadn't even thought of having sex with you." She shrank away. "No, baby." He pulled her closer and kissed her head and as far down her face as he could reach. "Not because I didn't want to. I mean not because I didn't think you were beautiful, but I wasn't sure if you were injured, and I didn't know anything about you. I don't usually have sexual thoughts about people to whom I'm administering first aid."

He deliberately made it sound like a ridiculous proposition and she couldn't prevent a small giggle. "So… how then?"

He pulled her tighter again. "Well…" he began, then paused, unsure of her reaction if the truth widely differed from her usual way of being. "Tell me about Fiona. About how you saw her, as a woman I mean—her sexuality."

"Are you asking me if she was kinky? Because of what Les said? She wasn't a lesbian. Although… I don't know, she might have been with women. Nothing she did ever surprised me, but she never mentioned women. And she never made a pass at me."

"But she was quite open sexually? I mean she wasn't shy with men? Maybe she liked things that some people might call kinky?"

"Yes. I suppose so. She certainly did heaps of… stuff I've never done."

"Was that because you didn't want to?"

"Not only." Elly paused before elaborating. "I didn't have

anyone to do… stuff with anyway, even if I had wanted to. No one ever suggested anything, and then I was with Les and he never did."

"Did you ever think about it, though? Doing 'stuff', I mean. If you'd had someone to do it with…"

"Maybe." She managed to sound noncommittal despite a tremble in her voice. "I might have thought about it sometimes."

"And do you remember what happened yesterday?" he asked again, nuzzling her hair.

"I think so. But, like I said, it's like remembering a movie rather than something… rather than real life. Does that make sense?" She raised her head to look up at him, her eyes puzzled by the memory of the strangeness of being both herself and someone else at the same time.

He kissed the tip of her nose and smiled encouragingly. "Do you think you were acting out what you'd heard your friend tell you—what you imagined she might do, as it were? Or do you think they were your own fantasies and you used the persona of another person to give you the courage to act them out?"

He waited patiently. They'd only known each other a couple of days and he was asking her to bare her soul to him, but it had been an intense emotional roller coaster from the moment he stopped in the dark to rescue her. Her trauma had temporarily overshadowed his own, and he'd been able to lose himself in tending to someone else in distress. He felt closer to her than he had ever felt to anyone. If he'd been asked before today if he believed love at first sight was a real thing, he might have said he didn't; now he felt so entangled with this beautiful woman he wasn't sure.

But what was love at first sight other than a strong attraction which developed into a lasting relationship? If a relationship ended, the initial attraction was called by a different name, and Gavin didn't give a hoot what name was given to it; all he knew was that he felt as though he might have been holding this woman in his arms, not for two days, perhaps not even two years, but maybe two decades or even two lifetimes.

She wriggled a little and he loosened his hold, but she pressed herself back against him as if afraid she might drift away if she wasn't tethered to him. He squeezed her gently.

"Can you tell me, baby? Do you remember wanting me to take your temperature?" She nodded. "Did you like me playing with your bottom?" She nodded again, then shuddered, gasped and buried her face against his chest as another memory flooded her mind. He chuckled softly. "Do you remember what I did to you there? You liked that didn't you? Does it seem shocking now?" As he spoke quietly to her, his hand ran down her back and stroked her bottom. "Had anyone ever done that to you before?" She shook her head. "Would you like me to do it again sometime?" He heard her take a deep breath and then she gave a tiny shrug. His mouth parted in a tender smile. *In time. In time.*

"And there was something else." He continued to stroke and nuzzle and kiss her to maintain the connection. "Do you remember? You wanted me to take my belt off? Was that you too?"

He waited so long for her answer, he began to think he wasn't going to get one. Then she spoke.

"When I was a little girl, my favourite stories always had a big, strong hero saving a sad princess. I'd imagine I was the princess, and the hero was someone important, who all the people loved and obeyed. I had to obey him too, and he'd reward me if I was good and punish me if I was bad."

"Was he a substitute father, do you think? Yours didn't live with you when you were growing up, is that right?"

"Yes. Dad left when I was a baby. It was just Mum and me. But my hero didn't feel like a parent, and mostly, when I made up my own stories, I had a make-believe happy family with a mother and father who were so happy and proud the hero was going to marry me."

"Did you think you were a bad person? That you deserved to be punished?"

"No. I didn't feel bad, and I never did anything really wicked even in my imagination. I wasn't afraid of the hero. He was stern but not cruel. Sometimes I would imagine deliberately doing something naughty, like disobeying him, so he would punish me. And…" her voice trailed away.

"And what, precious? Tell me."

Elly gulped a deep breath and then said as quickly as she could. "He was almost always a doctor. When I was little I thought of a doctor as a man who looked after me, kept me safe, and made me better when I was sick, and whenever I went to the doctor, I had to do whatever he said, even like taking my clothes off and keeping still while he examined my body. My own doctor was never in my fantasies, though. I made someone up. Is that weird? Do you think there's something wrong with me?"

"No, my love. No. Honestly. I don't think there is anything at all wrong with you. It is completely understandable why you would have thought that, and lots of people have sexual fantasies about doctors and nurses. Were your fantasies sexual, do you think?"

"I didn't know about sex when they started; I was too young. They just made me feel warm and safe and nice, but as I got older I guess they became sexual."

Neither spoke for a moment as Gavin digested the information she'd shared.

"Come here," he said at last, wriggling them both up so he was sitting with his back against the headboard with his arm still around her and her head on his shoulder.

"Is that why you were attracted to Les? I mean, he's not a

doctor, I don't think, but did he seem to be like the hero in your fantasies?"

"No. He isn't a doctor," she said hurriedly. "But he was older, he had money, and he took control of me and my life. At first I thought him bossing me around showed he loved me and that he was a strong man who knew what was best for me. I found it exciting. And he bought me presents and told me I was good, and then sometimes he would be cross and yell at me or not talk to me or not see me for a while. I thought it was like in my childhood fantasies. I was pretty dumb, eh?"

"Not dumb, baby. Not at all. Just young and inexperienced. And unlucky enough to come across a man like him."

"And when we first met, he was so romantic, attentive and kind, he swept me off my feet and I was married and pregnant before I realised it had all been an act. By then he had me where he wanted me and it was too hard to get out."

"So…" Gavin began to say something, but paused. His voice was thick and he had to swallow hard before he could speak again. His body tensed and he nuzzled into her hair. "Did Les destroy your little girl's fantasies? Was it Fiona who wanted me to look after her and take her temperature yesterday and called me Daddy and wanted me to spank her, or was that you, Elly?"

He waited, but there was no reply. "Sweetheart?"

"I guess it was me," she finally admitted in a tiny voice, then looked up at him with a frown, took a deep breath and said firmly, "but I don't want anyone else to ever be horrible to me or Joey again like Les is. I don't want to be bullied. Or frightened. Or hurt. I'm over it. I'd rather Joey and I live alone for the rest of our lives."

Gavin rubbed his head against hers. "Of course you would. And the last thing I want to do is anything that would frighten you or hurt you… or Joey. I want to take care of you." He smiled. "But, if you want me to, I'd love to be your play Daddy and for you to call me Daddy, and I'll reward you if you are good and punish you if you are naughty." He felt her tense, but held her firmly so she couldn't wriggle away. "Don't pull away, baby. I'm not going to pressure you. I'm just telling you what I would like to do if it's something you would like too. I think we mesh together perfectly, but I'm happy to take it as slow as you need. Okay?" She bobbed her head and he loosened his arms as he felt her relax. "And I promise I would never punish you in anger and never harm you and we'd have a safe word so you could stop me if you wanted to. I want you to feel totally safe and protected. Is that kind of how it was in your fantasies?"

She blushed and ducked her head. "I guess so."

"And did the punishments include spankings?"

She nodded.

They sat together in silence for a few moments, then Gavin massaged the back of her head. "I want to make love to you again, but this time with you as Elly, not Fiona."

"But didn't you like me yesterday because I was Fi? Maybe it was Fi you were attracted to, not me."

"I'd be lying if I said it wasn't a shock to discover I'd spent the day with two different women in the same body. But, while I enjoyed Fi's sexual confidence and freedom and I'm sure I would have liked her enormously if I had met her, my heart was stolen by the sweet little girl I saw peeping through. That was you, Elly. Not Fiona. It's you, and only you, I want to be with. Okay?"

"Yes." Her head was still buried so he couldn't see her face, but he felt her press herself against him and her arm tighten across his chest.

"And this time I want you to be my sweet, precious Elly who is rewarded when she is a good girl and punished when she is a naughty girl. Shall we do that?"

He gave her as much time as she needed, and when he saw the bashful bob of her head, he smiled to himself, then adjusted his features into a more serious expression, tilted her face up and kissed her gently, deeply and tenderly.

"Well, now we've got that straight," he said speaking in a lighter, more playful tone when the kiss ended, "as I'm your Daddy, I can now also ethically be your doctor, and as Doctor Daddy I believe a thorough physical examination of my beautiful and precious patient is called for, don't you?"

She giggled and hid her face as he pulled his arm away and stood up.

"Stand up, please." He held out his hand, then took hers and tugged gently when she hesitated. When she was standing next to him, he brushed her hair over her shoulders so it fell down her back. "Wait there." He left the room but returned seconds later with two towels. "I'm going to fetch my bag from the car, and while I'm gone you are to undress and hop up on the bed. You can cover yourself with these." He handed her the towels, gave her a stern look to show he was giving her an order and left her to it.

Chapter 12

When he returned, she was sitting on the bed, her bra visible above the towel she was clutching around her middle, and only her outer clothes piled on a nearby chair. She looked at him apprehensively, as he regarded her sternly.

"In future, if I ask you to undress I will expect you to remove all your clothes, and I will consider it punishable disobedience if you don't." He relaxed his features and lightened his tone. "But as this is your first offence and you might have misunderstood my direction, I'll let you off. Next time you won't be so lucky. Come on now, there's no need to look so worried. You've been examined by doctors before. I know."

Gavin kept his tone chatty and relaxed as he put his bag on the bed next to her, opened it and extracted his otoscope, a tongue depressor and a steel dish.

"Keep still," he said, poking the tip of the otoscope into each of her ears in turn and looking down into her ear canals. "Good girl." He checked both her eyes and then asked her to open her mouth wide as he removed the speculum from the end of the otoscope and put it on the bedside table. "Say ahhh," he ordered as he pressed her tongue down with the wooden depressor and shone the otoscope light down her throat. "All good," he said with a doctor's professional smile of encouragement. He popped the used tongue depressor into the dish, put the otoscope next to its speculum, fetched his stethoscope from his bag and hung it around his neck.

Elly felt a lifetime of tension begin to ease as his big, healing hands proficiently checked the lymph nodes under her ears, at the base of her neck and in her armpits. She'd been lost and frightened for most of her life, and even more so since Fiona's death, but right now, right here, with this gorgeous doctor examining her so carefully and meticulously, she could imagine that a place of peace and happiness did exist for her and that, if she could trust him, Gavin could take her there.

"I'm going to listen to your chest," he said, putting the stethoscope into his ears. "Lean forward." She bent from the waist and felt the cold end of the stethoscope on her back. "Big breaths." Holding her hair out of the way, he moved the stethoscope around as he listened to her lungs. "Okay, you can sit up." When she was sitting straight again, he listened to the front of her chest above her bra.

"Remove your bra, please." His tone was as professional as if he was actually attending to her in the hospital, and it was so convincing, Elly had slipped her bra off before she had time to feel shy. As he listened to her chest again and held her left breast gently out of the way while he listened to her heart, she felt her will surrendering to him. Her skin prickled with awareness of how deeply arousing she was finding his enactment of her childhood fantasies. This was exactly how she'd pictured it, except Dr. Gavin Minchin was a thousand times more handsome and sexy than her imagined doctors.

"Lie down on your back, please."

Elly swung her legs onto the bed and lay down, and Gavin spread the towel discreetly over her panties before his hand gently probed and kneaded her abdomen. Elly's eyes were fixated on his face as he placed the palm of one hand on her belly and tapped the back of it with his other hand as he moved it around. He stopped and his forefinger traced a tiny scar.

"You've had your appendix removed."

"Yes. I was twelve."

He smiled at her as he took off his stethoscope. "I'm going to check your breasts now. Can you put your right arm above your head?"

His exploration was clinical and precise as he used the pads of his three middle fingers to move methodically round her left breast and up into her armpit. The effect his examination was having on Elly, however, was anything but clinical. Bent down over her, he was so close she could feel his breath and smell his faint musky male scent. Her eyes followed his hairline and noticed a small mole above his left ear visible through his clipped hair.

"Good. Good. Other arm up, please."

As he moved his attention to her right breast, she struggled to conceal the quickening of her breathing and the slight trembling of her hands, hoping he hadn't noticed the tiny beads of perspiration she could feel on her upper lip.

"You breast fed Joey, did you?" he asked as he rolled one nipple between his fingers.

"Yes."

He nodded as though approving her answer, and then played with the other nipple watching it harden. "You have good sized nipples for breast-feeding." He paused, then murmured so quietly she could barely hear and wasn't sure if he was talking to her or to himself, "It's a beautiful thing— mother and child." Almost hypnotised by the soft feel of his hand playing with her breast and the low murmuring of his voice, Elly's eyes closed and her body went limp.

After one last reverential squeeze of each breast, he pulled the towel up to cover them.

"Can you bring both your knees up and cross one leg over the other, please?" he instructed her as he removed a small rubber-tipped hammer from his bag. "I'm going to check your reflexes before I examine you internally."

Elly tried to do as she'd been told, but it was like her mind had been disconnected and she could no longer control her body.

"Quick now," Gavin said in a stern voice. Elly noted his new sense of urgency, and realised the doctor was not as detached as he'd appeared. The knowledge that he was finding their play as sexually arousing as she, excited her further, rousing her body from its sensual languor. She quickly crossed her legs, wanting this part over as quickly as possible, so the next part could begin.

Having seen the corresponding leg twitch as he tapped each knee in turn, he put his reflex hammer away. "So far," he said with practised clinical formality, "you seem to be in excellent health, but I need to do an internal examination, so you'll need to slip your panties off. You can cover yourself with the other towel if you wish."

He turned to his medical bag and Elly, watching him remove rubber gloves and a jar of gel, felt a sudden rush of hot blood to her groin and the gush of her own natural lubricant as she anticipated what was about to happen. Her breath caught at the embarrassing thought that the doctor would see she had been sexually aroused by his examination, and she momentarily froze. Slipping his right hand into one of the gloves, he turned, aware she hadn't moved.

"Take your panties off."

Elly swallowed hard and licked her dry lips, but still couldn't move.

He scowled, then raised his eyebrows and relaxed his

mouth allowing it to twitch at the corner. "You can have a jelly-bean when we're finished if you're a good girl," he said with a wink, then paused, shrugged, and added, "or a spanking now if you are a naughty girl. Which is it to be: jellybean or spanking?"

Despite a spanking sounding infinitely more exciting than a jellybean, Elly hastily pulled off her increasingly damp panties, screwed them up in her hand to hide the evidence, and lay down, breathing heavily and preserving as much of her modesty as she could with the towel. Feeling like giving herself a good slapping for being too cowardly to admit to Gavin through disobedience that she did want him to spank her, she chewed the inside of her lip in frustration.

Having overseen the removal of her last piece of clothing, he finished putting on his gloves and set the gel, otoscope, a metal dish and tissues at the end of the bed next to her feet. She was now so hot, wet and swollen, her hands were twitching at her side, yearning to ease the ache in her belly and the throbbing between her thighs. She closed her eyes as the need to feel his fingers inside her became more overwhelming by the second, and a groan of frustration at how long he was taking escaped.

"Are you all right?"

He knows! She felt a surge of blood rush to the other end of her body as her face turned red, and she had to look away as she heard him quietly chuckle.

He picked up the otoscope, turned it on so it would function as a torch, pulled a chair to the end of the bed and sat down. "Slide further down the bed, please. Pull your knees up and drop them down to the side."

Feeling as though she was watching herself from a distance, Elly obeyed. The towel was covering her, but she knew he was face-height and only centimetres away from her most guarded secret, a place she'd not properly seen herself, and any second now he was going to lift the towel and she would be fully exposed in the most intimate way possible. A tiny shudder of doubt rippled through her. What if she was as ugly and disgusting as Les had repeatedly told her she was? How could she bear the shame and humiliation if Gavin saw her and also thought she was repulsive? He had seen so many naked women, he would know instantly if she was misshapen or deformed or if there was something else about her that was hideous. She suddenly wanted to cross her legs to protect herself, but even if she'd been able to move her body, it was too late. She could feel Gavin slowly peeling back the towel, and an exquisite bolt stabbed up through her middle and her muscles contracted as she imagined she could feel his breath on her.

"Aha. Perfectly formed, plump and firm," he muttered as he gently put one finger either side of her outer lips and starting at the top gently squeezed his way down causing her to sharply suck in her belly and her breath. "Ah, receptive, sensitive and responsive to stimulation. Excellent. And from what I can see, you are able to produce a more than satisfactory amount of lubrication, but I'll examine that more closely in a moment."

He hadn't recoiled in horror. In fact, he seemed to be complimenting her. Utterly mesmerised by the conflicting forces of shame and excitement, Elly couldn't move, couldn't speak, could scarcely breathe. She was acting out her most exciting sexual fantasy. She knew it was happening, but still half-expected to wake and find it was a dream, and the tiny nagging voice, trained by Les, warning her that Gavin couldn't possibly want her after he'd seen her like this would not fully be quieted.

Another bolt fired through her as she felt Gavin's finger gently probe the entrance to her wet, slippery tunnel, and then move up between her inner and outer lips on one side and then repeat the process on the other. He carefully spread her natural lubricant until his fingers were sliding easily, opening her folds as his eyes inspected her shape and colour. He parted her inner lips to expose the hiding place of her clitoris, then gently squeezed the flesh around it so the hood opened and closed.

Almost all of Elly's previous sexual experience had been with Les: short, rough, pinching and pulling foreplay, hurried, sweaty panting as he thrust into her, and then the discomfort of having him collapse on top of her when he was spent so she had to fight for air. Fiona had told her it didn't have to be like that, that sex could be extremely pleasurable, but Elly had found that hard to believe, and at first, when she thought herself in love with Les, she had felt disloyal even thinking that perhaps he might not be a good lover.

But now... this... with Gavin... The contrast between his touch being simultaneously both clinical and detached, and deliberately sensuous and arousing was driving Elly crazy. Instead of her being pushed so hard she wanted to pull away, Gavin was deliberately holding her back so she was mentally begging for more as the exquisite pleasure flooding her body became so intense it was verging on unbearable and her fingers clutched at the bedding. After ensuring his gloved finger was well lubricated, he rubbed it up and down directly on her clitoris. Her body shuddered violently, and she couldn't suppress a moan as she fought the urge to pull away expecting it to be painful and unpleasant as it had been in the past.

Taking his hand away, he gave her a few seconds to calm down. "Good girl," he said, standing up and watching the heaving of her breasts while he stroked the outside of her hip to maintain contact. "You're vulva is not only perfectly formed and a delight to behold, it is also highly responsive. I don't know what doctors have told you in the past, but it is my clinical opinion that, for the benefit of your health, it should be stimulated manually, orally and via intercourse regularly and frequently. Has this been happening?"

Her eyes had opened and a surge of happiness rushed through her at his reassurance that he found her attractive and desirable, then lowered in embarrassment as she had to admit to her previously woeful sex life.

"No," she said in a small voice.

"Hmm." He nodded his head seriously, sounding displeased. "It has been neglected then. Well, that needs to change starting now. Do you see a problem with that?"

"No."

"No who?" he demanded. "Speak up, Elly, so I can hear you."

"No, Doctor."

"Good. We'll finish the examination and then begin your course of treatment immediately, won't we?"

"Yes, Doctor." Her whole body was hot, trembling and glistening with perspiration.

"You look flushed," he noted, wiping his finger through beads of sweat on her belly. "And hot. I'm afraid I'm going to have to take your temperature once I've finished your internal examination. Look at me, please, so I can see your face while I do this."

Chapter 13

S till standing, Gavin coated his gloved fingers with
lubricant, placed his left hand on her belly and looked
into Elly's eyes as he slid one finger slowly into her. She
gasped, moaned and closed her eyes.

"Open your eyes, Elly. It's imperative I see your reaction
and I shan't be disobeyed again. You're beginning to make a
habit of it and I shan't let it go again." As he spoke, he slid his
finger slowly out and in while watching her intently. Her nerves
on fire and her muscles jelly, Elly shuddered and moaned with
the unbearable intensity of sensation. Her eyes closed before
she realised they were going to and could try and stop them.

"You've closed your eyes, Elly, despite my warning you
about disobeying me again. I can't keep letting it pass. You
shall have to be punished this time."

"No," Elly groaned, forcing her eyes open and looking
into his.

"Yes, but how severely depends on whether you disobey me
again. Keep your eyes open."

She watched him as he bent down towards her pussy so he
could see better as he positioned one hand to hold her open

and then prepared to insert the fingers of his other hand. When he was ready, he looked back up into her face. Her eyes were now wide open and her chest tight and still with anticipation. The tension was too much and she cried out as she felt the erotic intrusion of his finger. She saw the muscles in his cheek bulge in and out as he rubbed his teeth together, and his nostrils flare as he stared at her. With a grunt, he invaded her again, this time with two fingers. She moaned and mouthed a silent "please", but he held her eyes with his, daring her to look away. He gently moved them around inside her and she couldn't stop her hips from rising up slightly and pressing against him.

"Relax," he ordered in a hoarse growl.

"What?" she whimpered, and then arched her back in surprise as he manipulated his hand and forced three fingers in.

"Relax! Or your punishment will be more severe."

With a small sob, she took a deep breath and forced herself to relax and accommodate him. With his hand in as far as he could go, he pressed gently on her belly as he rubbed his fingers against the upper wall of her tunnel, sending a raft of sensations through her. "Please," she begged, feeling tears of frustration welling up. "Please."

"Please, what, Elly?"

"Please." It was all she could say.

"Tell me. Say it. Tell the doctor what you need."

She looked at him with stricken eyes, willing him to know that she needed him inside her, to bring her to orgasm, to give her the release she was craving.

"I see." He removed his fingers. "Roll onto your front, and put a pillow under your hips." As he spoke, he took a pillow and pushed it under her as she rolled over, a look of puzzlement on her face.

He took the thermometer from his bag and removed it

from its tube. Her eyes popped open as she realised what he intended to do, and she put one hand behind her, protectively over her bottom.

"Move your hand." She wriggled and whimpered. He stared sternly at her. "You don't seem to realise, that I, as your doctor, am in charge. You are not to resist any examination or treatment I prescribe, is that clear? Anything I do will be because it is in your best interest."

She nodded, her eyes not filled with fear but with longing: longing for everything his attention promised and longing for the release she would get from surrendering to him. He understood and reassured her with a slow blink of his eyes and a small nod of his head.

"Trust me. Move your hand." This time, she slid it slowly away and her bottom was his. "Before I take your temperature, I'm going to punish you. You have refused to follow the doctor's orders twice now, and that is strictly forbidden. I expect you to take your medicine now like a good girl."

She nodded, laying still ready to accept whatever punishment he prescribed.

"Have you been spanked before? I'm not talking about a beating; I mean having your bottom lovingly spanked until it's rosy red because you have been a very naughty girl."

"No." Her body was tense, her nerves alive with expectation, her sex swollen, dripping and aching with a deep warm need that spread through her belly and down her thighs.

Gavin rubbed her bottom which clenched tighter at his touch. "Relax," he ordered her. "You are too tense. Three deep breaths in through your nose and slowly out through your mouth." He continued to stroke her cheeks as she breathed as he'd told her to and she felt the tightness gradually leave her bottom. "That's better." She finished her three breaths and looked back at him standing next to her bottom. "While I administer your spanking, you are to think about three things:

firstly, as your Doctor Daddy my top priority is taking care of your health and well-being and I will do whatever I deem necessary because I care about you; secondly, you were disobedient during your medical examination, and such misbehaviour will always, without exception, be punished with a spanking; and thirdly, you are to keep your bottom relaxed and still until I have finished your punishment. If you move or start tightening your bottom, your spanking will start again from the beginning. Is that clear?"

As he spoke, Elly's eyes had opened wider and wider in surprise. She could scarcely believe what she was hearing. Somehow in the middle of the hell her life and been, she had fallen into a deep sleep and woken up in a different world where the most gorgeous man she'd ever seen instinctively knew her secret fantasies and was fulfilling them without her needing to ask. And he had promised to take care of her forever.

She was jolted from her reverie by the palm of Gavin's large hand connecting with the soft, spongy flesh of her bottom. Her reaction was immediate and instinctive: she yelped, tightened her muscles, and half-rolled over away from him. Then remembered his instructions and his warning. She sheepishly glanced sideways at him, hoping he hadn't noticed and quickly rolled back into position.

"Fortunately, naughty girl," he reprimanded her, "starting again this time only means one extra smack. I wouldn't do it again, though, or I might decide my hand, especially as I am wearing gloves, is not providing a sufficiently salutary lesson and find something a little more convincing."

"No. I won't move again," Elly hurriedly promised. She didn't know what he might consider to be 'more convincing', and wasn't sure she wanted to find out.

"See you don't."

Elly watched him raise his hand and smack it down hard

on her bottom again. It stung, and she flinched and curled her fingers into a fist but otherwise kept perfectly still. He smacked her again. And then again. Each time his hand connected with her bottom, she flinched and blinked as the sting burned her increasingly sensitive flesh but, to her surprise, the pain he was inflicting was also powerfully pleasurable, both physically and emotionally. Unable to take her eyes off him, she was utterly mesmerised by the sight of him dominating her in this way as she lay surrendered and submissive to him. Her heart was full to bursting as she felt herself opening to him like a flower in the sun. She was his to command, and in this moment he could take whatever he wanted.

While her inner self was deliciously and happily acquiescent, her outer self was registering ever more acutely the heat and sting the flat of his hand was inflicting on her bare flesh. She became aware she was grunting increasingly loudly with each new smack on her burning skin, as he spanked her relentlessly. Then, in response to an even harder swat, she heard herself cry out, her exclamation accompanied by a sob. The spanking stopped immediately, and as he rubbed her chastised buns, she realised she was trembling with the exertion of keeping still. Her bottom was aflame and the heat had spread through her lower belly. She moaned, her body crying out for the release of possession. Gavin smiled at her, and after giving each punished, rosy cheek one last squeeze, he brushed sticky hair from her damp forehead.

"You look uncomfortably warm. I hope you haven't developed a temperature." He picked up the thermometer and removed it from its tube, then unscrewed his jar of lubricant and scooped some out with the thermometer. He spread some of the gel onto one gloved finger and the rest over the end of the thermometer. Watching him, Elly felt her taboo opening relaxing as it prepared itself for the erotic intrusion she knew was coming. She closed her eyes and buried her face as he used one hand to push her cheeks apart and his other to slip in the thermometer. She froze, shocked by both the lewd invasion and the realisation that it was pushing her ever deeper into a place where she completely surrendered her power. She was a willing sacrifice laid on his altar, her body offered up without resistance.

After the required interval, he removed the thermometer, looked at it, wrapped it in a tissue and placed it in the bowl, then put the bowl on the cabinet next to the bed.

"Your temperature is quite normal, and there's just one last thing before your treatment begins." He put more lubricant on his gloved finger and then held her cheeks apart and slid his finger deep into her. So under his spell was she, her body so relaxed and open to him, she offered no opposition other than a low, throaty rumble at the unfamiliar pressure. He withdrew his finger slightly and then pushed it back in, and then again, each time probing deeper. His cheek hardened as he clenched his teeth, watching her involuntarily moving her hips as he thrust harder and faster.

"Perfect," he muttered. "I think it's time for your treatment to start. Roll onto your back, please, slide down to the end of the bed, pull your knees up and spread your legs wide."

Elly rolled over and watched him undressing as she put herself in the position he'd demanded. He was standing at the end of the bed, his chest now bare and glistening with beads of sweat.

"Open your pussy for me, beautiful," he said, looking at her face. "Use your hands to show it to me wide open."

No longer able to feel embarrassed, Elly reached down and held herself apart. Her heart was pounding and her breath coming in gasps. She was desperate for him. "Please," she murmured. "Oh, please."

He smiled. "Don't worry, my precious patient." He slid his jeans off and pulled down his boxer shorts to show her he had the equipment needed to satisfy her desires. "Your Doctor Daddy is going to provide the special treatment you need to make you feel better."

He sat in the chair at the foot of the bed, hooked her legs over his shoulders, gripped her hips and buried his face into the hot, salty treasure between them. She cried out and her hands fluttered at her sides as his tongue thrust into her and then retreated and dragged itself up until his mouth closed over her clit. He wasn't gentle. He had been all over her body, outside and inside, and now he was going to complete his mastery of her. His mouth was relentless, licking, rubbing and sucking, demanding her subjugation, demanding she come for him and, with a guttural cry, she did, her hips writhing against his persistence. Moving his mouth out of the way, he lowered her legs back onto the bed, stood up, took the packet he'd dropped on the bed, ripped it open and rolled the sheath over the glistening tip of his penis.

"Move back," he growled, and Elly scrambled up the bed. Kneeling on the bed, he pushed her legs apart and positioned himself between her thighs. Putting his hands under her hips and leaning slightly forward, he pulled her onto his cock, thrusting hard and deep. In this position, he was solely in charge and he wanted her to be in no doubt about it. He withdrew until he was almost out, paused, and then thrust in hard, his eyes glinting with triumph when she gasped and her head tossed from side to side. Raising himself to get a better angle, he pumped hard, fast and relentlessly. He kept breaking his rhythm to prevent her from joining in, so she was at his mercy as he continued his onslaught, driving her on until he felt her contract hard around him, and her hips rose up as she cried out.

"That's my girl," he muttered, by no means finished with her yet. Rolling onto his side, he moved between her legs, sliding his cock in as he tucked his arm under her and pulled her to him. He looked into her eyes, grinding his teeth with triumphant pleasure seeing her total surrender, and as he began moving inside her again, his mouth closed over hers and they were locked so tightly together, only a slippery layer of perspiration separated them.

"Are you my girl?" he asked when he could speak again.

"Yes." Her reply was barely more than a breath.

"Am I your Doctor Daddy? And will you take whatever medicine I prescribe?"

"Yes," she whispered again, her eyes rolling back and her eyelids closing as he pushed into her.

"Including this?" he asked, running his finger down her bottom and pressing it against the tight opening. "Relax," he ordered, as she instinctively constricted her muscles to resist the intrusion. "Let me in. Now."

With a soft sigh of capitulation, she relaxed, acknowledging his supremacy by opening to his finger and pushing against it to aid its entry. A tiny shudder was her only reaction as it forced its way deep inside her. She was his prisoner now, his cock pushing up into her as his hand behind her, his finger inserted, pulled her hard against him, and his tongue mimicked their actions as his mouth crushed hers.

In all her years with Les, even as his wife, she had never before experienced this feeling of being so utterly claimed and mastered. He had transported her to a place where thought no longer existed, where the only awareness she had was of being captured and imprisoned, dominated and possessed. Her belly had turned to hot liquid, washing back and forth which each deep thrust, like waves coming to shore. As each wave rose higher through her body, her chest filled and tightened until breathing became unnecessary and she waited, patiently and without fear, for death. The tide of burning fire rose ever higher until finally it overwhelmed her and, as her body convulsed again and again, her heart burst and she could feel her pain being washed away in a flood of tears.

"That's my beautiful girl. That's my beautiful girl," she could hear him intoning, clasping her to him and rocking them both as he moved inside her, forcing the last drop from her orgasm. As she returned from her ecstasy, he held her mouth fast with his while he slid out of her, then flipped her over, pulled her hips up and plunged back in from behind. Without showing her any mercy, he grasped her cheeks and pulled and pushed them in rhythm with the thrusting of his hips. Then letting go, he leaned as far forward over her as he could, one hand on the bed on either side, and triumphantly plundered her exhausted body, riding her harder and harder until his body spasmed over and over and his face contorted in a loud cry of victory as he reached his own glorious end. Paralysed and panting, there was a moment where they stayed locked together and motionless, and then with him still inside her and his arms tightly about her, they collapsed side-by-side on the bed, him holding her from behind.

As the sound of his final ecstasy echoed away and their breathing subsided, he pressed his mouth against the back of her neck as he slowly slid out.

"Come here, beautiful, beautiful, girl," he murmured, and she rolled over into his arms. He scanned her face for confirmation all was well and, seeing the joy in her eyes, he kissed her so sweetly and gently, she thought her heart would burst. "I think I should stick around and make sure you take your medicine regularly, my precious, precious patient. What do you think?"

"Yes, please, Doctor Daddy," she replied softly, for the first time in her life feeling truly safe and loved, and that she had finally found her way home.

Chapter 14

"You're sure you're going to be okay?" Gavin asked through her car window as Elly buckled her seat belt and started the engine.

"I'll be fine. Honest. I just need to get Joey. I hate Les so much. I can't believe he pretended to kill Joey to scare me."

Gavin's face clouded with anger. He looked up over the roof of the car to compose himself, and when he looked back at Elly the murderous rage in his eyes had dulled. "I'm going to stop him hurting you, Elly. You and Joey. I promise." He leaned through the window and kissed her lips, then stroked her face. "Okay?"

She smiled a still uncertain smile and nodded. "Okay."

He kissed her again. "We'd better get going. I've got your address in my maps, so I should be able to find it easily enough. You follow me as close as you can, and I'll watch in the rear-view mirror to make sure I don't lose you. If you need to stop for any reason, flash your lights and I'll pull over."

After a few more kisses, he got into his car and led the way from the shack back to the road. Exhausted by their lovemaking, they'd fallen asleep early the previous evening and slept soundly until Elly, waking in the middle of the night, had reached over and woken him by stroking and squeezing him until he was hard. With a grunt of pleasure and a kiss, he'd stayed her hand, and left the bed long enough for a necessary trip to the bathroom and to don a condom. Back under the covers, he pulled her on top of him and slid her down onto his erection, encouraging her to pleasure herself while he lay back enjoying it and admiring the look and feel of her heavy breasts as they danced to the rhythm of her ride. When they were done, they'd kissed and snuggled until drifting off to sleep again.

Glancing at Elly in the rear-view mirror as they headed away from their love shack, Gavin wondered what she was thinking. For him, after leaving town expecting to spend a few quiet days by himself dealing with his anger and grief, the last two days had been surreal. He wasn't a man who put much faith in miracles, nor even meaningful coincidences, but if such things existed, this surely must be one. His gut had been twisted in knots by his inability to save one little boy from unspeakable cruelty, and out of the blue another little boy in need of help had crossed his path. Whether it was random chance or divine providence didn't matter.

It wasn't only about Joey, though. Whatever the connection was that he had with Elly, it existed before he knew Joey was alive and that he was her son, not Fiona's. He glanced into the mirror to check she was still following and because he needed to keep making sure she was real. He'd never imagined how quickly his life could change. Two days ago he was heartsick, alone, unable to contemplate returning to his work at the hospital, and considering driving off into the sunset and letting the winds of change blow him about like a tumbleweed.

And even as he was picking Elly up from the side of the road and putting her carefully in his car, he had no idea that within a few short hours she would become central to his life, yet here he was—feeling strong again, no longer alone, even looking forward to returning to work and reorganising his life to include a ready-made family: his beautiful Elly and her son, whom he was still yet to meet.

He glanced at her again. She was still there. Still real. A huge wave of emotion radiated from his gut, feelings he'd never experienced before or, at least, never as intensely, and it wasn't only lust despite the immediate stirring in his groin whenever he saw her or thought about her. She had already revealed a myriad of facets and he found her complexity intriguing. He admired her devotion to her son, and the courage she'd found to leave her abusive husband. He was saddened by her childhood suffering and the recent loss of her best friend. He was enchanted by her sweetness, and stirred by her vulnerability and need for protection. And he was excited by her sexual fantasies which meshed so neatly with his own in a way he'd not believed possible.

Two days ago, he'd been adrift and despairing; now he was re-energised with a new sense of purpose. He had a mission: to rescue Elly and Joey and provide them with a safe haven for the rest of their lives. His mouth tightened as he thought of Les: a bully and a coward, who terrorised and abused a fragile woman and frightened little boy, but who ran away from anyone able to defend themselves. Once Les saw Elly had a new protector, he had better slink away or Gavin would find a way to deal with him.

He glanced up again. She was too far behind for him to clearly see her face, but he could see the mass of curls falling behind her shoulders. He wondered again what she was thinking.

Elly saw Gavin checking in his mirror to make sure he hadn't lost her. He'd been doing it regularly and it felt like a lifeline, reassuring her she wasn't alone, that they were still connected despite being in separate cars. She felt like pinching herself to make sure she wasn't dreaming, but knowing she had spent twenty-four hours thinking she was Fi, she couldn't be sure that even knowing she was awake meant she could trust what she thought was real.

She'd gone to the beach on Tuesday night expecting to collect Joey, and instead thought she'd seen him killed, lost her senses and been in danger of dying herself, adopted Fi's identity, started an affair with the gorgeous doctor who'd rescued her, regained her memory, acted out her deepest sexual fantasies, and now Gavin was escorting her home after vowing he wanted to take care of her and Joey forever.

She hadn't had many good things in her life. Her childhood had been spent in poverty with an inadequate mother, and she was an outsider at school, constantly teased and bullied.

She'd found her first real happiness when she'd met Fiona and become an honorary member of her family, the only blight having been to stand helplessly by as her mother spiralled out of control. She had prayed, wished and hoped someone, something would save Jenny from the drugs and alcohol. But nothing did. Her death was sad and sordid, and Elly had vowed to herself that she would not emulate her mother. She would marry a good man like Fiona's father, Jeff, and have a happy, normal family.

Then Les came into her life. "No one's perfect. I'm certainly not," was her stock answer whenever Fiona tried to warn her. Jeff and Moy had been married for decades and Elly was sure that by the time she and Les had been married as long, they would have developed the same close, loving and companionable relationship Fiona's parents had.

By Joey's first birthday, though, she knew in her heart that Les wasn't fit to clean Jeff's boots and would never be the loving husband and father at the centre of her longed-for happy family. Her dream was over, but she could still ensure Joey had a better childhood than she'd had: he had a father, they weren't living in poverty and she tried to be the perfect mother.

If she could just stop making Les angry, everything would be all right, but there was no pleasing him, and when he lost a lot of money on bad business deals and his friends started dropping away, he took it out on her and Joey. The instant he struck Joey, staying with him was no longer the lesser of the two evils and she left.

While Fi was alive, she could pretend she hadn't turned out like Jenny: a single mother living in poverty. She'd tried everything to get a job, but she hadn't worked in nearly a decade and was competing with younger job seekers with more up-to-date skills. On their own after Fi died, they'd had to manage on her welfare payments as Les refused to give her money unless they lived with him. As far as the authorities were concerned, he was paying child maintenance, and he'd used his standard threat to stop her from informing them of the truth: he'd sue for sole custody on the grounds that she was an unfit mother and he'd win because he could afford the best lawyers and she couldn't.

His own ambition of being a rich, successful business man had evaporated in the smoke of a couple of big, dud deals, and he had grown angrier and more bitter as he approached forty and was confronted by his growing irrelevance in the world. Elly had watched him becoming increasingly callous but was still shocked by his latest cruel trick. Knowing there was no limit to what she would do to protect Joey, he was warning her there was no limit to what he would do to get her back.

She saw Gavin look at her in his mirror again. It was kind

of him to want to protect her, and her heart filled with love and gratitude. He was a good man like Jeff, a man who would be a loving husband and father in a normal, happy family. If only she had met him before she'd married Les—but then she wouldn't have Joey. Les was the price she paid for Joey, and if the only way to keep Joey safe was to submit to Les' demands, then that's what she would have to do.

The thought of having to live in the same house and bed with Les filled her with horror, but this mess was of her making and she would have to see it through at least for another fifteen years until Joey was an adult and able to look after himself. If she avoided upsetting Les and did as he said, he might leave Joey alone. With a sigh of sorrow of what might have been with Gavin, she resolutely determined to cut all contact with him lest Les find out and… Panic rose in her chest. She didn't know what he might do but was terrified of finding out.

By the time Gavin pulled up outside her apartment block and waited for her to turn in, Elly's resolve to break off with him had hardened into concrete. She pulled into her parking space, got out and walked back to meet him.

"Thank you for seeing me home. I'll be fine from here."

"I'm coming up."

"No. I have to put these things away, change into clean clothes and get ready for Joey. There's no point you being here."

"What do you mean 'no point'?" Gavin's voice dropped and his eyes narrowed. "Of course there's a point. I want to be here when that prick turns up. I'm going to tell him exactly what will happen to him if he even thinks about pulling another stunt like that."

"No." Elly pushed her hands desperately against his chest. "You can't. Please. I don't want to make him angry. You don't know what he's like. What if he really does hurt Joey next time? No. You have to go. I'll tell him Joey and I want to go back. That I made a mistake. That I don't want a divorce. He'll calm down if he knows we're going back. It's what he wants. And he'll be better this time, I'm sure, now he knows I've left once and could do again."

"Don't count on it, baby. From what you've told me, I doubt he's going to change. He'll keep bullying you because it's how he makes himself feel important. You have to put a stop to it."

"No." Elly's face turned white and her eyes filled with tears. "I can't. You don't understand. I'm afraid for Joey. And if Les sees you here, he might take Joey away again and not give him back. Please, please, leave. Don't let him see you. You have to go." She looked nervously both ways up the street. "He's going to be here soon. What if he's early?"

Gavin put his hands on her shoulders to hold her still and spoke firmly. "Okay. I can see you are worried that he might not let Joey out if I'm here, and I wouldn't put it past him to drive off either. We don't want that. I'll wait down here until after he's been. He's never seen me so won't know I'm watching. If he tries to leave with Joey, I'll stop him, otherwise, I'll stay out of sight until he's gone."

"No," Elly began but Gavin cut her off with a quick kiss.

"Stop arguing. I'm not leaving here until I know Joey is with you, you're both safe, and your dick of a husband has left. End of story. And don't worry, I'm not going to confront him. If he behaves himself, he won't know I'm here, but if he tries anything, I'll stop him. Not another word. Just get yourself upstairs and get ready. You can't let Joey find you in a state. Quick now. Doctor's orders." He smiled to soften his words, but Elly looked no less anxious as she collected her and Joey's things from the car and disappeared through the entrance to the lift and stairwell. Gavin got back into his car and idly played with his phone while waiting for Les to arrive.

Ten minutes later, he saw Elly appear on her balcony and

look down. Without acknowledging him, she went back inside. Gavin was furious and sickened by the way Les had treated her and it broke his heart to see her so afraid but, much as he took pleasure in imagining all the ways he could torture the abusive bully if he got his hands on him, he'd promised Elly to stay out of it and he meant to keep his promise—at least for now, until Joey was safely back.

He was still imagining kicking Les into the following week when a red Mazda MX-5 sports car with its roof down pulled into the visitors' car park. A man in a shiny silver suit, designer sunglasses, and cream shirt with the top buttons undone to show off a chunky gold chain and a thick mat of chest hair jumped out. He gesticulated impatiently to his passenger and, as he climbed out, the man cuffed the back of the little boy's head to convey to him that he was being too slow, and he was irritating and inconveniencing the adult.

Joey's head was down and he appeared listless as he waited for Les to collect his bag from the back seat. Furtively, he raised his eyes to the apartment in which his mother was waiting for him, and Gavin knew that, were the child not so afraid, he would dash joyfully upstairs to throw himself into her arms. Then his whole body perked up as he saw Elly exit the building and come towards them. His little feet were running on the spot and his head swivelling from his father to his mother, but still he didn't dare run to her.

Gavin looked on in disgust; Joey had been trained to await his father's permission to hug the mother he hadn't seen for a week. Gavin's fist itched with an almost irresistible longing to punch him in the face but, apart from violating his own moral code, it probably wouldn't help and would likely frighten Joey even more.

Elly didn't wait for Les' consent, however, and swooped on Joey scooping him up into her arms to hug and kiss him. Les said something and appeared to be trying to stop her and make her put her son down. She pulled away from him but he grabbed her upper arm hard enough to make her visibly wince, and spoke roughly. As their voices grew louder, Gavin was able to hear them through his open window as he got ready to defend her if Les didn't leave her alone immediately.

"No wonder he's a little sissy boy," Les said with a sneer and another clip around the boy's head. "Put him down, ya soppy cow or you'll make him as weak and pathetic as you are."

"I didn't think I was ever going to see him again," Elly said, clearly on the verge of tears.

Laughing at her distress, he let go of her and took out a cigarette and lit it. "You liked my show then, did you? I thought it was time I taught you a lesson. Now your skinny dyke friend is dead, good riddance, and you're not listening to her crap anymore, you and Joey are coming back home where you belong. We can take some of your stuff now and I'll send someone tomorrow to pick up the rest. Joey wants to come, don't you?"

He put his hand on Joey who pulled away and buried his face against his mother.

"Go on, kid, tell your mother you want to live at my house, not in this poky little flat," Les barked, trying to pull him away from Elly, but Joey clung on more tightly. Les glanced nervously around fearing someone might see him being rejected by his son. He grabbed Elly's arm again, pulled her towards his car and tried to shove her and Joey in. "I've had enough of this. Get in the car. You can get your stuff later."

Resisting as hard as she dared, Elly looked wildly around for an escape. She looked up toward her flat, back at Les and his car, and then surreptitiously to where Gavin was parked.

"I... I..." she stammered, her earlier resolve to acquiesce vanishing faced with the actuality of surrendering them both to this odious man when it was so clearly not what Joey wanted.

"Do as you are goddamn told and get in the car, or would you prefer the back of my hand?"

Elly wriggled sufficiently free to put Joey on the ground out of Les' reach. "Run upstairs, baby. Quick." He sped off without a backward glance.

His face red with fury, Les wound one hand in Elly's hair and used his other to twist her arm up her back. "That wasn't very clever, was it? You want to go upstairs? Let's go upstairs where we can—talk—in private." He pushed her arm hard on the word 'talk' and she cried out, her knees buckling with pain.

"No," she managed to gasp, resisting his attempt to shove her towards the apartment block entrance. "You go home. We'll follow in my car. I promise."

"You're a lying piece of trash," Les growled into her face, still twisting her arm behind her. "Didn't you take my warning seriously? Maybe I'll give…"

"No, Les. *I'll* give *you* a warning, and you had better take it very seriously indeed."

At the sound of the deep male voice behind him, even more sinister for being quiet and controlled, Les released his hold on Elly and spun around to find Gavin scowling at him with undisguised revulsion. He looked up at the intruder in surprise and shock, then understanding and fury, and whirled back to Elly.

"Have you been fucking around, you slut?" he shouted and then spat on the ground next to her before turning to Gavin. "Fuck off, mate. She's my wife and this is none of your business, so you'd better keep your nose out of it or you'll find out you've bitten off more than you can chew."

His bravado was fake and Gavin knew enough about human nature to smell the other man's fear. He was like a small dog, ferociously chewing on a guinea pig, and then, when confronted by a much larger dog, barking and snarling while checking out escape routes in case his bluff didn't work.

Gavin stared at him through narrowed eyes and bared his teeth as he pushed his hands into his pockets. Les' eyes glanced down, and he licked his quickly drying lips as he rightly understood Gavin's gesture to mean that he considered Les to be so small a threat he didn't even need to keep his fists ready. "No, mate." Gavin puffed himself up so he towered over the other man. "I'm not going anywhere. And she's not your anything."

"She's my wife," Les snarled but in a slightly less aggressive tone now also carrying the hint of a whine as he took a half step back.

"That doesn't give you any rights over her, and she wants a divorce." Gavin turned his back contemptuously on the other man and spoke to Elly. "Go up to Joey, baby." He nodded his head in the direction of her apartment, but her feet were rooted to the ground.

Les' face had turned purple and his body was shaking with rage. He desperately wanted to launch himself at the invader and pummel him into a bloody mess, but it was obvious he was physically no match for the mountainous younger man. As he stared at Gavin, his mind was ticking over. This was a situation he couldn't win, but he knew what he lacked in size and strength, he made up for in cunning and viciousness. He'd leave now if he had to, but he'd get his revenge, they could both count on that. He spat on the ground again, but far enough from Gavin for it to be a matter of debate as to whether or not he was actually spitting *at* Gavin, put his hands on his hips and swaggered.

"Okay, have it your way." He shrugged and held up his hands, palms up, in surrender. "I see she's got you pussy-whipped, but she does have a juicy cunt. I know. Better than anyone…" He paused to ensure Gavin took in the full thrust of his meaning then turned to Elly. "You and I aren't finished. He's my son, and I mean to get what's mine, one way or the other. You can come too. Or not. Your decision. But that offer closes soon. And don't think you aren't going to pay for this," he added with a nod at Gavin.

"Go to Joey," Gavin again ordered Elly, and this time, with no more than a quick glance at Les, she fled. A look of homicidal fury flashed across Les' face as he saw Gavin take control of Elly and her obey him. He gripped the door handle of his car ready to open it, then turned to Gavin for a parting threat.

"Remember, cowboy, if anything should… happen… to her or the boy, you'll only have yourself to blame." Mimicking Gavin's display of alpha male contempt, he turned his back on his rival as he started to open his car door.

In an instant, Gavin was pressed hard against the smaller man's back, his hands gripping the car on either side of him, squashing him and bending him over the door.

"You low-life grub," he growled, his mouth so close to Les' ear he could have bitten it. "You should be in jail for what you've done to Elly. And you don't deserve a son. Now go away and leave Elly and Joey alone, or you will answer to me. And if the slightest thing should happen to either of them, or you even think about harming them, I will personally cut your balls off and shove them in your pocket. Now get out of here and don't come back."

He stepped back and watched with a look of pure disgust as a white-faced Les got into his car, started the engine, reversed out of his parking space, yelled, "You're going to regret this, mate," and sped off.

Alone in the car park, he wiped the sweat from his forehead onto the back of his hand, took deep breaths to slow his galloping heart, and swallowed hard as he felt bile rising up from his stomach. He'd never seen Tyler's abuser, but Les had ripped open the wound the little boy's death had caused, and for a moment Gavin thought he was going to throw up. Forcing himself to keep taking slow, deep breaths, he bent forward, his hands on his knees. He couldn't see Elly or meet Joey until he was calm. In through the nose, out through the mouth, three, four, five... His heart slowed, his stomach subsided and the roaring in his head quietened.

Hearing a noise above, he looked up and saw Elly and Joey on her balcony looking down at him.

"All right if I come up?" he called in his most casual voice, giving them a quick wave, then disappearing out of view and heading up the stairs before Elly could refuse.

Chapter 15

"Y ou all right?" Gavin asked an ashen-faced Elly who was holding the front door open for him. "How's Joey?"

"He's okay. He's watching TV." She stood back to let him in, then closed and locked the door.

"Hi, Joey," Gavin said to the little boy sitting tensely on the edge of the couch staring at a cartoon on the television. "I'm Gavin. Your mum's friend."

Joey showed no sign of having heard. Elly was about to speak to him, but Gavin held up his hand to stop her. "It's okay. I suspect he's had enough of being pushed around by men for the moment."

"What did Les say?" she asked softly, glancing nervously at Joey.

"Nothing worth repeating. Look, why don't we get out of here? Does Joey like burgers? We haven't eaten yet, and it wouldn't surprise me if he hasn't either. Let me take you both out for lunch and then to a playground or something. I think the fresh air would do us all good. It will give him a chance to get to know me a little bit on neutral ground. He might feel safer, and we might get a chance to talk a bit in private. What do you say?"

"Do you want to go out for lunch, Joey?" she asked, walking over and sitting on the couch next to him.

He looked up eagerly. "Can I get one of those flying things?" He glanced nervously at Gavin before dropping his eyes to the ground.

Elly looked up at Gavin too. "It's a toy they're advertising with the kid's meal."

"Sounds great," Gavin replied enthusiastically with a grin. "I think I might get one for myself."

Joey looked at Gavin, surprised his choice appeared to have approval. He turned hesitantly to Elly, still sure wrath was about to descend on him from somewhere. She hugged him and smiled encouragingly. "Come on, then."

Restrained and without the natural ebullience of a secure, confident child, Joey took her hand as they followed Gavin down to his car.

Seated in the restaurant a short time later, having placed their orders and now waiting for their food to arrive, Gavin discreetly studied Joey from across the table. A skinny, sweet-faced boy, with short brown hair, he sat as close as he could to Elly and ignored Gavin, only breaking his silence a few times to whisper in his mother's ear. Gavin understood. He genuinely liked children, and knew that if he wanted Joey to feel secure around him, he had to give him time and space. Consequently, he didn't question the boy, or say anything requiring a response. He copied Joey's order and was rewarded with that same look of cautiously pleased surprise he'd got at the flat. When their food arrived, he took out the complementary flying disc included and studied it appreciatively.

"I got a blue one."

Joey took his green one out and almost held it up, but didn't speak.

"Wow, you got green. That's a cool colour. I wonder if a green one would fly better than a blue one."

Joey fidgeted and looked quickly at Gavin and then away. Gavin knew he wanted to say something but wasn't ready.

"We'll take them to the park after lunch and see how they go, shall we?" Before Joey had to worry about answering, Gavin turned his attention to Elly. "If that's okay with Mum."

"Of course." She smiled gratefully at Gavin and mouthed 'thank you' out of Joey's eyesight.

"Mmm, yum," Gavin said, munching his food. "This burger is yummy. How's yours?" He again directed the question to Elly, and was heartened to see Joey beginning to relax and be less afraid to look up from the table.

"Well, I can't wait to have a go at flying my disc," Gavin said as Joey finished his burger and seemed to be losing interest in his remaining chips. Gavin and Elly had both finished eating and were talking about music while they waited for the slower-eating Joey. "Shall we go to the park? You can bring your chips with you if you want or leave them here if you've had enough."

Joey was still eyeing him suspiciously, unsure whether or not this strange man was suddenly going to start ordering him around or scolding him the way his father did, but Gavin didn't even look at him, just collected up the rubbish and took it to the bin. Free of pressure, Joey picked up his disc and chips and headed for the door, then turned to wait for the grown-ups.

They found a park nearby with a playground and plenty of room to throw their discs. As soon as Gavin had parked the car, Joey jumped out, ran onto the grass and hurled his disc, but he didn't hold it flat and it fell straight down. He tried again with the same result. He tried once more and when the disc again tumbled to the ground at his feet, he glanced nervously at Gavin who was joining him and stomped angrily on the misbehaving disc.

"Good try," Gavin said. "I saw you throw yours like this." He demonstrated with his own disc but without letting it go. "But it didn't go as far as you wanted, so maybe there's a different way to hold it that would make it go further. What do you think?" He squatted level with the boy, and asked the question seriously, pausing to let Joey know his opinion was valued. Joey was staring at him, goggle-eyed; he'd been expecting a clip around the ear for failing to make his disc fly and instead he was being consulted on the physics of throwing them. He nodded furiously and snatched his disc up from the ground, discreetly wiping the dirt off. He turned it around in his hand, then looked back up at Gavin.

"How else could we hold it?" Gavin asked. "Like this maybe?" He held it flat and waited for Joey to copy what he was doing, then threw it gently so it sailed only a short way before falling. Joey followed his example and jumped up and down in delighted excitement when his flew further than Gavin's before floating to the ground.

Inspired by his success, he forgot to feel self-conscious and soon he and Gavin were flying their discs all over the park. After one particularly long throw, Joey looked joyfully up at Gavin, for a brief moment without the trouble that had been clouding his eyes. In this moment, he was a happy little boy having fun, apparently without a care in the world.

Eventually tiring of his disc for the present, he ran to Elly.

"Can I play on the playground now?" She looked at Gavin.

"It's fine by me," he said. "I don't have anywhere else I need to be. You can run ahead, if you want, Joey, and your mum and I will follow at an old person's pace."

"Okay," he said eagerly, handing his disc to Elly. "Can you take this for me?"

"Thank you, Gavin," Elly said earnestly as they watched Joey sprint to the playground and ambled slowly after him.

"You're so good with him. He's always so nervous when Les is around, but look how relaxed he is with you already."

"He's a good kid, and it's obvious he adores you and feels safe with you. You weren't serious about going back to Les, were you? Not after the way he's treated you both."

Elly stopped and swung around to look directly at him. "I don't want to." Her eyes were darkened by the same troubled shadow Gavin had seen in Joey's, and she was shaking. "It's the last thing I want to do, but I'm scared of what he'll do if I disobey him, and I don't trust him anymore when he's alone with Joey. I have to be there to protect Joey as much as I can even if…" Her voice died away unable to voice her darkest fears. "And maybe he won't this time," she finished lamely, looking ahead at Joey in the playground and then resuming walking towards him.

"He will, and you know he will," Gavin said sternly, walking with her, then softened his voice. "I know you loved him once. He was handsome and charming, and you were young and innocent and lonely; you were an easy target. I can see how he would have drawn you in. It's not uncommon for people who are abusive and controlling to keep that side of their personality hidden until they've gained the other person's trust and established an emotional and financial hold over them, which is pretty much what Les did to you, isn't it?"

Elly nodded. "I feel so ashamed. I was so stupid. I didn't see him for who he is, and I wouldn't listen to Fi. She knew. It's my fault Joey is in this mess. I have to protect him as much as I can." Her shoulders heaved with a barely suppressed sob. Checking Joey wasn't watching, Gavin gave her a quick hug.

He was about to reply but was interrupted by her phone ringing. She stopped again, pulled it out of her pocket and looked at the screen. The colour immediately drained from her face. "It's Les."

"Don't answer," Gavin said firmly. She put the phone back

in her pocket. "Listen, baby," he said. "I'm not going to push you around—I'm not Les, but my gut tells me I should just forbid you from going back to him. I can't kidnap you and Joey, much as I'd like to. The decision has to be yours."

"But what choice do I have? I don't even feel safe at the flat anymore. He's not going to leave us alone. How can I keep us safe? Who knows what he'll do next?"

An alert from her phone underlined her words. She took it out of her pocket and looked at it. "It's a message from Les. It says: *Hey, Sweetie. I'm looking forward to coming over tonight like you asked. I'm so happy you've missed me. I've missed you too. Can't wait for us to talk things over and make up in bed. If you want to play dirty games, you picked the right man. You won't know what hit you.* And there's a wink emoji. See?" Her eyes welled with tears of fear, frustration and resignation. "He'll keep harassing me until I agree. He was scared of Fi, but he's not scared of me. And there's no point going to the police. They can't do anything. Look at this: *You won't know what hit you.* It's a threat, but he's made it sound like an exciting date. He's too clever."

They reached the playground where Joey was happily running, climbing and jumping as he explored all the equipment. Gavin had been silent while thinking things over, but as they sat on a nearby bench he spoke.

"You can't stay at your flat; Les will keep harassing you. Come and stay with me. Les won't know where you are. I live by myself, my house has three bedrooms so there's plenty of room, and you and Joey can each have your own bedroom. And you need to take out a restraining order. I know they aren't always effective and it will probably make him even angrier, but it will put his behaviour and your fear on record so nobody can ask later, if it ever comes up, why you didn't do anything. And I think you should also file for divorce immediately."

"But I can't afford a lawyer and he will get some fancy

lawyer who'll portray me as a terrible mother with no job who can't support her son and Les will get sole custody and I won't be able to see Joey anymore and…"

"Shh," Gavin said, gently shaking her shoulders to snap her out of her rising panic. "He's not going to get custody." His voice broke and he had to collect himself before he could speak again, his voice harsh and rough with emotion. "That's not going to happen. Ever. I'll pay for the lawyer if need be."

Elly looked at him in surprise. He was looking away from her, but she could see a vein throbbing in his temple, a flush darkening the skin on his neck and cheek, and the tendons in his neck straining against the tightness in his throat.

"What is it?" she asked, briefly forgetting her own troubles. He took a deep breath, sighed, shrugged and then turned back. Without looking at her, he leaned forward resting his elbows on his knees and faced the ground in front of him. She waited, also looking down, as her shoe scuffed the dirt. "You know," she said at last. "We've been so caught up with me and my stupid life, I hardly know anything about you. Well, apart from you being a doctor." She blushed. His head still down, he grinned.

"What do you want to know?"

Elly shrugged. "I don't know. Nothing in particular— except, maybe, I wanted to ask you if you have any children. I think I remember you said you didn't, but you're so good with Joey and you seem… I'm not sure… I don't know quite how to describe it… sort of intensely protective. Would it sound silly if I said it's almost like you're on a mission where he's concerned?" She gave a small self-deprecating laugh, inhaled shakily as she looked away, her hands gripping the edge of the bench either side, and then spoke clearly. "Why aren't you at work? It wasn't an ordinary holiday, was it? Why do I feel it was more than that? I feel like I should remember something."

Gavin shrugged and tilted his head on its side without

raising it so he could see her. "Do you remember on Wednesday when we were at the shack, I told you about Tyler, the little boy who died at the hospital?"

Elly frowned, and cocked her head as her eyes darted back and forth searching for the memory, but she drew a blank. She screwed up her mouth, shrugged and looked at him. "Not really. Maybe it sounds familiar."

Gavin lifted himself up and leaned against the back of the bench, folded his arms and rested his right ankle on his left knee. Staring at Joey playing happily on a swing, he clenched and rubbed his teeth together, took a deep breath and exhaled it slowly.

"It's only a kind of holiday," he acknowledged. Elly listened as he told her about Tyler again, and nodded as his words triggered a memory of her having heard the story before.

"I couldn't bear that there was nothing I could do for him." Gavin's throat caught and he coughed to clear it. Elly had turned her face away as his story unfolded, not wanting to make him self-conscious as he struggled with his grief and anger, but as he finished, she reached over and put her hand over his. He flinched at her touch, then looked down at their hands and took a slightly calmer breath.

"You want to make sure the same thing doesn't happen to another child." It was a quiet statement. "And helping Joey might ease your own pain about Tyler."

He ducked his head low to hide his emotional struggle. Elly squeezed his hand comfortingly, and that made it even harder for him not to cry.

"Do you have any family?" Elly asked lightly. "I don't even know that about you."

He shook his head, his heart filling with gratitude to her for changing the subject and breaking the shackles of his grief, at least about Tyler.

"No." He managed a rueful smile. "I guess we're both orphans, alone in the world."

"No brothers or sisters? Neither of your parents still alive?"

He shook his head.

"Oh, I'm sorry," Ellie said quickly. "I didn't mean…"

"Shh. It's okay. You don't have to apologise. I know you didn't mean," he said, making a little joke to assuage her guilt. Her lips twitched in an attempted smile.

She patted his arm. "We're a pair of sad sacks, aren't we? You don't have to tell me, if you don't want."

"I do want," he replied, putting his hand over hers and squeezing it. "Mum and Dad were both thirty-three when they met, and both wanted big families, but neither had found anyone they wanted to marry until they met each other. They decided they must have been meant to meet long before but had missed each other at the appointed time and place." He chuckled. "It was like they were trying to solve a mystery; they'd think of all the places they'd ever been to see if their paths could have crossed."

"Oh, that's so romantic," Elly said in a cracking voice. She cleared her throat. "Did they ever find anything?"

"No, but they loved the game, and I reckon they knew almost as much about each other's lives as they did about their own."

"So how come you're an only child?" Elly asked after a pause.

"Oh, yeah." Gavin chuckled. "Sorry, I got lost remembering all the time I spent listening to them talking about where they were living and working and shopping and going out, and all the people they knew. Handy if I ever decide to write their biographies. But… anyway… So, they married six weeks after they met and I was born ten months later. They tried for another baby pretty much straight after I was born, but I was over a year old by the time Mum got pregnant again.

Then she miscarried. They kept trying but she didn't fall pregnant easily. When she did, she miscarried again. Three more times in total, and then she was diagnosed with uterine cancer."

"Oh, Gavin, that's awful. I'm so sorry. Your poor mum. How terrible for all of you. I guess you were pretty young?"

Gavin sighed and didn't speak for a moment. "Yeah, I was five when she was diagnosed. I was too young to understand much other than that Mum was sick. She had a hysterectomy which of course meant no more babies. The dream of a houseful of kids went up in smoke. They were sad, but I think what Dad cared most about was that he still had Mum, and Mum was mostly grateful to still be alive. They got on with their lives, I got spoiled and life went back to normal... until the cancer came back three years later."

"Oh," Elly said sadly, understanding without him having to say more. He sighed.

"It was horrible. Dad was devastated. Watching Mum go through that was when I decided I wanted to be a doctor. I was sure that if I'd been a doctor, I would have been able to fix her. I thought her doctors weren't trying hard enough; that there must have been a way to make her well. A pill or a medicine or something. Now, of course, I know it's not that simple. Progress is being made, but it's more a succession of small advancements rather than one big miracle cure."

"I'm sorry," she said gently. It felt inadequate, but what else could she say? "And your dad?"

"He was lost without her." Gavin's voice was tight, his words clipped. "She died at home. Dad refused to be apart from her and wouldn't let anyone else take care of her. He nursed her to the end. He had his own plumbing business which he put on hold and then picked up again afterwards. But he was never the same. He was as good a father to me as he could be. He was always kind and, physically, at least, always there. I became obsessed with becoming an amazing doctor who would miraculously save people, and all I did was work—so much so, I even worried my teachers." He shrugged and looked at her with a wry smile. "I made it into medical school." He looked away again. "Dad died not long after I graduated. He went to bed one night and that was it. He never woke up. I think he believed his work on Earth was done and he was free to join Mum once I didn't need him anymore." He gave a half-laugh, half-snort. "I guess that sounds a bit fanciful."

"Not to me," Elly said gently. "Especially not after what else you told me about them. I think it sounds beautiful. Sad. But beautiful." She paused. "And you've never married? Sorry. I feel like you might have told me this before, but I can't remember."

He shook his head. "Nope. Never married. I guess I went into my shell after Mum died, and I stayed there for a long time. As a teenager and then at medical school, I put all my energies into work, and what little free time I had I spent mostly at the gym or pool trying to make up for spending so much time sitting on my arse with my books. I had a couple of girlfriends, and then met Sara, another intern, when I first started working in a hospital. We hooked up and were together for nearly three years, although it didn't seem that long because we both worked such long hours and different shifts we barely saw each other. It was easy, I suppose. Then Sara decided she wanted to do a stint overseas, but I wanted to finish my surgical training. We talked about waiting for each other, then realised neither of us cared that much about breaking up, so we did."

Elly swung her legs back and forth under the bench as she listened to him.

"Have you thought about work? Will you go back to the hospital?"

This time he did look at her, with an intensity that sent a shiver through her.

"Aha. You remember me saying I'd been thinking about driving into the sunset. I was, it's true, but I think I want to go back now. Especially if you'll let me take care of you and Joey. Come and stay with me. No strings. You'll be free to do whatever you want, but you'll be safe and not alone."

Her eyes darted either side of him, but before she could answer, her phone signalled another message. She read it and shuddered.

"Okay. We'll come."

"What did it say?"

She read it aloud: Hey Doll. I'll be there at 7. Hope you're ready for me. Did you like my last surprise? I can do way better than that. And next time I'll make sure Joey is there to fully experience it."

Gavin leapt up, his fists clenched at his sides. "That vicious, cowardly scumbag. Don't answer. Get Joey and we'll go back to your place so you can pack what you need. You *are* coming home with me, and that's final."

Chapter 16

While Elly and Joey packed, Gavin made an appointment to see a lawyer, and by the time the three of them sat down for their first meal together in Gavin's house that evening, Elly had applied for a restraining order against Les, had initiated divorce proceedings, and had sent Les a message telling him not to go to her flat because she and Joey weren't there, and he would be hearing from her lawyer in due course.

Les had rung immediately, but Elly hadn't answered. She had Joey with her and, as Les didn't know where she was, she didn't have to worry about him turning up at her door.

When they had first arrived at Gavin's comfortable suburban home, Joey had been hesitant and confused.

"Why are we here, Mummy?" he'd whispered.

"We're just going to stay here with...?" She'd looked questioningly at Gavin who mouthed *Gavin*. "With Gavin for a little while. Would you like that? There's a garden like at Nanna Moy's."

"Can I see the garden?"

"Sure," Gavin had interrupted. "Follow me and I'll show

you."

"Do you like to kick a ball?" Gavin had asked, squatting down level with Joey's face after they'd done a quick tour of the backyard. "There's plenty of room. And I could put up a basketball hoop if you'd like."

Joey hadn't replied, but he had at least looked hesitantly hopeful, and it seemed to Gavin that the little boy might have shed one thin layer of fear and uncertainty. He smiled, stood up, put his arm around Joey's shoulder and gave him the briefest of hugs. Joey initially flinched at his touch, but Gavin had already moved away before it felt threatening, and he clumped behind Gavin with a little more confidence as they went back inside to find Elly on her phone.

"I'm just calling Nanna Moy," she whispered to Joey as Moira answered.

Joey bobbed up and down without moving his feet. "Can I talk to Nanna Moy, Mummy?"

"Hi, Moy. Yes. Yes. I'm fine, and Joey is fine too," Elly said, answering Moira's questions. "He's right here. He wants to say hello."

Elly handed her phone to Joey who put it to his ear.

"Hello, Nanna Moy. Yeah. Yeah. Nah, not really," he responded without enthusiasm to questions about his holiday, then his face brightened. "Guess what, Mummy and I are staying at the man's house, and it's got a dime garden and I might be able to get a puppy now, can I Mummy?"

Elly retrieved the phone and heard Moira chuckling.

"I'm not sure I followed all that," Moira confessed when she discovered she was talking to Elly again. "Man? House? Puppy? And what on earth is a 'dime garden'?"

"Les was trying to force us to go back and live with him, so Gavin said we could stay at his house so Les wouldn't know where we are. I think 'dime' means good. Joey is delighted he's got a garden to play in. No. No. We haven't talked about a puppy… Yes, Joey and I will come and visit you soon. And maybe you can come and check out the dime garden, too. Okay, Moy, see you. Love you."

"Moy says you're a good man," she told Gavin joining him in the kitchen.

Gavin smiled and stole a sneaky kiss while Joey wasn't watching. "I think you should listen to her. She sounds like a lady who knows what she's talking about."

After dinner, Gavin cleaned up, and Elly helped Joey shower and get into his pyjamas.

"Are we going to stay here forever?" he asked as Elly helped him into the spare double bed she was going to share with him for their first night and tucked him in. "Is Daddy going to live here?"

"I don't know how long we'll be here," Elly answered honestly. "Do you think you will like living here for a while?"

Joey nodded seriously. "Having a garden is dime."

"That means good, doesn't it?" Elly said with a smile.

"Uh-huh," Joey nodded. "Will Daddy be coming though?" Elly could see the anxiety in his eyes.

"No. I don't think so. Would you like him to?"

Joey looked down and shook his head.

"Then he shan't. And you don't have to see him for a while if you don't want to."

"Won't that make him mad?" Joey asked anxiously, breaking his mother's heart. How could a father be so cruel to his little boy, she wondered for the millionth or more time.

"It might." She kissed his forehead, pulled the covers up snuggly around him, and cheerfully added, "But if we don't see him, we shan't know, shall we?"

Joey seemed reassured and she left him to sleep, switching off his light but leaving the hall light on and his door ajar. In the living room, Gavin was waiting for her. He'd put on some quiet music and poured two glasses of *sauvignon blanc*.

"I thought we might drink to your first night under my roof," he said, standing up and handing her a glass. "To my new little family." He clinked her glass and took a sip. Elly blinked, still unable to shake the feeling that this couldn't be real.

"You look a bit stunned, beautiful. Come and sit with me," Gavin said, sitting on the couch and patting next to him. Elly joined him and sipped her wine. "Tomorrow," he went on, "we can organise the other room for Joey. I'll clean my stuff out and we'll get him his own bed. We can go back to your flat and pick up some more things if you want."

Elly blanched. "What if Les is watching?"

"We'll go very early, and we can check for his car. I don't think he will have camped out last night. He seems to me like a man who values his creature comforts a bit too much."

"What about school, though? He's bound to turn up at Joey's school."

Gavin nodded thoughtfully. "Yeah, that could be a problem. Should we ask Joey how he'd feel about changing schools? There's a primary school not far from here. We could go on Monday, have a look and talk to them. And Joey can have his old schoolmates over for a play until he makes new friends. How does that sound?"

Elly looked squarely at him. "Moy was right; you are good a man, Doctor Minchin."

"Am I?" he asked with a self-conscious grin. "And that's Doctor Daddy to you."

Elly blushed, and Gavin put down his drink, took hers and put it down, and pulled her into his arms. "Am I allowed to kiss you? If Joey doesn't see."

She smiled and nodded, leaning forward as his mouth covered hers, but the first real kiss they'd managed since leaving the shack earlier that morning was interrupted by the ringing of her phone. She broke away from Gavin and turned to where it was lying on the table near them, then ignoring it, she turned back to Gavin, snuggling against him and resuming their kiss. It rang again.

"It's probably Les. I should have blocked him," she said, picking it up and looking at it. "No. It's Moy. Hi, Moy. What's up?" As Elly answered the call, Gavin saw her pleasure turn to dismay. "Oh no. Oh, I'm so sorry. I can't believe he did that. Are you all right? Are you sure? I'm really, really sorry. But it is my fault. It's me he's after. Okay. And call the police if he comes back. Promise? Okay."

The call ended and she turned to Gavin, who'd leapt to his feet and was pacing up and down, muttering, "What? What's going on?"

"Les went to her place. He thought I'd be there or Moy would know where I was. No, he didn't do anything," she replied to his urgent unspoken question. "He's too cunning for that. But as he was leaving, he told her he was worried about her living alone without a man about, and he's going to keep dropping in and hanging about to keep an eye on her. But he'd feel less like he needed to if he knew I was visiting her regularly, and to let him know if I went over so he could come and make sure. And he said if she told him where I was, he'd leave her alone."

"That bastard. Somebody needs to teach that guy a serious lesson: that he can't go through life bullying vulnerable people. I guess tricking you into thinking your son had been blown up shows how low he's prepared to go. Goddammit. I wish we had some evidence of that to take to the police."

"He's too clever," Elly said, miserably shaking her head. "He never puts anything incriminating in texts. I can show he called me, but I don't have any proof he told me to be at the beach. And I bet even if they could salvage the boat, they wouldn't be able to connect it to him."

Gavin nodded. "He still has to be stopped. He's done

enough damage already to you and Joey. I can't let him do any more."

"What are you going to do?" Elly asked tremulously as Gavin took her phone, scrolled through it and then held it up to his ear, his nostrils flaring and his face a mask of anger.

"No. This isn't Elly, but I'm speaking on her behalf," he growled when Les answered having seen Elly's number and thinking it was her who'd called. "This is your last warning, dirtbag. If you go anywhere near Elly or Joey or Moira or anyone else she knows, you will wish you hadn't. Your reign of terror is over. If you're smart enough to know when you're beaten, you'll disappear quietly—forever. If not, you'll face the consequences."

Elly could hear Les trying to talk back, but Gavin said his piece, hung up and blocked Les' number. He put his arms around Elly and held her against him until she'd stopped shaking, then sat them both back on the couch, his arm around her and her head on his shoulder.

"Finish your wine, precious," he said gently, "and forget about that arsehole for the moment. He won't go back to Moira's tonight and he has no idea where you are, so he can't turn up here. You can relax. You're safe."

Elly finished her wine in a gulp and handed her glass to Gavin who put it on the table. She snuggled back into him, her body slowly releasing the tension it had been holding for so long. Suppressed tears found their way to the surface, welling in her eyes and then spilling over to cascade down her cheeks. Gavin held her tighter and kissed her hair as she began to cry, his own eyes burning from the pain they'd all suffered. Her body shook against him as she silently sobbed into his chest, and he rocked them both gently, staring at nothing and licking the salt from the tears that trickled down his own cheeks onto his lips.

Chapter 17

Pulling up in the doctors' car park on Wednesday, having requested and been granted two additional days leave to get Elly and Joey settled, Gavin turned off his engine and sat for a moment staring at the higgledy-piggledy, brick complex in front of him. The Emergency Department at the front was in the original section of the hospital. It had been modernised inside, and the double doors leading in were now self-opening, but high-tech modern ambulances unloaded the sick and injured at the same place their predecessors had done for more than a century.

Behind this entrance, Metro Dora had grown steadily up and out. Like a giant mother ship, its stairs and lifts, wards and corridors, laboratories and kitchens bustled with people in uniforms, impassive but not indifferent, confidently striding together deep in conversation, wheeling the sick and injured on gurneys and in wheelchairs, or pushing food trolleys and cleaning carts from ward to ward.

Scattered among them and dressed in civvies were the outsiders: people not sick enough to be admitted visiting outpatient clinics, and those not there for their own health but bringing emotions and news from the world to their bedridden family members and friends. New arrivals with concerned faces moved about the hospital hesitantly, feeling their way through the maze as they stopped to read signs and ask directions in hushed voices, while the faces of those whose lives had been centred around frequent visits showed the strain of prolonged grief for a loved one who would never recover, or the tired joy of a harrowing ordeal reaching its end as preparations were made for the joyful homecoming.

Walking toward the entrance, Gavin felt Tyler's presence rising within him. Pausing to honour a life so cruelly and brutally cut short, he feared for a second that he had overestimated his recovery but, as the familiar ache filled his chest, he realised it was no longer anger and despair but love and hope. Tyler was at last sleeping peacefully and couldn't be hurt again. "Fly free, sweet child," Gavin whispered, then fancying he had Tyler's blessing to move on and help others, he walked briskly across the car park, in through the doors that opened before he got there and, after swiping his card across the reader, through the *Staff Only* door.

"Hi, Doctor Minchin," a senior member of the nursing staff greeted him, pausing briefly. "Welcome back. We've missed you."

Gavin read the unspoken question in her eyes. He looked around, taking in the remembered sights and sounds and smells, then smiled and nodded. "Thanks, Millie. It's good to be back." The concern clouding her face vanished. She smiled back and patted his arm before hurrying on.

Time passes faster in hospital emergency departments than just about anywhere else on earth, all too frequently almost faster than anyone can keep up with, and evening shifts usually fly by fastest of all while still seeming to never end. Fortunately on this day, it wasn't more frenetic than usual when Gavin arrived, and he was able to ease in and reply in brief snatches to his co-workers as they welcomed him back.

By the time he dashed to the cafeteria to grab some dinner in a lull around 6:00 p.m., he'd seen an elderly lady who'd fallen while gardening and sustained a Colles' fracture of her forearm, a young woman having an asthma attack, a young man who'd dislocated his shoulder clowning about, three people injured in traffic accidents, an elderly man so tired of life he could barely stand, and three abdominal pains, one requiring only analgesics and reassurance it was nothing serious, one that was investigated via an ultrasound before the patient was allowed home, and one suspicious enough for the patient to be admitted for observation and investigation.

Sitting at a table with a plate of curry and rice in front of him, he took out his phone and checked his messages finding one from Elly saying she'd collected Joey after his second day at his new school and they were home safely.

Having been reassured his father didn't know where either his new home or his new school were and therefore couldn't turn up, Joey had lost some of his ever-present anxiety, and Gavin was getting an inkling of the boy's real personality when not oppressed by his bullying father. Elly had also relaxed a little but wasn't so easily able to dismiss Les from her mind. Consciously, she couldn't see any way he could know her whereabouts, but that didn't stop her heart racing whenever she heard a car approaching down their quiet street, or heard footsteps on the pavement outside, or imagined she heard the front gate open. When she'd collected Joey from his school, she'd glanced nervously around as she'd waited under the tree in the grounds for his class to be out, and bundled him quickly into her car as soon as he'd appeared.

"Hey, Gav," a deep voice said as a man placed his plate of rissoles, chips and salad on Gavin's table and pulled up a chair. "Mind if I join you?"

"Hey, Ron," Gavin replied with a smile and flourish of one hand while returning his phone to his pocket with the other. "Be my guest."

"So, what do you know?" Ron asked casually, gently fishing. He was the one person Gavin had confided in about his emotional and psychological struggle over Tyler, and it was he who had finally convinced Gavin he needed to take a break and offered him the use of his shack, the shack in which Gavin and Elly had spent two nights. Both men knew his question was a diplomatic way of asking Gavin how he was feeling being back at work.

"Yeah, good," Gavin answered, looking directly at the older man across the table who nodded in response and raised a querying eyebrow to show he was interested if Gavin wanted to expand. Gavin shrugged and grinned, not sure where, or if, to start, but Ron recognised something in his expression.

"What's this?" he said with a chuckle. "What have you been up to?"

Gavin grimaced and snorted. "It's almost so bizarre, you probably won't believe me if I tell you. I can scarcely believe it myself."

"Try me."

Without going into intimate details, Gavin gave his friend a quick outline of the previous week. Ron ate his dinner, nodding at intervals to show he was listening.

"So Elly and her kid are living with you?" he asked when Gavin had finished. Gavin nodded. "Is her ex still hanging around? He sounds like a piece of work."

"He doesn't know where Elly and Joey are for the moment, but I doubt we've heard the last of him. Control freaks aren't known for giving up easily, and I don't think he's got much else in his life apart from bullying his wife and kid. My take is that he's a guy who thought he'd be Mr Big one day, but is now having to face the truth that he's a pathetic nobody, and he's taking it out on others."

Gavin pursed his lips and put his hand over his chin while he rubbed his cheek with his forefinger, then sighed and scooped up a spoonful of food.

"I'm expecting him to show his ugly face at some point and, to be honest, I'm not sure how far he'll go. He's used physical violence before and that stunt with the boat shows he's no less into emotional violence. It's hard to know how to stop these jerks. I mean, Elly's applied for a restraining order, but too often they're not worth the paper they're printed on, and she's told him she's suing for sole custody. If Les seriously wanted access to his kid, he'd be trying to prove he's a good father. My bet is that he sees Joey as a way to get at Elly, and he doesn't give a flying rat's arse about making him suffer."

"Someone should cut his balls off?" Ron said with a grin, tilting his head and raising his eyebrows.

"What?" Gavin looked confused for a second, then laughed. "Quoting me back to myself, hey?"

"I may have heard you say that once or twice. And to be honest, I'd happily do it myself if he turned up under my knife. Seriously though, Gav, are you okay? Do you know what you've got yourself into? And why?"

Gavin looked at him for a moment. He knew what Ron was asking, and it was a question he'd asked himself. "Fair question. I guess the best way to answer it would be to say, I would have wanted to take Elly home with me even if her first story, that she had no kids and was single, had been true. Don't worry mate, I've asked myself the same thing: is Tyler the reason I'm getting involved, and the answer is no. I'm sure of that."

Both men ate silently, then Ron, who'd been eating while Gavin had been talking and had finished his meal first, pushed his plate away. "Well, let me know if there's anything I can do to help. I'd better get a move on. I'm due in surgery again shortly."

"How is OR? Still surviving without me?"

"Barely managing," Ron said with a laugh, then winked. "But I much prefer it to anywhere else; I like my patients asleep. They're less trouble."

Gavin chuckled as Ron stood up. "I guess there's something to be said for that. Definitely less trouble than some in Emergency."

"That they are." Ron sat back down. "Hey, Gav, I don't suppose you'd consider coming back for a while, would you? Dicko's leaving and we haven't found a replacement as yet. Fortunately, he's been able to stay on a bit longer but I think another week is about his max. I could talk to the Boss. I'm sure she'd be rapt to have you. It'd give you chance to refresh your skills and, who knows, you might enjoy the break."

Gavin paused in thought. "It's been a while…"

"I know. It's a shame. You were good. Best registrar I've ever had." Ron held his hands up defensively as Gavin opened his mouth to respond. "It's okay, mate. I know you weren't sure if you'd made the right choice and needed to have another crack at Emergency. I get that, and I don't know if you've made up your mind whether you want to settle there or not. All I'm saying is, if you think you could hack OR again for a while, you'd be doing us a favour, even if it's just filling in until we find someone permanent. I'm sure the Boss can convince Prof to give you leave from Emergency. But, it also goes without saying that I'd back you all the way if you decided you wanted to apply for the permanent registrar position. But that's up to you. No pressure. At least would you consider helping us out?"

Gavin sucked on his teeth, then grinned and nodded. "You know what? It sounds good. Honestly, I think I'm pretty much done with Emergency, and I'd be lying if I said I hadn't been tossing around the idea of moving back to OR. I thought I'd probably have to leave Dora, though, so I've kind of been stalling making a decision. I'm pretty happy here. Your offer must be another of those signs I don't believe in, hey? Nah, nothing, mate. Don't worry," he said, grinning and waving his hands as Ron looking at him questioningly. "But thanks. I appreciate it. Yeah, see what the Boss says and if she can get Prof to agree, and let me know. Now I'd best get going too, or I might not have a job in any department."

The two men shook hands and headed back to work, and not much more than a week later, Gavin was once again a surgical registrar in the OR. He was surprised how easily it was all coming back to him, and he felt certain now that this was where he wanted to be. As a resident, he'd flipped a coin between specialising in surgery or emergency; surgery had won, but after four years, he felt he had to make sure he'd made the right choice. As much as he had enjoyed the pandemonium and unpredictability of emergency over the last year, lately he'd been feeling the lure of surgery calling to him again and, now he'd taken the plunge, he could see himself staying.

At home, he and Elly and Joey continued to settle into life as a cosy little family. Freer than she had been in years, Elly was able to begin some projects she'd been forbidden from doing while she'd been under Les' control. She started a short online course to upgrade her skills so she could look for a job, and Gavin surprised her with new art materials and created a small studio area for her in the outside shed.

Deciding Joey had enough to deal with for the moment without seeing his mother in a new relationship, Gavin and Elly had reluctantly agreed to temporarily put their romance on hold. Their first priority was maintaining stability for Joey, and considering they still barely knew each other, it was enough they were now all sharing the same house without adding extra stresses. While there had been the odd occasion when, alone in the house, Gavin had pulled Elly across his knee for a bare-bottom spanking and they'd been unable to resist making love afterwards, for the most part they spent the small amount of time they had alone together talking, going to a movie, or pottering in the garden. To their joy, they discovered that not only was their sexual attraction simmering beneath the surface as hotly as ever, but there was an equally strong mutual liking and respect.

"You're my best friend, you know," Gavin had said to her one day as they struggled together to move a weighty planter to a new spot in the garden.

Elly had blushed with pleasure. She'd been thinking the same thing, but had been too shy to tell him. "You too."

The calm environment also had a healing effect on Joey who was gaining in confidence and looking happier with every passing day. He idolised Gavin, wanting to be with him whenever he could, and Gavin felt the same, never tiring of playing with him, taking him to the park, kicking balls, watching television, helping with his homework, and sharing long conversations.

Joey had also settled well into his new school, and was starting to have regular play dates with his new friends. He had also maintained his friendship with Liam, his best friend from his previous school, and the two boys had been delighted to see each other when Liam had come for his first play date at Joey's new home. Elly's heart had overflowed to see Joey proudly and happily showing Liam around before they disappeared into the garden to play with a ball.

Days went by and drifted into weeks with no trouble from Les. The restraining order, granted by the court, forbade Les from contacting Elly directly, decreeing that all communication between Joey's parents be directed through their lawyers. One such communication was that Les would not only be fighting her application for sole custody, but that he had made a similar application with the court, and it seemed that, for the moment at least, he was taking his lawyer's advice to avoid doing anything that might jeopardise his application.

By the time Elly had been living with Gavin for a little over a month, a mild, wet spring had triggered a profusion of flowers, not just in their garden but all over the city. The avenues of jacarandas were slowly turning purple, and it seemed every garden was a chorus of daisies, opening to the sun in the morning and then carefully tucking their colourful costumes away at night to keep them fresh for the following dawn.

"It's Fi's birthday tomorrow," Elly said as she and Gavin shared a late nightcap, snuggled together on the couch. Even though he was always late home from the hospital, it had become a ritual for her to wait up for him unless he let her know he was delayed and wouldn't be home until the wee small hours. "I'm going to Moy's for lunch and then we're going to visit Fi and take her some flowers."

"That's a lovely thought." He nuzzled her hair. "You will be careful, though, won't you, precious? I know Les hasn't bothered us for a while, but I don't think we should assume we've heard the last of him. Keep a careful eye out, and don't take any chances if you see anything suspicious. You have my number on speed dial, if you get worried. And don't hesitate to call the police."

"I'll be careful, and I'll be with Moy. I don't think Les would dare bother us while we're together, and besides he won't know we're going."

"All right. I'm sure Moy will keep careful watch too, but I don't trust Les. I was kind of expecting to hear from him when you rejected his last offer of reconciliation, but Craig reckons it wasn't a serious suggestion anyway, more something some lawyers do so it's on file that an attempt was made."

Elly shuddered. "I hope Craig is right. Les can't seriously have thought I would agree to a reconciliation. Why would I want to go anywhere near him? Ever. He knows he lost the hold he had on me ages ago, and the only reason I would consider going back was if it was in Joey's best interest. And it would never be that."

"No. It wouldn't. But the court case is coming up, and once it's over, and you've legally got sole custody, and Craig seems pretty confident it's unlikely to go any other way, that should be the end of it. Les may be allowed to see Joey occasionally but, according to Craig, it will almost certainly be supervised access, and he probably won't even get that if he does anything stupid in the meantime."

"You're such a good man; do you know that? I will never be able to thank you enough for hiring Craig. I could never have afforded a lawyer, and certainly no one as good as Craig."

"You don't have to thank me, precious. Getting that prick out of your life will be thanks enough."

"I hate him, you know, but I can't wish I'd never met him; if I hadn't, I wouldn't have the two most important people in my life now."

Gavin chuckled. "That's true. Certainly Joey, and if he hadn't made you go to that beach that night, I would never have found you. Am I the second person you're referring to here? I hope I am, baby girl." He looked sternly at her. "Think carefully before you answer. I can always take you out to the Woodshed and spank that deliciously plump bottom of yours with my switch again if you give me the wrong answer."

Elly laughed and rubbed her hand on his chest. It was a private joke. They didn't have a fireplace so there was no need for a woodshed but, when Gavin had made her studio in the garden shed, he'd also made a sign which said *Woodshed* and hung it on the door. When it was ready, he'd told her to put on a skirt and taken her in, put her over his knee, taken her panties down and spanked her with a switch he'd made from thin, supple branches from the garden. He'd told her he needed to take his woodshed for a test run, so he would be punishing her for all the misdemeanours she'd committed since her last spanking that he didn't know about.

He'd made her laugh despite stinging her bottom with the switch, and she loved her Daddy time with him so much, that by the time she was squirming and begging him to stop, she was wet and hungry for him. And when he pulled her up, she fidgeted impatiently as he pulled his track pants down, slipped on a condom and then pulled her down onto his cock. She was straddling his legs and facing him so he could play with her breasts while she rose up and down until he grabbed her around the waist and forced himself up into her as they climaxed in unison.

"I did mean you, Daddy," she said now, kissing his neck and hiding her face. "But I did like going to the Woodshed, too."

"Me too." He kissed her again for a long time, then reluctantly pulled away. "Well, my precious girl, it's getting late, and we've both got busy days tomorrow, so I'd best tuck you into your bed, but as soon as this court case is over, I want you in my bed. Permanently." His voice was gruff as he tilted her face up so she had to look at him. "I think Joey will be okay with it now."

Her eyes shone with happiness and her kiss told him she wholeheartedly agreed.

Chapter 18

Joey was nowhere to be found when Elly arrived seven minutes late to collect him after school the following day. She searched frantically, calling his name and accosting parents, children, teachers, anyone: *Where's Joey? Have you seen Joey? Have you seen my little boy?* He'd come out of his classroom, those who'd seen him agreed, and stood by the tree where he expected his mum to be waiting for him. And then he'd vanished.

Pale and shaking, she paced the corridor outside the headmistress' office and dialled Gavin's number only to be whisked straight to voicemail. *I'm unable to take your call. Please leave a message.* Hanging up, she rang the hospital receptionist who promised to get a message to him, but warned that, if he were in the operating room, he might not be able to return her call for hours.

Driven by a raging helplessness, Elly stomped outside and prowled around the buildings and gardens, then up and down the street, not knowing where Joey was, when the police would arrive or how long it would be before she could talk to Gavin. Her phone rang.

"I didn't think you'd call," she babbled hysterically when she heard his voice.

"I was in the OR but we'd just started. My assistant can cover for a few minutes but I can't be long. What's up, baby?"

"I was only a couple of minutes late. There was an accident and I got held up on the way back from Moy's, and now he's gone."

"Joey?" Gavin felt his scalp prickle. "What do you mean gone? He wasn't at school?"

"People saw him waiting under the tree straight after his class came out, but when I got here, he'd gone. I don't know where he is. I can't find him."

"Do you think Les took him?"

"I don't know. I don't know. I called him and called him but he wouldn't answer. What am I going to do?"

"Have you called the police?"

"The headmistress did. They're on their way."

"Okay. Well, wait for them, and do as they say. And try and keep calm. He's probably wandered off in a dream and will turn up any minute. I'll be with this patient another hour or so, but I'll call as soon as I can. Leave me a message if you hear anything, or call the hospital to give me a message if it's urgent. I love you, baby."

Putting his phone back in the pocket of his coat in the change room, Gavin put fresh gloves on and hurried back to his patient.

"Kid wasn't waiting at school where he was supposed to," he explained as he took over from his assistant. "I'm sure they'll find him. They're going to let me know when they hear."

Ignoring the sympathetic and worried eyes looking at him from above their masks, he pushed thoughts of Joey from the front of his mind and focused his team on the patient whose life was in their hands. Right at this moment, he had to be the priority, and for the next hour Gavin managed to keep his mind away from his private life. He would hear if there was any bad news.

"That was a great job," his assistant said as they prepared to close. The operation had gone smoothly without complications and without further interruptions. "I can take over from here if you want to check on your kid," she offered, having noticed Gavin glancing at the clock and sensing how torn he was between his responsibility to his patient and his concern for Joey's welfare.

Gavin looked at her gratefully. "Thanks, Denny." He looked around at the other members of the surgical team. "Thanks, guys. Awesome job." They nodded and murmured 'thanks' and 'good luck' as he hurried out.

Ha! His mind pounced on the first crack as his concentration on the preceding operation broke apart. *I love you, baby.* It pushed the memory through. *You said that. You said, I love you, baby.* It was the first time either of them had mentioned love. He hadn't known he was going to say it right then. He might even wish to have chosen a more romantic moment for the first declaration of his love for her, but it was too late. It was said, it couldn't be unsaid, and his heart told him it was true.

His single-use gloves in the bin and his soiled gown and cap in the dirty linen basket, he fished his phone from the pocket of his jacket and checked his messages. Five from Elly. The police had arrived, taken statements and then sent her home saying they'd continue the search for Joey who was still nowhere to be found. He was about to call her when he was paged from Emergency. He called the desk, but couldn't get through. Frowning and muttering at the waste of his time, he hurried along the corridors, wondering who didn't know he'd moved from Emergency to OR.

"Oh, Doctor Minchin," an ER nurse said as he marched up to the desk.

He was about to demand why he'd been paged when he noticed her expression. "What is it? What's going on?"

"I'm not sure. We've had a little boy turn up. He wouldn't say anything except Gavin. We asked if that was his name and he said 'Doctor Gavin', so we wondered if that could be you."

"Joey! My God. Is he all right?" The colour drained from Gavin's face and he stumbled after the nurse as an image of Tyler suddenly flooded his brain. "No. No," he muttered, all but running the last few steps to the bed the nurse was indicating and pushing through the curtain. A little boy, pale as a ghost, his face tight with pain was cowering on the bed nursing his arm. Seeing Gavin, he struggled to raise himself, but fell back with a cry. Gavin saw the helpless plea in his huge eyes, and for one ghastly second the image of Tyler fighting to raise his hand as he died filled his mind. He closed his eyes, took a deep breath and pushed it away, clenching his hands to control their shaking.

"Joey." Gavin's voice was deeper than usual but he kept it even. He had to be as calm as possible for Joey's sake, and managed a reassuring smile as he gently stroked the little boy's head. "What happened, son?"

Joey stared mutely up at him with frightened, pleading eyes. Pulling a chair close to the bed, Gavin sat down so he was level with, rather than towering over, him.

"You've hurt your arm, have you, mate? How did you manage that?" he asked gently, hoping a simple question would break Joey's shocked paralysis, but it had the opposite effect as an expression of abject terror contorted the child's face even more. Gavin grabbed Joey's small, trembling hand and held it tightly in his big one and stroked the little boy's clammy forehead.

"It's okay, mate. Don't be frightened. We'll fix your arm. We'd better tell Mummy you're here, hadn't we? She's been looking all over for you. She'll be so happy we've found you."

A huge tear rolling down his cheek was Joey's only reply.

"That's a good lad," Gavin said, gently wiping away the tear.

He looked at the male nurse standing by the bed. "Hey, Brett. Has someone called his mother to let her know he's here?"

"No, he doesn't have any identifying information on him, and he was by himself when he appeared out of nowhere. Apart from 'Doctor Gavin', we haven't got a word out of him. We don't even know how he got here, or why whoever brought him here and disappeared didn't take him to the kid's hospital in the first place. There's an ambulance waiting to take him to Rafe's now."

Gavin's mouth set grimly. "I think I know why he's here," he muttered, standing up and pushing the chair back against the wall.

"Do you know him? Do you have a contact you want me to call?" Brett asked, but Gavin had already pulled out his phone. "Call Elly," he ordered it before adding, "Thanks mate. I've got it," to the man watching him closely, stunned by Gavin's expression which, usually so compassionate, suggested a man with murder on his mind.

"Joey's here at the hospital," Gavin said into the phone when Elly answered. "He's only just arrived. It's okay. Don't panic. He doesn't seem to be badly hurt, but I'd say his arm is broken. No. No one knows what happened or how he got here. He just turned up and so far he hasn't said anything. He's being transferred to Rafe's to get his arm seen to. I'll go in the ambulance with him if I can get away. I'll have to clear it with the Boss. It's a light load this evening, so I think it'll be okay. Get a taxi if you don't want to drive, and I'll go now or come over as soon as I can. Okay, baby. Will you let the cops know, or shall I call them? Right. Good girl. Don't worry. He's going to be fine. I've got to go. His lift's arrived."

An orderly had appeared and while he checked Joey's things were on his bed before being wheeled out to the ambulance, Gavin called upstairs and got clearance to leave.

"I'll just dash upstairs and get my things," he said to the orderly. "Don't go without me."

Hearing Gavin was leaving him, Joey burst into tears. Gavin quickly squatted down by his bed and looked into his eyes.

"It's okay, mate. You and I are going to go in an ambulance to another hospital so we can get your arm fixed, and Mummy is going meet us there. I'm just going to get my coat before we go. I'll be right back." He turned to the orderly with a wink and spoke sternly. "Don't you dare take Joey anywhere before I get back. Okay?"

The orderly grinned and sat down. "Sure thing, Boss. We're not going anywhere. We'll wait right here, won't we, son?"

With a reassuring smile for Joey who had stopped crying, Gavin dashed off thankful that a doctor rushing through a hospital was not an unusual sight. Within minutes, he was back downstairs with his coat and holding Joey's hand as the orderly pushed the gurney to the desk where they stopped.

"Joey was reported to the police as missing," Gavin told the charge nurse. "They've been looking for him, so they'll probably want to know how he turned up here with a broken arm. I'll be at Rafe's with him and his mother if you need me."

"Okay, Gav. Thanks for the heads up. I'll organise a report for the police. Good luck."

Gavin managed a tight smile and nod before, holding the little boy's small, trembling hand all the way, he accompanied Joey and the orderly to the waiting ambulance.

The next few hours passed in a blur of answering questions, filling out forms and waiting. Another thorough examination of Joey when he arrived at Rafe's found no physical injuries apart from his arm and some nasty bruises on his hip, one leg and his unbroken arm. A distraught, white-faced Elly had arrived in a taxi shortly after Gavin and Joey had been discharged from their ambulance, but reassured her son's injuries were not life-threatening and she would be able to take him home once his arm had been put in plaster, some pink crept back into her cheeks.

In the ambulance, Gavin asked Joey again who he had been with and how he'd broken his arm, but Joey's only response was clenching his mouth tightly shut and turning his face away, his little body rigid with internalised anxiety.

During the evening, two police officers arrived, but Joey again refused to speak, curling himself into as tight a shivering ball as his sore body could manage at the first sight of the uniforms. Agreeing he was clearly already traumatised and it would be pointless and cruel to pressure him any further, the police officers moved well out of his sight before taking statements from Gavin and Elly.

"I reckon his brute of a father is involved," Gavin told them. "He must have found out which school Joey had moved to and waited for the opportunity to snatch him. He's a sick bastard. He must have been stalking him, waiting for the chance to pounce. Where is he? Have you spoken to him yet? Elly has called him over and over but he hasn't answered or called her back."

"No, we haven't located Mr. Sutton as yet. He's not at his home. We know about his history. We have Mrs. Sutton's report about the boat explosion and we know she's taken out a restraining order against him, but so far there's nothing linking him to Joey's disappearance and injury today. And we'll need the medical report before we know if we're dealing with an accident or assault, but we will be carrying out a thorough investigation, and we will be interviewing Mr. Sutton as soon as we can. You can count on that."

It was after midnight and they were all exhausted by the time the doctors and police had finished with them and Joey was ready to leave. With neither of their cars at the hospital, they took a taxi to Metro Dora to pick up Gavin's car, and he drove them all home from there. Joey, who'd been sedated, barely stirred when Gavin carried him inside and helped Elly undress him and tuck him into bed.

"Glass of wine before you turn in?" Gavin asked as they left Joey's room.

"Please." Elly followed him to the living room and collapsed on the couch.

"Poor baby," he murmured moments later as he handed her a glass of Shiraz and sat down beside her. He reached over and gently stroked her cheek. "You're so pale, and your eyes are all puffy."

"At my best, then." Her attempt at a smile failed dismally. "It's no good, Gavin," she said, her face threatening to crumple again. "This is all my fault."

"What? How can this possibly be *your* fault?"

"I should never have left Les. While I was with him, he didn't physically hurt Joey… apart from that one time, but he's been threatening to hurt him ever since I left. He knows that's the best way to get to me. He keeps saying all he wants is to have his son living with him. If I give him that, he'll leave Joey alone. I'm sure he will. He'll let me live there, too, and I have to be with Joey; it's the only way I can be sure to keep him safe."

"So you're pretty sure it was Les? You can't give in to him, Elly. Going back is not the answer. What would he do to you? You'd never be safe and, besides, now he's had one go at Joey he could easily have another, whether you're with him or not."

Gavin slipped his arm around her shoulders and kissed her hair. "You going back to him is not the right thing to do. I know that absolutely. I can't forcibly prevent you. I wish I could. But you must at least promise me, you won't rush into anything. Wait and see if the police can find enough evidence to put him away. He won't try anything else for the moment. He'll know he's being watched."

Elly lay her head on his chest and nodded. "All right. Joey's not going back to school until next week. We can stay locked up in here till then. I don't know if Les knows this address, but there's so much security around the house, I don't think even he would risk showing his face. But once Joey is ready to go back to school what are we going to do? We can't keep switching schools, can we?"

"No. I don't think that's the answer," Gavin agreed, wrapping his arms around her and bending to kiss her lips. "But I can't bear to think of you and Joey living with that monster and I don't want to live without you. Either of you. You're my little family now and I want you both here with me. Is that what you want? I mean, if Les didn't exist, would you want to be here with me? Joey's happy here, isn't he?"

Elly raised her head and looked at his tense face with sad eyes, then put her hand gently on his cheek and managed a small tired smile. "My heart will be with you forever, Doctor Daddy, wherever I am, and if I didn't have to protect Joey, I would stay here with you for as long as you let me. And so would Joey. He worships you. You're the best father he could ever have and I don't think he's ever been happier than he's been here with you." She sighed. "Maybe the police will arrest Les and lock him up and throw away the key," she said, but without conviction.

"Let's hope so and, if they don't, we will find another way to stop him." Gavin kissed her again. "Now, Doctor Daddy says it's time you went to bed. You look absolutely worn out, baby girl. We'll see what the police have to say tomorrow."

He stood up and walked her to her bedroom, taking her

into his arms when they stopped and kissing her deeply and sweetly so she could taste his longing.

"Good night, baby. Daddy is going to find a way to fix this. I promise. I'm not letting you go. I meant what I said on the phone, you know. I do love you. And Joey. And I will find a way to protect you, so try not to worry and get some sleep. I'll be right here if you need me."

Chapter 19

The next day brought no good news, though. When the police arrived late morning to try again to talk to Joey, they told Gavin and Elly they had spoken to Les and he seemed to be in the clear.

"He said he took his car out of town for a drive yesterday afternoon and stopped for fuel around half past three," Senior Constable Pam Ryan told them. "We checked the CCTV from the petrol station, and a red Mazda MX-5 pulled in at the automated pump at 2:47 p.m. The driver got out, paid at the pump with Mr. Sutton's card, filled his tank, then continued on out of town."

"Are you sure it was him?" Elly asked, tears of disappointment rolling down her cheeks.

Snr Cst. Ryan sympathetically patted her hand. "There isn't much room for doubt. We could see the licence plates and it was definitely Les Sutton's car, and it was his card that paid for the fuel. His size, colouring etcetera matched Mr. Sutton's, and Mr. Sutton showed us the clothes he'd worn the previous day and they matched the CCTV as well. There wasn't a close-up of his face, but I'm afraid there doesn't seem to be much doubt it was him. I don't know who took Joey but I don't think it was Mr. Sutton. He might have organised it, but at this stage we have no evidence of that either. We're focusing on finding the actual kidnapper at the moment. If we can do that, we might be able to get the full picture, but so far we don't have much to go on. We don't have any witnesses who saw Joey being taken, no suspicious car, nothing out of the ordinary at all. I'm afraid unless some other information comes to light, we're pinning our hopes on Joey. Has he said anything yet?"

Elly shook her head. "He won't talk about it. Whoever did it must have threatened him with something terrible if he said anything."

"What about the hospital?" Gavin interjected. "Didn't anyone see who left him there?"

The second officer, Constable Peter Rowland, who'd been in charge of following up at the hospital, shook his head. "No. We had one report of a black SUV near the hospital around the time Joey turned up, but no make, model or number plate and nothing to suggest it was actually connected to Joey. Whoever dropped him off knew about CCTV, and knew how to avoid being obvious. It looks as though the perp waited until there was a group of people going in and got lost among them. After they'd walked past a row of chairs, Joey had magically appeared on one of them. We found the family and spoke to them, but none of them saw Joey. I left my card and they promised to call if they remember anything they think might be useful."

"How can a little boy be stolen from his school and then dumped at a hospital and no one see anything?" Elly demanded. "How? I don't understand."

"It's unfortunately not uncommon at all for people not to notice things happening even right under their noses," Snr Cst. Ryan replied. "They're not expecting a crime, so they don't see it if it's done quietly and without a fuss. And this all happened in the space of only a couple of minutes. Whoever left Joey there walked in, sat him in the chair and disappeared. That was it. But perhaps Joey might be able to tell us something that will help."

"I'll fetch him," Elly said, going to Joey's bedroom where they'd left him to play while they spoke to the police. He allowed her to lead him into the living room and sit him on her lap where he curled up. Without speaking, he shook his head in response as Snr Cst. Ryan asked if he knew who'd taken him from school, what car he was in, how his arm had been broken, and how he'd got to the hospital.

"You can't remember anything, Joey?" Snr Cst. Ryan prodded gently, but Joey turned his face against Elly's chest and clutched at her top.

"I think that's enough," Gavin said. "Elly why don't you take him back to his room. I'll see our visitors out."

Joey immediately wriggled off his mother's lap and fled, and Elly thanked the police and said goodbye before following him.

Gavin saw their guests to the front door and opened it. "I'm sorry. I don't think there's any point trying to push Joey at the moment. It might even make him less willing to talk. I think it's best if we give him some space. Elly and I will try and encourage him to talk about what happened and let you know if he says anything."

The two police officers nodded. "Yes. I think that's for the best, too," Snr Cst. Ryan agreed. "He's more likely to open up to you and, if he does, he may be more ready to talk to us. Give us a call if he says anything, or you hear or remember anything that might help. And we'll keep in touch and let you know what's happening at our end."

"I don't care what they say," Elly said to Gavin after the police had left. "And I don't know how he did it, but I know it was Les. He must have swapped cars or something, and he's too smart to get caught on camera if he doesn't want to. They're never going to be able to pin it on him, are they?" Her voice had risen almost to the point of hysteria and Gavin pulled her into his arms and hugged her as hard as he could without hurting her.

"Don't give up, baby. If they can't get him, I'll think of something to make him go away. I promise."

Her head jolted up and she looked at him with wild eyes. "Don't do anything to get hurt. I couldn't bear it. You might be twice his size, but he's mean and nasty."

"I won't get hurt," he promised, his mouth tight and a steely resolve glinting in his eyes. "Now I'd best get to work. I've set all the alarms, so it will light up like a Christmas tree and sound like an air raid siren if anyone comes near the place. Will you be okay while I'm gone?"

Elly nodded. "Yes. I'm waiting for Les to let me know he did it and demand I go back, but I don't think he'll *do* anything else before then. I don't know how he's going to contact me because he's blocked on my phone. He will though. I know he will."

And he did. Three evenings later, she received a phone call from Snr Cst. Ryan.

"No. I'm sorry," she replied to Elly's eager question. "We don't have any new information about who kidnapped your son, but we're doing everything we can to try and track the person down. No, I'm calling to let you know that Les Sutton came to the station a little while ago. He said he can't contact you because of the restraining order, and he's worried about his son and wants to know how he is. He asked if I could pass a message on to you."

An icy wave washed over Elly triggering a rash of goose-bumps and setting her teeth chattering. "A message? What?"

"He insisted I write it down word for word and then read it to you. He seemed concerned I might not get it right."

"I bet he did," Elly mumbled, bracing herself. "I know what it says."

"Do you want me to read it?"

"No," Elly blurted out, and then more quietly and with resignation in her voice, added, "No. Thank you, but I already know what it says: that if I don't go back to him worse will happen."

"Goodness, no. It doesn't say that," Snr Cst. Ryan said with a surprised snort.

"Well, that's what it means. Let me guess, it says he's devastated by what happened to Joey and desperately wants to see him to make sure he's all right. He misses us and wishes he could look after us, and he's worried something worse might happen. Won't I please go home so he can take care of his family. How did I do?"

Elly heard the other woman suck her teeth. "Yep. Not exactly word for word, and he also asked if you would let him talk to Joey so he can hear for himself that he's okay. But, other than that, you pretty much got the gist of it, and you're saying that's a threat?"

"Yes. He's saying something worse will happen if Joey and I don't go back, but he's clever. No one else is going to read that note and see anything but the natural concern of a loving father and husband. And I guess I look like the bad parent because I've walked out and am refusing to let him see his son, and I can't even keep Joey safe." She burst into tears.

"I'm sorry, Elly, but you're right about the note not appearing to be threatening on the surface, but if you believe you're in danger from this man, you have my card. Call me if anything at all happens—if he contacts you again, turns up, anything at all. Okay? I'll hang onto this note in case it's useful in the future. But he is clever. You're right about that, too. Now that I think about it, he didn't touch anything in here either. I offered him a pen, but he asked me to write it down, so we have no DNA, fingerprints or record of his writing. We can get all those things later, but it shows a man who is careful to cover his tracks in a way most people wouldn't even think to do."

"Did he say anything else?"

"I don't think so," Snr Cst. Ryan answered slowly, clearly trying to remember any other details. "Oh wait, he did. I didn't think it was important at the time—it sounded like something a father might say, but maybe it means more to you."

"What?"

"Something about him being glad Joey was still able to play with his old friends, like… Liam, is it?"

Elly gasped and her heart stopped.

"Are you there, Elly? What? Do you think he meant something by that?"

"Yes. He was telling me he knows where we're living. Joey had Liam over a little while back for a play date. Somehow Les must have followed Liam here or got the address from him or something. That's how he knew where Joey's new school is. He must have been spying on us, or had someone else doing it for him."

"Right. Well, I can organise for a plain car to be on the lookout for any suspicious vehicles hanging around in your street. I suggest you be as vigilant as you can as well. If you notice a car parked nearby that doesn't seem to belong or is hanging around more than usual or there's someone sitting in it—that sort of thing, call me straight away. If you can get a number plate, so much the better, but only if it's safe. Oh, and while I've got you on the phone, I don't suppose Joey has said anything yet?"

"No," Elly replied, her voice breaking with the pain of watching her baby suffer. "He clams up and won't move, like he's frozen, if I mention it. The rest of the time he's trying to be as normal as possible, but I can see how much he's struggling. I've made an appointment with a child psychologist to see if I can find out how to help him. I can't see him saying anything soon about his arm, but if he does, I'll let you know."

Home from the hospital later that night, Gavin listened with a grim face as Elly told him about Les' message.

"My God," he said when she'd finished. "Look at you." He wrapped his arms around her and held her trembling body. "You're shaking. You're pale. You've got dark circles under your eyes, and you've lost weight, haven't you? This can't go on."

"I have to go back. It's not fair on you and Joey if I don't."

"No! No, baby. The only thing not fair is what that prick is doing to you and Joey. He has to be stopped. We'll find a way. I promise." He kissed her softly, then nestled his head against hers. "I'm afraid Doctor Daddy has not been taking proper care of you, precious. Hop into bed and I'll bring you a cup of chamomile tea and something to help you sleep. And starting tomorrow, I'm going to watch your diet and make sure you're eating properly."

"But Les…"

Gavin cut her off. "You leave Les to me."

The only other time Elly had seen such a dark expression on Gavin's face was when he'd told her about Tyler and what he'd like to do to the man who had beaten the poor little boy to death. She shuddered, terrified by what the future seemed to hold. She already had the burden of guilt for Joey's injuries to carry, and she couldn't bear the thought of anything happening to Gavin as well. Les was, after all, her responsibility; it was time she did what needed to be done.

Chapter 20

Les was feeling pretty good as he sat behind the wheel of the black SUV, the window down, his elbow resting on the door and his gold bracelet glinting in the sun. Today was finally going to be the turning point. He could feel it in his bones.

Things had not been going well for him for too long, and he didn't like it. Bad luck with business deals had cost him money and prestige. He knew his colleagues were no longer taking him seriously and were lampooning him behind his back. He needed a win, a big win to get his mojo firing again, and the biggest win would be having his wife and son come crawling back to him. How could a man be respected if his wife walked out on him? And took his son. A son belonged to the father. How could a woman teach a boy to be a man? Les snorted at the thought. No wonder Joey was such a wussy, wimpy milksop, spending all that time with his stupid, hysterical mother.

Now he could put that right. He was looking forward to getting Elly home, too. His house was a mess and he was damned if he was going to pay a cleaner. Why did he bother to get married if he still had no one cleaning his house? She'd better get stuck into the cleaning straight away, and do it quickly and do a good job or she'd feel the back of his hand.

But most of all, he thought with a leer, he was looking forward to sex, and lots of it. She was nearly thirty, had fat thighs, her tits had sagged since she'd had the kid and she was without doubt the worst fuck he'd ever had, but young women were all lesos these days apparently, not interested in men, and he was tired of having to pay for it. That's what a wife was for, plus she owed him big time for humiliating him, and he was looking forward to making sure she paid in full. He'd always wanted to see what it would be like using vegetables as dildos. The image of her naked, on all fours with a cucumber sticking out of her arse filled his brain and stirred his cock. That would teach the whore. He had to control himself, though, and pretend to be nice to her until he got her behind locked doors. She was as dumb as an ox thinking she'd be able to waltz back when she felt like it without paying for her treachery, but her stupidity made it easy for someone as clever as him to manipulate her.

He grinned as he breathed in the ocean air, then laughed out loud, getting an immediate hard on picturing the look on that jumped-up Doctor Minchin's face when he found out what a loser he was, and that he, Les Sutton, had won. His laughter morphed into a sneer. That tosser honestly believed Elly wanted him to protect her when she was trying to get away from him. Snatching her back from under his nose would be an amusing start to the revenge he intended exacting on Minchin, and he would not be letting him off lightly. He could bide his time, he wasn't foolish enough to rush, but at some point in the future, when he was least expecting it, Doctor Minchin would get what he had coming.

What made Minchin think he had the right to strand Elly and Joey out here in the middle of nowhere to keep him, her husband and the boy's father, away from them? Elly had made a big mistake telling Minchin she wanted to go home—one more thing he would have to punish her for. And that arrogant prick couldn't handle her dumping him after all his bragging and big-noting himself about how he was saving her. Les wished he could see Gavin's face when he came looking for her and found she'd done a runner and chosen her husband over him.

He hadn't been surprised by Elly's message asking him to fetch her. From the moment he'd heard that skinny bitch friend of hers had died, he'd known it was only a matter of time before Elly would come crawling back. She would have done so already, he was sure, if Doctor Arsehole hadn't butted in trying to be the big hero.

He was heartily sick of other people sticking their noses into his marriage. It was bad luck the doctor had happened on Elly right after she'd seen the boat blow up and realised Les meant business. She would have come straight back to him then if that bozo hadn't effectively taken her prisoner and prevented her. But Les knew his wife. He knew Joey's broken arm would be the last straw. He hadn't planned for that to happen, it was just a stroke of luck, but he knew once it had she'd get away from the doctor and back to him as fast as she could. He'd had to bide his time for too long, but now that patience was paying off. By this evening, he'd have his wife and son back under his roof and under his control, and he could start whipping them into shape. His fading erection fired back up and he licked his lips as his mind savoured the promise of those words 'whipping them'.

He knew he was getting close to his quarry. Adrenaline had started pumping through his body, his palms were sweating, his breathing had quickened and blood was rushing to his head reddening his face. He was tired of driving, and had begun cursing Elly for being too stupid to provide proper directions when he saw the turn-off to the shack.

"Just as well," he muttered out loud as he swung his car into the drive, got out, stood with his back to the car door and flicked his foot behind to push it shut. He loved that move. He hoped she was watching through the window. He puffed out his chest, stretched up to his full height and strode to the front door. Pinned to it was a note: *The doors not locked. I'm in the shower.*

He pushed the door open and went in.

"I'm here, doll face," he called out, heading towards the sound of running water. "Washing your pussy all clean for me, are you?"

He opened the door and entered the bathroom. Immediately, small goosebumps popped up on his arms and the tiny hairs on the back of his neck sprung up. Something was wrong. He pulled back the curtain to see the shower recess empty and the water running pointlessly down the drain. At that moment, he felt himself grabbed from behind, his arms pinned to his side, and a bag pulled over his head and tied at his neck with a drawstring. Momentarily feeling he couldn't breathe, he panicked and froze long enough for his arms to be pulled behind his back and held tightly. He struggled and let out a torrent of abuse, but the silent assailant holding him was much bigger and stronger, and the person who'd finished securing the bag and who also hadn't spoken, helped pushed him into the bedroom and onto a plastic sheet covering the bed. Grabbing an arm each, they tied his wrists to the bed head, then, dodging his flailing feet, grabbed and secured them to the other end so he was spreadeagled and fastened tight.

He thrashed around trying to wriggle free as he continued swearing, threatening and demanding in a loud voice to be released, but there was no reply. He paused and listened. Nothing. He couldn't see or hear anyone. He suddenly realised all other noise in the room had stopped.

"Hello?" he called out. "You pricks still here? Hey, Doctor Fuckface? I know it's you. You wait until I get out of here. You're going to wish you were never born. I've got friends, you know." He waited for a reply, straining his ears for the slightest sound, but there was nothing other than a bit of wind outside. A different kind of panic overtook him. What if he'd been left here to die? No one knew where he was. No one would be looking for him, except men, hard men, to whom he owed money, and if they found him... he shuddered to think. He started frantically struggling again, but his restraints were too tight. His bladder was full after his long drive and sweat broke out on his forehead as the pressure became insistent.

"Hey," he yelled again. "I need a piss. Let me up or I'll piss on your bed." He tried to make it sound like a threat, but couldn't disguise his panic that he might actually pee in his pants. He would be utterly humiliated if he wet the bed like a baby, and rage replaced his fear. No torture was too bad for anyone who made a bloke piss his pants. He couldn't think of a lower act. That's probably what they wanted him to do, so they could laugh at him, but he wouldn't give them the satisfaction. He'd hold it forever if he had to. Unfortunately, thinking about it was increasing his need to go, and the pain in his abdomen was getting stronger making it harder to ignore.

He started yelling again, dredging up the filthiest of insults and the cruellest and most disgusting of threats, but there was still no response. Not a sound. His bladder ached and a wave of nausea was rising up from the pit of his stomach. He swallowed hard as he felt it moving up into his throat. His whole body broke out in a cold sweat as he pictured his corpse being found covered in urine and vomit and... he groaned and shook his head. Imagine if that was how he was remembered... dead, covered in maggots, and lying in a pool of his own vomit and excrement. Frustration, fear, and a sense of failure swamped him, and the watery tears of self-pity which began rolling down his face had the same effect as if a tap had been turned on. He moaned in utter despair as he felt his muscles surrender and warm liquid fill his pants.

Someone moving nearby jerked him awake. It took a second for him to work out what was wrong; then he remembered. His arms were aching from being held stretched above his head, and he was cold, painfully cold. He felt damp discomfort in his trousers which was exacerbating the coolness of the air and his lack of a jumper or coat over his polo shirt. His nose twitched at the unwanted and unpleasant smell of drying urine. With the bag over his head obscuring the light, there was no way of knowing how long he'd been there or what time it was. His stomach was growling annoyance at having had nothing in it since an early breakfast, and he could feel the first warnings of his bladder refilling.

He fought against his ties again, but his arms and wrists were sore and aching, and all strength seemed to have vanished from his legs. A giant sob rose in his throat. He couldn't understand why anyone would want to do this to him, or how they could be so cruel. He was literally being tortured; the pain in his arms was bad, but he had manfully endured worse agony in the past. What was truly unbearable and what was unravelling him was his total lack of power and subsequent helplessness, and the complete stripping of his dignity.

He heard movement again. At least he was no longer alone.

"Let me go," he whined before he even realised he was going to speak. "Please." His voice was almost a whimper. "Let me go."

No one replied. He heard more footsteps and then a clanking sound like cutlery banging together, and at last a man's voice, but not one he recognised.

"Are you going to cut one ball off or both? I say take both balls and while you're at it cut his dick off as well."

Les' blood froze. "No. No. No." He thrashed his head from side to side. "No. You can't!" He wrenched at the cords holding his hands, desperate to get one free to protect his genitals, but it was useless. Then he felt hands undoing his trousers and pulling them down.

"Yerk," he heard the voice say in disgust. "He's wet himself, the dirty little bugger. He stinks."

"Why are you doing this?" Les cried in anguish. "Don't. I'll do anything. What do you want? Tell me what you want, for fuck's sake, and I'll do it. Do you want Elly? You can have her. Dirty bitch. I never liked her anyway. I don't want her. I only came to get her because she begged me to. She said she couldn't stand the sight of you and she wanted me back. I felt sorry for her, but she's stupid, ugly and cold as a fish's arse. You're welcome to her. Let me go and she'll never see me again. I swear. Or Joey. I don't even believe he's my kid. Look at me! How could I produce such a snivelling, little crybaby? I don't want them. You can have them. Good riddance."

"At least both his balls, then?" the voice said. "I say take his repulsive little white worm as well. I doubt he'd even notice it was gone."

Les felt something cold prod his testicles and then lift up his flaccid penis and flop it about.

"I'm cold. What do you expect? And of course it'll shrivel if it hears you threatening to cut it off." As soon as the words were out of his mouth he wished he could take them back. He sounded pathetic even to his own ears, and obviously to the other people in the room judging by the laughter. He now knew there was definitely at least two men with him. He'd bet anything one was Gavin Minchin. He'd recognise his voice, he was sure, but so far only one man, not the doc, had spoken.

"Listen, Gav," he said in what he hoped was a man-to-man voice. "She's my wife, okay, but, and I mean this, you're welcome to her. I reckon I know her better, though, and I'd bet a stack on you being able to get much hotter pussy; I do, all the time, and I'm not even a doctor. If she's fooled you so far, she won't much longer. You'll see. She's nothing. Just trash. Always has been, always will be. I bet she didn't tell you her mother was a junkie? She probably would be too if I hadn't picked her up out of the gutter. I mean I did my best to give her a good life, but there's no pleasing her. In bed or out. I bet you're already finding that one out." His eye automatically winked lewdly even though he still had a bag over his head and no one could see.

What sounded like a knife being sharpened, froze him, and he started thrashing and blubbering again. "Don't do this. What do you want from me? I'll do whatever you want. Do you want money? I can give you money. Business has been bad lately but I still have a little. Tell me how much you want. I can get whatever you say. You can have my car, too. Not that heap of crap out there. The red flash. You can…"

"Shut up, you odious little man." The unknown voice, steady, low, and serious, shut him up. "I've heard all about how you pretended to kill your son to frighten your wife, and I know it was you who kidnapped the boy and broke his arm. Any man who abuses a child deserves to have his balls cut off, and I have a scalpel here in my hand. It could be simple, quick and painless, but instead it's going to be slow, messy and agonisingly painful."

"Nooo," the man on the bed wailed, tossing his head from side to side. "I didn't mean for him to break his arm, honest. I accidentally pushed him a bit harder than I meant and he fell down a few stairs. Do you think I'd deliberately push my son down the stairs? But he wouldn't shut up with his crying and whining even after I'd told him a dozen times. A man can only take so much and, besides, he has to learn. "Ahh!" A yell of anguish erupted from him as he felt a sharp metal point pricking his scrotum. "Nooo," he screamed, wrestling desperately with his restraints again. A foul smell rose up from the bed.

"Aw, geez, Lezzy, you haven't crapped yourself now as well, have you? What a pitiful, disgusting excuse for a man you are."

"Let me go," Les moaned, mortified by his body's treachery. He was pretty sure he hadn't made a big mess. It was mostly gas, but what might happen if that guy stuck the knife in his genitals again? "Please. I'm begging you. I'll do whatever you want."

"Oh, I know you will, Lezzy, my boy, because, if you don't, by the time you leave here you'll have to sit down to take a leak."

Chapter 21

"What then?" Les asked eagerly, terrified he was going to be castrated or worse, but sensing the first ray of hope he might be able to cut a deal. "What do you want me to do? I'll do it. Anything. Just tell me."

A hand rifled through his pockets and took out his phone.

"Password?"

"What do you want my phone for?" Les' voice had a new panic. "That's private and personal. You can't go through my phone. It's mine."

"Fair enough. I'll trade you."

"What do you mean?" The panic had been replaced by an uneasy suspicion. "Oww!" The knife nicked his scrotum for a second time. "No, please," he begged, panting breathlessly.

"That's the trade. I get your password and you get to keep both your balls – for the moment at least. Otherwise, one's coming out now."

"No. No. Give me the phone. I'll do it. Promise. Untie one of my hands and my feet. You can leave one hand tied."

"Nope. Password or snick... plop... Your choice."

"No. No. No." Tears were cracking the captive man's voice.

"Okay. You're wasting our time and we're in a hurry. No password means you've chosen the knife. Let's get started. You brought the upholstery needle to stitch him up after, didn't you mate?"

"No!" Les screamed, then muttered, "Six, nine, six, nine," under his breath as he choked back sobs and wished he'd chosen a different password.

"Ha. I might have guessed a sleazebag like you would have something like that, mightn't I?"

The hatred Les was feeling towards the owner of that voice had permeated his entire being. He wanted to kill him, crush him, squash him like a bug under his shoe. He couldn't do anything at the moment, but as soon as he was free, he would take his revenge for being humiliated, terrified, and disrespected. Whoever this guy was, he was now destined to meet a cruel and painful end.

"Aw no, you filthy piece of scum," the voice said and Les' heart sank. He'd hoped the intruder wouldn't know his way around that model phone. "Here, mate, look at this." He was obviously showing his accomplice what he'd found.

"They're legal," Les said sulkily. "It says they're all at least eighteen."

"Well, they sure don't look it. Either the site is lying and they are underage, or they are eighteen-year-olds who look underage. You're disgusting whichever it is."

"I haven't done any harm. They're legal. I'm no pedo. All blokes like young dollies. But let me go, and I'll delete them. I swear."

"Nope. You are going to make a recording on your phone admitting what you've done."

"What? What have I done?"

"I'm sure the list is as long as your arm, but the two I'm most interested in are you luring your wife to an isolated beach and blowing up a boat to make her think you'd killed her son and, ignoring a restraining order, kidnapping her kid from his school and dumping him at the hospital with a broken arm."

"How can I be sure it won't get to the police?" the cold, smelly, abject figure on the bed asked nervously from behind his still hooded head.

"It will. That's the idea. But that's too bad because you making that recording is the only way you are getting out of here with these."

Les squealed as he felt the sharp point of a knife prick him again, once in each testicle and once in the tip of his penis. "You're bluffing. You'll never get away with it."

"Nope. Not bluffing. And I reckon we'll get away scot-free, but, even if we don't, you'll never grow them back, will you? Hey, mate, give us a hand, here; mop up the blood as I cut him."

"No. No," Les bawled. "I'll do it. I'll do it. Don't cut me."

"Right then. Make yourself comfortable. It has to sound natural and relaxed." This time as the captor was speaking he was removing the hood over his prisoner's mouth but fastening it so it couldn't slip off his eyes. "Make sure your voice is clear. We want to be able to understand every single word."

Les squinted in the tiny bit of light that found its way under the hood as it was raised above his mouth. His eyes darted around in an attempt to see his assailants, but the light disappeared as a thick wad of cloth was placed across his eyes and secured with a tie behind his head. He heard a chair being pulled up next to the bed.

"Right, dirtbag. What's your wife's name?"

"Elly."

"And your son's?"

"Joey."

"So, you can start with 'Hi, Elly, this is your piece of garbage husband'. Then tell her all about the boat, how you found out her new address and stalked her, how you kidnapped your son, and how you broke his arm. Now be quick. We're leaving soon, either with your confession clearly recorded on your phone, or with your balls and your dick in your pocket. Your choice."

Ninety minutes later, the recording was done to the kidnappers satisfaction, Les had been dragged outside and cleaned up a bit with a bucket of cold water, his trousers were up, the shack was tidied, the plastic sheet was in the bin, and all traces of the recent party had been removed.

He was then bundled into the backseat of the SUV, his seat belt buckled, and his hands tied together on his lap and the rope holding them passed under his legs and fastened so he couldn't raise them. A towel was hung across the window so no one could look in and see the passenger with the bag over his head.

"Where are you taking me?" he asked, as his captors prepared to set off in convoy. He sensed only one man in the car with him and guessed the other one was driving their vehicle which must have been parked out of sight.

"Home," came the unexpected reply. "I'll stop a couple of blocks away and release you and you can drive the rest of the way yourself."

"Can I have my phone back?" Les' voice was shaking from an adrenaline surge at the first flicker of hope his ordeal was over and he'd survived.

"Nah, sorry, mate. That's going to the police. I'm guessing they'll be around to collect this car for forensic examination and, no doubt, once they've seen your nasty little collection of pics, they'll be searching your house and computer as well. I don't think I'd like to be in your shoes."

Les started shivering violently and wriggling to get free. "No. Don't call the cops. Please. Can't we make another deal? If this is about Elly, I've already said I won't see her again. I'll tell my lawyer to give her custody of the brat. Let me go. Please."

"Sorry, mate," the driver said, starting the engine and following the other car out onto the road. "You've got nothing else we want now. I reckon you should be grateful your balls are still in their bag and not in your pocket. If it had been down to me, they'd be gone."

"Look, I tell you what," Les tried again desperately, "if you give me some time to get... organised before the police come, I'll give them the phone myself. I'll make a written confession about blowing up the boat."

The driver laughed. "I'm sure you will, but so what? I don't know how much of a crime the police will consider that to be even with a doctor's report detailing the shock it caused your wife and the effect that had. You could have killed her. You might get charged with assault, but I can't be sure it would stick. You frightened the hell out of her taking her kid from school—exactly like you meant to—but again I'm not sure that'll send you to jail for as long as you deserve to be there. The porn, though, that was a stroke of luck. The cops will take that seriously, and I'm guessing there's more at the house."

Les was silent for a while, then eventually he forced himself to speak. "It's not the girls. I told you, the sites say they're legal."

"What was that, Les?" the driver asked, enjoying Les' misery. "Speak up."

"It's not the porn; that's legal. I swear. But there's other... stuff."

"Stuff, eh? Good stuff? Bad stuff?"

"I needed the money," Les whined. "It's the first time. Honest. But if they find it, I'll go to jail. Maybe for years. Let me get rid of it. That's all I ask. I'll pay you. Or you can have some. It's good stuff if you want to try it. Or you could sell it."

The driver screwed up his face as though he had a bad

taste in his mouth. "Drugs? I don't want your filthy drugs or your filthy money, and I don't care if you go to jail and die there. You've been terrorising and abusing your wife and son for years, and now you've pushed the kid down stairs and broken his arm. How long before you kill one of them? He could have died then. Your wife could have been killed or seriously injured by the explosion, or she could have been hit by a car or died of cold lying on the side of the road. That she wasn't is down to her good luck."

"All I wanted was my wife and kid at home. What's wrong with that? She shouldn't have left in the first place. I'm her husband."

"You're a brute, a bully and a disgrace. No wonder she left."

"I don't want to go to jail. I've heard about what happens in jail."

"It's all true. Now shut up. I'm sick of listening to you." He turned the radio up, keeping an eye on his prisoner by periodically glancing in the mirror.

The rest of the trip passed uneventfully until the driver pulled into a small, empty car park attached to a sports ground not far from Les' house. The second car arrived almost immediately and parked next to the SUV. Les' driver got out and opened the back door.

"The police should be at your place shortly. You might have time to grab a bag and get to the airport if you hurry. At least that's what I'd do in your situation, I reckon. Go somewhere far, far away and not come back because I'm betting you'll be arrested before you pick up your luggage if you set foot here again."

"Yes. Yes. I'll go. Promise. Give me a head start. Half an hour. That's all. Go on mate, be a sport."

"I wouldn't count on the cops not getting there sooner," was the last thing Les heard before his captor half undid the ties holding him, jumped into the passenger seat of the other car and sped away, leaving him to untangle himself. By the time his hands were free, his blindfold off, and he was ready to dash home and hide his incriminating evidence, he was alone.

"So, all we have to do now is call the cops, drop the phone off and go home," the driver said to his fellow kidnapper as they drove slowly around the block and back in the direction of the car park they'd just left.

"Yeah, but I reckon we should give him a few minutes."

"How come?"

"So he can scarper. If he's got any sense, and the jury is still out on that one, he'll jump on the first plane with an available seat, get out of here as fast as he can and never come back. I suggested it to him in case he couldn't think of it himself."

"Really? You think he might leave the country? That seems a bit extreme. I doubt the confession tape will get him into too much trouble, but that and the threat to deknacker him might scare him off if we're lucky. There's the porn, but he reckons that's legal—and I hope he's right, for the girls' sake, not for his."

"Yeah, I hear you on that one, but even if the porn is legal, he made it plain he's got other stuff to worry about."

"He said that? Like what?"

"Drugs I'd say. He was seriously worried."

A slow whistle greeted this news. "Well, that is a stroke of luck I wasn't expecting. Still can't say I'm surprised. That would be jail time for sure, wouldn't it?"

"I reckon so, but we don't know how much; maybe only a couple of years depending on what it is, how much and so on. If we give him a few extra minutes to get to the airport, though, he just might leave the country and never come back. And if he's stupid enough to hang around, the cops will get him eventually. There's nothing to lose. So, what do you think?

Through a drive-through and grab a coffee before we make the call?"

"Sure.

Ten minutes later, an anonymous call was made from Les' phone to Crimewatch and the phone then secreted in the predetermined hiding place in the park.

"Done and done. Now how about giving me a lift to my car and let's get home. I need a long hot shower after being in that filth's company all day."

The two men took off their gloves, shook hands for a job well done and headed home.

Chapter 22

Joey was tucked up, fast asleep in bed, and Gavin and Elly were in the lounge when the knock on their door came later that evening. Gavin opened it to find Snr. Cst. Ryan on the doorstep looking both pleased and apologetic.

"I saw your lights on. I hope it's not too late to disturb you, but I have some news I thought you might like to hear."

"No. No. It's not too late. We were just watching TV. Please, come in. I'm sure Elly will want to hear any news." Gavin opened the door wider and gestured for her to go through to the living room while he closed the door and followed.

Hearing the police officer's voice, Elly had jumped up.

"There's some news," Gavin explained, then spoke directly to their visitor. "Please sit down. Can I get you something? Tea? Water?"

"No, thanks. I shan't stay long." The officer sat down, clasped her hands in her lap and leaned forward.

Elly sat down and wrapped her arms across her chest, her eyes fixed on the other woman and her mouth opening as she listened to Snr Cst. Ryan explaining how an anonymous tip had led the police to Les' phone and his confessions of domestic violence, and about the subsequent search of his house that uncovered dubious pornography on his computer, a stash of drugs and cash, and a collection of stolen property.

"Poor Les," she said when the story was finished. "He wasn't a criminal when I married him. He was a wheeler and dealer, but the deals were legal, I think. He wanted money, but even more, I think, he wanted to be a big man so people would admire and respect him. It's kind of sad he wound up nothing more than a small-time crook."

"You must have a very forgiving nature if you can feel any sympathy for him after all he's put you and Joey through," Snr Cst. Ryan replied.

Elly shrugged, embarrassed by the compliment and by revealing her feelings. "Have you arrested him? What's going to happen to him now?"

"No. He managed to get on a plane before we could stop him. We located the black SUV in an airport car park a couple of hours ago. A warrant has been issued for his arrest on multiple charges, and all the airports around the country have an alert for him. If he tries to return, he'll be arrested before he gets through customs. We'll try and get him arrested when he lands, but there's no extradition treaty so they aren't usually helpful unless the crime has been committed in their country. There's not much else we can do unless he's arrested in a country with which we have an extradition agreement. But at least," she'd added with a smile, "I don't think he'll be bothering you again."

"Why would he have made a confession tape and left his house full of incriminating evidence though?" Elly asked with a frown still trying to make sense of what she was hearing.

Snr Cst. Ryan made a 'who knows?' face. "It looks like it might have been another one of his elaborate charades, this time to avoid his creditors. One of the officers searching the house found a half-written note that said: *I was kidnapped and tort*. It was on the floor with a pen nearby presumably to make it appear that he'd been interrupted, but there's nothing to suggest he was kidnapped. The house was a pigsty, but there was no evidence of a struggle. Plus we know he drove to the airport, withdrew money from an ATM, bought a ticket and boarded a plane, and he was alone the whole time. I'm inclined to think he was staging his disappearance for the benefit of the people to whom he owed money."

Elly shook her head. "Why would he run away without getting rid of all the illegal stuff? It still doesn't make sense."

Snr Cst. Ryan patted her hand. "It must have to him, and fear can make people behave erratically. I'd say he was leaving in a hurry because he knew someone was after him, or maybe he was creating an elaborate excuse as to why he left and can't return. Leaving incriminating evidence instead of getting rid of it would tie in with his story about being kidnapped. We know he wasn't kidnapped, though. He emptied his bank account at the airport of as much cash as he was allowed to take, and it looks like he has an overseas bank account, so he'll have money to keep him going. He's no doubt hoping the people after him will believe he was kidnapped and murdered and stop looking for him while he finds a place to hide overseas."

"What about his alibi, though? How could he have kidnapped Joey?"

"The anonymous tip, which came from his phone and probably from him, included the licence plate of the black SUV which we believed was used. We tracked its owner who confirmed Mr Sutton asked to swap cars with him on the day Joey was kidnapped on the pretext of needing a bigger car to move some things. Mr Sutton paid him $1000 to run an errand for him out of town, gave him his credit card and told him where to stop for fuel and when, and supplied him with an identical set of clothes to the ones hanging in Mr Sutton's wardrobe. Apparently Mr Sutton told him he was supposed to pay some creditors on that day but didn't have the money. He'd managed to negotiate an extension by making up a story about picking the money up out of town. He told his mate he needed to show them proof he'd really gone."

"And he believed it?"

"Not entirely, but he didn't think he was doing any harm, so he was happy to pocket the $1000 and not ask questions. Mr Sutton could have come unstuck if the other man had seen any news reports about Joey's kidnapping, but the story didn't get much coverage, so I think Mr Sutton lucked out there. The other man also told us they had swapped cars in the past and more recently. Yesterday in fact."

"What now, then? Is the other guy going to be charged with anything?"

"No. We've got a full statement and, if he had no knowledge of Mr Sutton's intentions or actions, he hasn't committed a crime."

After Snr. Cst. Ryan had left Gavin listened quietly while Elly went over and over the story.

"Do you think he's gone for good?" she asked.

"It seems possible. If he comes back, he'll be arrested and I doubt he wants that. He'll probably use his money to buy a new identity somewhere and try and make a new life. There's not much for him here, but jail and angry thugs. You'll have no trouble getting sole custody of Joey now."

Looking down at her hands clasped in her lap, her thumbs banging against each other, Elly said nothing as Gavin put his arm around her shoulder and pulled her to him as he leaned back. Releasing her hands, she put one arm across his waist and laid her head on his chest.

"Am I free?"

"Free of him, by the look of it."

"I don't want to ever have to think about Les again. I will, I guess, because of Joey, but not for a while, and maybe we will never have to see him again."

"Do you want to be free of me, too?"

Her head sprang up. "No. No, Daddy. Do you want us to go if we're safe now?"

Gavin bent down and kissed her hard and long. "No. I do not. I want you to move into my bed starting tomorrow, after we tell Joey. I don't think he'll mind and I've got an idea which I think will distract him too. But, I'm sick of sleeping without you. I want to be able to feel you with me all night. If you think he's ready and you are ready, it's time we put an end to this half-relationship."

"We'll have to tell Moy that Les is gone. She'll be so happy. It's been a worry for her too."

"Yes. And it's Sunday tomorrow and I've got the day off, so we can go over then. We're going to have a busy day. Now, precious, I'm going to take you to bed with me and make love to you. You can slip into your bed after in case Joey wakes and looks for you, but after tonight you will not be sleeping in that bed again. Okay?"

Elly smiled up at him. "More than okay, Daddy."

"Mummy. Mummy."

Elly opened her eyes as Joey gently shook her shoulder. Her heart filled with love at the sight of his sweet, pixie face and earnest expression. She smiled, sat up and enveloped him in her arms.

"What is it, my sweet, sweet boy?" she almost sang.

"Can I play games, please?"

"Yes, my darling. You may. But first I want to have a talk

with you. The police lady came to see us last night and said your daddy went away on a plane. She also said he told them that he took you from school and pushed you on the stairs and that's how you broke your arm."

Joey burst into tears. "Did she come to arrest you, Mummy? Are you going to go to jail forever now?"

"No, no, baby. Don't cry." Elly smothered his face and hair with kisses. "Why would I be going to jail?"

"Daddy said if the police ever found out that he got me from school and pushed me and took me to the hospital, you would go to jail forever for not being at school when I got out. I don't want you to go jail, Mummy."

"Listen, sweetie. I promise you I am not going to jail. What Daddy told you wasn't true. The police know everything and they know I haven't done anything wrong. They just came to tell us your daddy has gone overseas and probably won't be coming back. Maybe not ever."

"Does that mean I don't have to see him anymore?"

"At least not for a long, long time."

"Goody. Can I play games now?"

"Yes, darling. You can play games while I get dressed and make breakfast, and then we're going out. We've got lots to do, and we're going to see Moy later."

"Goody. I love Moy."

"Me too, sweetheart."

"Is Gavin coming?"

"Yes."

"Goody. I love Gavin too."

Tears of happiness clouded Elly's vision. "And he loves you, my darling."

Joey frowned. "If Daddy is gone, are we going back to the flat now?"

"We could. Or we could stay here. Gavin said he would like

us to stay if we want to. What would you like most? Would you mind if we didn't live at the flat anymore?"

"I want to stay here with Gavin."

"That's good, sweetie. I do too. And would it be okay if I sleep in Gavin's room instead of in this bed?"

Joey didn't reply. Elly could almost hear him thinking such was the look of concentration on his face. Then he grinned.

"Sure. That'd be dime. You'd be like a real Mummy and Daddy then, wouldn't you?"

Elly chuckled softly and kissed him. "I suppose we would. You'll just have to remember to go into that room if you want to wake me instead of coming in here."

"I don't care." Dismissing adult concerns, he ran off to the TV and his video games.

Elly stretched luxuriously, her body still sweetly aching from Gavin's lovemaking and her heart full of happiness. As she collected her clothes and headed for the shower, she couldn't help bursting into song.

"Why are we here?" Joey asked, as they stood by a metal gate listening to a cacophony of barks.

"I heard there might be a puppy here looking for a home," Gavin said.

"A puppy!" Joey grabbed Elly's hand and danced around tugging on it. "Am I getting a puppy? Really, Mummy?"

"We're going to have a look and see if there's a puppy here," she replied, smiling at his enthusiasm.

A tall lady in khaki trousers and shirt opened the gate. "Oh dear," she said to Joey after she'd introduced herself as Vera, and ascertained the purpose of their mission. "You've hurt your arm, I see."

"Yes," Joey replied casually. "I fell over. It's broken but it will be all right."

Elly and Gavin's eyes met over his head, pleased he seemed able to talk about it without apparent psychological trauma, and proud he'd found a noncontroversial way to explain how it happened.

"We don't have any very young puppies at the moment," Vera told them stopping in front of a kennel in which a little brown and white spaniel was bouncing around, delighted to see them, "but Sissy is only five months old and super lovely."

"What do you think, Joey?" Elly asked, turning to discover Joey wasn't with them but was standing outside a cage three down from them. As she watched he moved close to the bars and squatted down. He'd been told not to put his fingers near the cages, so he kept his hands to himself and just spoke quietly to the occupant.

"Who's that?" Elly asked Vera.

"Oh, that's Rosco. Poor baby. But he's not a puppy."

Elly walked down to Joey and looked into the cage to see a medium-sized, short-haired black dog shivering in the corner and staring at them with one sad brown eye.

"This dog looks so sad, Mummy," Joey said. "Why is it so sad?"

"I suppose he's sad because he doesn't have a home and maybe he is frightened being with all the other dogs barking so loudly."

"And because he only has one eye? Where is his other eye?"

Vera, who'd joined them, squatted down next to Joey and called Rosco, holding out a treat for him. He slowly came over, crawling the last bit on his belly.

"He's a lovely boy, but he wasn't well-treated in his last home, and he is so timid now it's hard to find a home for him."

"Does he bite?" Joey asked.

"No. He is very gentle. He wouldn't bite anyone."

"Can I give him one of those?" Joey asked, pointing to the dog treats she was holding. She handed him one and he wriggled closer to the cage so he could put it close enough for the dog to be able to take. After eyeing him warily for a few seconds, Rosco inched close enough to take it from him and then sat down without running away.

"You're very good with him, aren't you?" Vera said. "Usually he is more timid with new people, but I think he knows he can trust you."

"Can we take Rosco home, Mummy? He needs us."

Elly looked at Vera who addressed Joey again. "Rosco might not want to play with you for a while. He might just want to hide somewhere, so you would have to be very patient until he got used to living with you and wasn't scared anymore. If you want a dog to play with, maybe you should think about a different one."

"But if we leave Rosco here, he will still be sad, won't he?"

"Yes, but someone else might come and give him a home. Someone that doesn't want a puppy."

"I don't want a puppy any more. I want Rosco."

And as if to signify the feeling was mutual, Rosco wiggled his tail for the first time and pushed himself against the bars so Joey could scritch behind his ear.

Before the adoption was allowed to be formalised, Rosco was brought out of his cage so they could meet him properly and take him for a walk. Vera showed Joey how to wrap the leash around his hand, so he couldn't accidentally let go and they walked him around the big exercise yard. Then Joey sat on the ground and Rosco immediately sat next to him. The adults, realising objections would be pointless, finalised the deal by filling out a mountain of paperwork and handing over the adoption fee.

"You're very quiet, mate," Gavin said to Joey, already strapped in, as he lifted Rosco into the back seat.

"I have to be quiet so I don't scare Rosco," Joey said quietly as Rosco lay on the seat and rested his head on Joey's thigh. "I think he trusts me already."

"I think he does, too," Gavin agreed, ruffling Joey's hair. "It's a nice thing you did, Joey, choosing Rosco instead of a puppy. I'm sure the puppies get snapped up in no time, but poor Rosco had already been there for a long, long time."

Joey stroked Rosco's head and smiled. "I love Rosco. Are we going to Moy's now? Can I show Rosco the backyard? Moy won't mind I've brought Rosco with me, will she?"

"Yes, sweetie, we're going to Moy's for lunch," Ellie said. "She won't mind Rosco coming too. She loves dogs, and I told her you were getting one today. She thinks you were getting a puppy, so she'll be surprised to see Rosco."

She was surprised, but as proud and delighted as the others that Joey had willingly foregone his dream of a puppy to open his heart to a sad, frightened dog in desperate need of love. Rosco seemed to instinctively trust Joey and they pottered around in the backyard together while Gavin, Elly and Moy sat at the outdoor setting and discussed Snr. Cst. Ryan's visit the night before.

"I don't care why he did it," Moy said when they'd run over all the events and possible explanations for them. "I'm just glad he's gone and won't be bothering you any more, love." She smiled at Elly and patted her arm. "Or Joey." Her eyes narrowed as she looked at the cast on Joey's arm, then she smiled at Gavin and Elly. "You two have done wonders for him. He seems a bit less anxious already, and considering what happened to him not much more than a week ago, I think it's amazing. So what's happening with you two now, then?"

This time it was Elly's turn to put her hand on Moira's arm. "I hope you won't mind too much, Moy, but Gavin has asked us to stay at his place, so I'm going to let the flat go. I know it's been in the family for a long time. I hope…"

Moira stopped her. "It's fine. Honestly. I'm so happy for you, love, and I don't really care about the flat anymore. I'm not sentimentally attached to it. Well, maybe a little bit, but without Fi or you there, I shan't miss it. And I was hoping you would stay with Gavin, and now it's official, I want to give you a sort of house-warming present." She disappeared into the house and returned with Fiona's photograph, *Magic Shadow Shapes*, and held it out to Gavin who put his hands up in protest.

"Oh. No. Thank you. That is so kind, but I can't accept it. I know how much you love it."

Moira smiled. "Please take it. I really, really want you to have it, Gavin. It would make me very happy if you would accept. I know it would be appreciated, and you can always invite me over so I can admire it at your place."

Gavin's cheek twitched as he rubbed his teeth together and swallowed. "Thank you, Moira. I will cherish this, I promise, and you are, of course, welcome any time with or without an invitation. You're family after all."

Moira pressed her trembling lips together. "Come on, then. Let's go inside and have lunch. Joey, bring Rosco and I'll find something for him to eat too."

Chapter 23

"You're looking a little pale, baby," Gavin said to Elly as they sat in the backyard drinking coffee. Joey was at school and they had the house and the morning to themselves until Gavin started his shift. Elly looked happily around the garden. She'd put a lot of work into it in the nearly six months she'd been living with Gavin, and it gave her pleasure to see it doing so well.

Her whole life was infinitely more pleasurable with Les out of it. There had been no word on him, and no other information had come to light about why he'd suddenly confessed and fled. As the days drifted by, Elly and Joey had continued to relax as they became more confident they were free of him and safe. Under Gavin's watchful care, they'd both thrived, until recently when Gavin had noticed a change in Elly. She seemed to have lost some of her bounce and, looking at her now, he could see she was paler than usual.

"What's up? Are you feeling ill?"

"I'm fine," she replied, but Gavin heard a heaviness in her voice and saw a worrying shadow in her eyes.

"Are you sure?"

"Yes, Doctor Daddy," she answered with a cheeky smile, but seeing he was still unconvinced she tried again. "I'm fine. Honestly. Maybe a bit tired. I think I might have a bit of a stomach bug, that's all."

"You haven't said anything about a stomach bug."

Elly shrugged and looked away. "I didn't think it was worth mentioning," she said with artificial brightness. "It's nothing. Let's go inside." She moved to pick up the cup, but knocked it over.

Gavin put his hand over hers to stop her. "Something is going on. I'm going to give you a thorough examination and see if I can get to the bottom of what's troubling you," he said in his professional voice, gently teasing her with a slight emphasis on the word 'bottom' so she blushed and dropped her eyes. He allowed himself a little smile of his own while she wasn't looking, then picked up both cups and stood up. "Come on. Go to the bedroom and get ready. I'll put these in the kitchen and fetch my bag."

"I'm all right. Promise. I don't need examining."

He looked stern. "Instead of arguing with me, I'd go and get ready if I were you, unless you'd like me to spank that bottom I was talking about before I examine you."

"No," she answered quickly, ignoring how dry her mouth had suddenly become and how fast her heart was beating. "But…"

Without another word, Gavin took her hand, pulled her up and led her into their bedroom, depositing the cups on the coffee table on the way past.

"Now get undressed while I fetch my bag, and I think you best get a slipper from the cupboard as well if you're going to be naughty."

Elly plopped down onto the bed and watched him go, wringing her hands. She didn't want to be examined. She hadn't been feeling well, and was terrified of what he might find. She knew she shouldn't keep anything from Gavin. She should have told him at the start—he was a doctor after all—but she couldn't get Fi out of her mind. One day she had been healthy and making plans for her future, the next she'd had a pain in her tummy and in a matter of a few weeks she was gone. Elly was terrified the same thing was going to happen to her. She'd thought that maybe if she ignored the niggling, it would go away. It hadn't done, though, and now she wasn't going to be able to hide it from Gavin and he was going to be cross she hadn't told him, and he was going to examine her and maybe tell her she was dying.

She was still caught up in her worst fears when Gavin returned with his black medical bag. He looked at her, fully-clothed exactly where he'd left her, and frowned. He put his bag down, undid the buttons on his shirtsleeves and rolled them up while Elly stared silently at him. He went into the bathroom and thoroughly washed and dried his hands, then came back out carrying a towel which he put on the bed. Elly hadn't moved.

He grimaced and squinted his eyes. "What's going on, baby?" he asked.

She looked down and shook her head.

"Nope. That's not going to cut it. I asked you a question and I want an answer."

"I don't want you to examine me," she mumbled. "It's just a tummy bug. Honestly."

"What is? You haven't said anything about not being well."

"I didn't bother because it's nothing."

Without speaking, he put his hand across her forehead then put his fingers on the pulse in her wrist.

"What have you been feeling? Have you been keeping something from me?"

Elly squirmed as she nodded her head. "Maybe a little. But it's nothing," she blurted out, quickly looking up at him with what she hoped was the expression of someone in the pink of health.

"Take off your clothes and sit on the edge of the bed this instant."

This was it then. She was about to find out she was seriously ill, dying even. She disrobed and sat down. She'd been undressed in front of Gavin so many times now that she usually wasn't self-conscious about her naked body, but she did feel horribly self-conscious about her unwell body.

Gavin opened his bag and put his stethoscope around his neck and the thermometer, gel and otoscope on the bedside table, and then sat next to her. She looked at his beautifully clean hands with their immaculate fingernails, his lovely thick bare forearms with their covering of black hair, the stethoscope around his neck, and then up to his gorgeous face and brown eyes which were looking down at her with concern.

"Tell me what you've been feeling," he asked gently.

"Nothing much. Hardly anything," she hedged.

"What exactly?" he probed again. "Headache? Dizziness? Pain? What?"

"A little bit sick a couple of times and a bit more tired than usual. I'm sure it's a harmless tummy bug."

"So you keep saying. I don't understand why you have kept it from me, though. Why would you do that?"

"I didn't want you to examine me."

"Why not? Come on, Elly. Tell me."

"I'm afraid you'll find something wrong," she whispered. "Like Fi."

"Ah, I see." He tucked strands of her hair behind her shoulder. "Poor baby, have you been worried? But that's no excuse for keeping it to yourself. If you don't feel well, you should tell Doctor Daddy straight away so I can help you. It was very naughty of you to keep it from me, wasn't it? You shouldn't be worrying about things on your own, and you shouldn't be hiding things from me. So, the doctor is going to examine you first, and if there's nothing to be concerned about, Daddy is going to put you across his knee and slipper your bottom."

"Oh." Elly didn't want a spanking despite his scolding having triggered a warm slick between her legs, but she wanted to be ill even less so she had to hope her fate was going to be a session across his knee.

Gavin stood up, picked up his otoscope and switched it on, then checked both her ears, unscrewed the end and shone the light down her throat while she said "Aaaahhh".

"That all looks fine," he said, putting the otoscope down and then using his fingers to check her lymph nodes. "I'll do your breasts while you're sitting up. Sit up straight and put your arm up behind your head." When she was in position, he pressed his hand gently against her breast. She winced, and he quickly looked at her with a slight frown.

"Did that hurt?"

"A little, maybe."

"What about here?" He pressed her breast again.

She nodded. He tried the other breast and the result was the same.

"How long have they been tender?"

"I hadn't noticed they were. I mean until now."

He checked each one thoroughly being careful not to press hard.

"Okay?" he asked. She nodded. "They seem perfect." He smiled and a tinge of pink coloured her cheeks. "I'm going to take your temperature. Can you get into position for me, please?"

Her cheeks darkened further as she lay on her side, her bottom facing him and her knees curled up against her chest, while he pulled on a pair of gloves, removed the thermometer from its case and scooped some gel from the jar.

"Ready?" he asked. "This might be a bit cold." Elly's muscles tightened involuntarily at the first touch of the cold gel and his finger pushing it into her tight entrance. "Relax," he ordered, and she felt the thin instrument slide in surprising all the nerve endings as it made its way through.

"Tell me more about how you've been feeling," he said, waiting to remove the thermometer. "Any pain in your belly? Nausea? Vomiting?"

"A bit of a sick feeling in my tummy sometimes. I haven't vomited. I thought I was going to a couple of times but didn't really."

"Anything else? Pain lower down?"

"A bit achy. Not too bad. And tired. No energy."

"Periods?"

Elly blushed again and bit her lip. "Okay."

"Normal?"

"Sort of."

"Elly. Tell me, please. Honestly. I'm your doctor at the moment, but I can easily switch to Daddy if you would prefer I slipper your bottom. Would you?"

"No."

"Come on, then. There's nothing to be embarrassed about."

"Sort of normal," Elly admitted reluctantly.

"Go on."

"Last one was a couple of weeks late and much lighter than usual." She was glad her face was turned away.

"Shorter?" She nodded.

"Okay. Good girl. I'll have a look in a minute and see what's going on. Stay still now while I take the thermometer out."

She closed her eyes and clenched her teeth as she felt him gently pull one bottom cheek open so he could see, then felt the strange sensation as the thermometer slid slowly out. Gavin looked at it, shook it, put it down on a tissue and took off his gloves.

"Normal," he said, smiling reassuringly at her as she looked over her shoulder at him. "Roll over so I can check your tummy."

"Anything?" he asked as he palpated her lower abdomen.

"Not really. It is a tiny bit tender… low down."

"Is it? Okay, slide down to the end of the bed and pull your knees up and then drop them down to the side. Let's have a look, shall we?"

He covered her lower abdomen with the towel, removed the end of the otoscope, put on clean gloves, took a small scoop of gel, pulled up a chair and sat down as she reluctantly spread her legs. She looked down, shivering slightly, as he gently ran his fingers over her most sensitive flesh to spread the gel, and then gasping softly as he slipped one finger inside her. The artificial lubricant wasn't needed, though; she might not have overcome her initial embarrassment at being so open to his view, but that only added to the arousal his intimate examination triggered in her.

Holding her open with one hand, he shone his light up her vagina and peered in.

"Mm-mm." He stood up, put the otoscope down and pushed two fingers into her as far as he could as he gently pressed her belly. His eyes were turned upward as he concentrated on feeling around inside her. Grimacing at the pressure, Elly watched him closely for any sign he might be concerned.

At last he removed his hand, and turned to her as he pulled off his gloves.

"I'm pretty sure I've found the problem."

"You found something?" she whispered fearfully, wondering how long she had.

He took a deep breath through his nose, nodded and pursed his lips, then let out his breath.

"I have. We'll do a follow up test to confirm my diagnosis, but I don't think there's any doubt that something growing inside you is causing your symptoms."

"A tumour?" All the colour drained from Elly's face and she could barely breathe as panic tightened her chest. Then she noticed Gavin was grinning at her. She frowned. "What?"

"Not a tumour, you goose," he said, still smiling. "You're pregnant, my darling. That's all. About four or five weeks, I'd say, but an ultrasound should give us a definitive date."

Elly sprang up and swung around so she was sitting on the edge of the bed, covering herself as best she could with the towel, as her head spun with the news. She was shocked that it hadn't crossed her mind that she might be pregnant, but they hadn't discussed having children other than as something that might happen in the future, and they certainly hadn't been trying for a baby. Plus they'd been taking reasonable precautions, and she hadn't missed a period altogether. She bowed her head as she tried to absorb this unexpected news, then felt him sit next to her.

"What's the matter, baby?" he asked gently, trying to push her thick curls out of the way so he could see her face. "Don't you want to be pregnant?"

She looked up at him, her eyes full of uncertainty. His smile had gone and his eyes were troubled as he clenched his teeth. "Do you want me to be?" she asked.

He took her hands in his. "I love you, Elly. Nothing would make me happier than for us to have a child together. That's truly how I feel, but it's your body so it has to be your decision."

Her heart melted at the depth of emotion in his eyes, and she could feel his hands trembling as he waited for her answer. "No," she said. "This is your baby too, and I want us to make all the decisions together, like names, schools, everything."

"Are you saying you want the baby?" She could feel him holding his breath.

She smiled and slipped one hand out of his so she could touch his face. "I couldn't want it more, and I can't wait to tell Joey. I hope he'll be excited. He's always said he wanted a brother, although he might have to make do with a sister."

"Oh, my darling," Gavin muttered pulling her to him and kissing her over and over again. "There's one more thing. It won't be too long now before you'll be able to get a divorce without Les' consent. When you do, do you think we could get married? I mean, would that be okay? Not okay, but I mean…"

"Yes," Elly said teasingly with a grin. "What exactly do you mean?"

Gavin slipped onto the floor on his knees in front of her.

"Will you marry me, Elly?"

Gavin was at work when Joey got home from school so they had to wait until the following morning to tell him their news.

"We've got something exciting to tell you," Elly began while the three of them were around the kitchen table eating breakfast. "Mummy's having a baby."

Joey stared at her, then at Gavin, and then back to her. "Will Gavin be the baby's daddy?" he asked with a frown.

"Yes, darling."

Joey's expression turned to horror and he pushed back his chair and ran from the room. Elly looked at Gavin in complete bewilderment. She started to get up, but Gavin stopped her.

"I'll go."

He found Joey face down on his bed.

"What's the matter, buddy?" he asked gently, sitting down

next to him. "Don't you like the idea of having a baby brother or sister? Is that what's wrong?"

Joey shook his head.

"What then? Can you tell me?"

"If you are the baby's daddy, I won't have one anymore," a little voice, muffled by bedclothes, explained.

"I see," Gavin said seriously. "Don't you want Les to be your daddy?"

"No, I hate him. I hope he never comes back."

"Mmm," Gavin pretended to be considering this information. "Well, what can we do about this?"

"I thought you were *my* new daddy."

"Did you?" Gavin sounded surprised. "Well, I would love to be your daddy. I can't think of anyone who's daddy I'd rather be."

Joey sat up and looked at him suspiciously. "What about the baby? Don't you want to be its daddy?"

"Ah." Gavin nodded. "Yes, I do. I can't think of anyone who's daddy I would rather be than you and the baby."

"Can you be both our daddies?"

"I can. If you'll let me be your daddy."

"And can I call you Daddy?"

"Of course. I would be honoured," Gavin said, scooping Joey into a bear hug and smiling up at Elly who'd come into the room in time to hear the last part of the conversation. He turned to her as she sat close to him on the bed, leaned over and snuggled happily into his neck, whispering, "And can I still call you Doctor Daddy?"

"You'd better," he whispered back. "Forever. Or else. And you will always be my precious patient, won't you?"

She nodded. "Forever."

The End

Chapter 24

Polly Carter

Polly Carter has been writing in one form or another most of her life. With more time on her hands after her children had left home, she was finally able to realise her long-held desire to write romance novels.

"I've always loved the idea of being a writer and taking my work with me wherever I go. I hate being stuck in an office, and being able to travel and work at the same time seems like the perfect life. And, of course, I love, love, and love writing about it."

Polly has four children and four grandchildren. She lives in Western Australia where she has spent most of her life. Her other passions include dogs, travel, reading (quantum physics, I know!) and occasionally painting.

You can email her here: PollyCarter@Australiamail.com
Find her on Facebook:
https://www.facebook.com/PollyCarterRomance
Or follow her on Twitter: @Polly_Carter1

Don't miss these exciting titles by Polly Carter and Blushing Books!
Danny's Secret Desire
Rescuing Rudi
The Lawyer's Secret Baby

Claimed By Daddy series

Daddy's Precious Jewel
Daddy's Precious Patient

Blushing Books

Blushing Books is one of the oldest eBook publishers on the web. We've been running websites that publish spanking and BDSM related romance and erotica since 1999, and we have been selling eBooks since 2003. We hope you'll check out our hundreds of offerings at http://www.blushingbooks.com.

Blushing Books Newsletter

Please join the Blushing Books newsletter
to receive updates & special promotional offers.
You can also join by using your mobile phone:
Just text BLUSHING to 22828.